THE VULGAR HEART

Unmarriageable
Book 3

Mary Lancaster

Books from Dragonblade Publishing

Dangerous Lords Series by Maggi Andersen
The Baron's Betrothal
Seducing the Earl
The Viscount's Widowed Lady
Governess to the Duke's Heir

Also from Maggi Andersen
The Marquess Meets His Match

Knights of Honor Series by Alexa Aston
Word of Honor
Marked by Honor
Code of Honor
Journey to Honor
Heart of Honor
Bold in Honor
Love and Honor
Gift of Honor
Path to Honor
Return to Honor

The King's Cousins Series by Alexa Aston
The Pawn
The Heir
The Bastard

Beastly Lords Series by Sydney Jane Baily
Lord Despair
Lord Anguish
Lord Vile
Lord Corsair

Dukes of Destiny Series by Whitney Blake
Duke of Havoc
Duke of Sorrow

Legends of Love Series by Avril Borthiry
The Wishing Well
Isolated Hearts
Sentinel

The Lost Lords Series by Chasity Bowlin
The Lost Lord of Castle Black
The Vanishing of Lord Vale
The Missing Marquess of Althorn
The Resurrection of Lady Ramsleigh
The Mystery of Miss Mason
The Awakening of Lord Ambrose

By Elizabeth Ellen Carter
Captive of the Corsairs, *Heart of the Corsairs Series*
Revenge of the Corsairs, *Heart of the Corsairs Series*
Shadow of the Corsairs, *Heart of the Corsairs Series*
Dark Heart
Live and Let Spy, *King's Rogues Series*

Knight Everlasting Series by Cassidy Cayman
Endearing
Enchanted
Evermore

Midnight Meetings Series by Gina Conkle
Meet a Rogue at Midnight, book 4

Second Chance Series by Jessica Jefferson
Second Chance Marquess

Imperial Season Series by Mary Lancaster
Vienna Waltz
Vienna Woods
Vienna Dawn

Blackhaven Brides Series by Mary Lancaster
The Wicked Baron
The Wicked Lady
The Wicked Rebel
The Wicked Husband
The Wicked Marquis
The Wicked Governess
The Wicked Spy
The Wicked Gypsy
The Wicked Wife

Unmarriageable Series by Mary Lancaster
The Deserted Heart
The Sinister Heart
The Vulgar Heart

Highland Loves Series by Melissa Limoges
My Reckless Love
My Steadfast Love
My Passionate Love

Clash of the Tartans Series by Anna Markland
Kilty Secrets
Kilted at the Altar
Kilty Pleasures

Queen of Thieves Series by Andy Peloquin
Child of the Night Guild
Thief of the Night Guild
Queen of the Night Guild

The Book of Love Series by Meara Platt
The Look of Love
The Touch of Love

Dark Gardens Series by Meara Platt
Garden of Shadows
Garden of Light
Garden of Dragons
Garden of Destiny

Rulers of the Sky Series by Paula Quinn
Scorched
Ember
White Hot

Hearts of the Highlands Series by Paula Quinn
Heart of Ashes
Heart of Shadows
Heart of Stone

Highlands Forever Series by Violetta Rand
Unbreakable
Undeniable
Unyielding

Viking's Fury Series by Violetta Rand
Love's Fury
Desire's Fury
Passion's Fury

Also from Violetta Rand
Viking Hearts

The Sins and Scoundrels Series by Scarlett Scott
Duke of Depravity
Prince of Persuasion
Marquess of Mayhem

The Unconventional Ladies Series by Ellie St. Clair
Lady of Mystery

The Sons of Scotland Series by Victoria Vane
Virtue
Valor

Men of Blood Series by Rosamund Winchester
The Blood & The Bloom

CHAPTER ONE

MISS HENRIETTA MAYBURY fanned herself vigorously. The heat inside the Theatre Royal, Covent Garden, was intense that July evening, not least because of the thousands of candles which lit the stage and the auditorium with equal brightness. A faint, smoky mist blurred Henrietta's view of the play, but it made little difference to her understanding, for she couldn't hear the dialogue either. The noise of the chatter from her own and surrounding boxes drowned most of that out. Then, there was the general background hum from more distant voices and the occasional shout from the cheap seats in the pit.

The whole oppressive atmosphere combined to make Henrietta feel just a little dizzy. A few twinges behind her eyes warned a headache was not far away. To distract herself, she transferred her attention to the audience—which was, after all, the main reason most people of her class attended the theatre. There was always a wonderful new fashion to observe, or gossip to acquire from seeing who accompanied or visited whom in their box. Or one could look down on the hoi polloi who rubbed shoulders with the few single gentlemen ogling the ladies from the pit.

Henrietta's slightly blurred vision was drawn to the boxes opposite, particularly to one in the row above her own, where she picked out a gown of such a vibrant shade of puce that it cut through the haze. Worn by a stout, middle-aged lady, it was indeed an extraordinary garment, trimmed with feathers of the same shade. A puce turban, sporting plumes so tall they bent against the ceiling of the box completed the awe-inspiring ensemble. Henrietta wanted to applaud the lady's courage, if not her taste, for the sight quite cheered her up.

The lady's companions were an older gentleman with bushy side whiskers, and a younger, elegantly dressed man with short, dark hair…who gazed directly at her. Of course, she should have immediately lowered her eyes and pretended not to see, but Henrietta was bored with the stifling conformity of her first London season, and some devil prompted her merely to stare back in order to put him rather than herself out of countenance.

He was not even a handsome man, nor particularly young, she guessed, but his harsh, weather-beaten face held a certain rough attraction, particularly when an intrigued smile began to form on his lips. Far from being embarrassed by her haughty glare, he inclined his head. Of course, even she could not acknowledge such a sign from a stranger. Recognizing with some pique that this was one staring contest she was not going to win, she let her gaze drift out of focus. Then she glanced along the rest of the row before returning casually to the stage.

It was still hot, still oppressive, and the incipient headache behind her eyes had intensified. After a further ten minutes, she leaned closer to her mother. "Mama, it's so hot in here, I'm just going to put my head out of the door for some fresher air."

"Well, don't go out into the passage," her mother warned. "At least, not alone. Do you feel faint?"

"No, no, I just need a breath of cool air." Henrietta slipped past her sister Thomasina, now Lady Dunstan, to the back of the box and opened the door.

A waft of slightly cooler air greeted her, and she stuck her head out into the corridor in search of more. Fortunately, it was empty, so she slipped outside and lifted her head and arms to catch as much breeze as she could. She closed her eyes, willing away the headache.

A small, high-pitched whine disturbed her. Opening her eyes in some surprise, she looked around her. A tiny puppy wobbled along the passage toward her, sniffing at the wall as it went, all but tripping over its too-large feet.

Henrietta smiled, surprised to realize how much she'd been missing Spring, her sister's pet dog, who'd gone with Charlotte to Lincolnshire since her marriage. She could not resist hurrying toward the little creature. "Hello there, little fellow, where did you come from?" she murmured, pausing at the stairs and holding out her hand.

The puppy wagged its tail but backed off, clearly unsure.

"Has someone hurt you, poor little thing?" Henrietta murmured in quick sympathy. She remained still, with her gloved hand held out. "I won't. Come and greet me civilly, which is more than Spring ever did."

The pup pranced forward a little, sniffed once at the very tip of her finger, and then bolted down the stairs, bouncing and tumbling.

"Oh, silly creature!" Impulsively, she ran after it. But her attention was more on the dog than her own clothing, and her foot caught in the tumbling train of her gown. She gasped, grabbing for the bannister to save herself.

Vaguely, she was aware of a male figure bounding upstairs toward her. Her floundering hand missed the bannister and then she was falling, head first.

She slammed into a man's hard chest. His arms closed around her, catching her and hauling her upright.

Bemused, unable to quite believe her inevitable disaster had been prevented, she gazed up into the face of the man who had bowed to her from the opposite box.

"You," she uttered in confusion.

"Are you hurt?" His voice was deep, his speech clear and clipped, like a man used to giving orders. He had eyes the color of the sea. Her hands still clung to his thick arms.

Hastily, she released him. "No…no, I don't believe I am, thanks to you."

She flushed, just because she could feel the heat of his body, and tried to step back. He released her, but slowly, perhaps to be sure she wouldn't fall again, and stepped down on to the stair below.

She smiled a little uncertainly, smoothing her ruffled gown. "I'm most grateful, sir. Oh! The pup! Where did it go?"

"What pup?"

"A tiny little thing with a floppy ear. I was following it down-stairs… I've no idea how it got into the theatre, but I fear someone has mistreated him because he seems very thin and timid for a puppy. Though, of course, there's no point in comparing him to Spring."

"To *what*?" A faint frown of bafflement tugged at the man's brows.

"My sister's dog," Henrietta said, starting down the stairs again, this time looping her train over her arm as she should have done in the first place. "He bounces—" She broke off as she caught sight of the puppy watching her through the spars of the bannister from the landing. "Ah, *there* you are!"

It seemed to be playing, in a nervous kind of way, because alt-hough it waited for her, as soon as she offered her hand, it made to scamper off again. But she was ready for it this time and merely scooped it up.

Triumph turned quickly to concern. "Oh, dear, he's mere skin and bones. The poor little thing is starving."

The pup wriggled, licking her detaining hand and then chewing her finger with needle-sharp teeth. Henrietta laughed.

Her savior stood at the foot of the stairs, regarding them with amusement. "Now what do you plan to do with it? Take it to the play?"

"Oh, the devil, the play!" she uttered, quite improperly. "It will be the interval any moment and Mama will scold me into next week! Perhaps I could give the pup to the doorman to look after until we leave…"

"Allow me," her savior offered.

Henrietta regarded him doubtfully. Despite his swift action in saving her from a nasty fall, he did not look to be a terribly *safe* person. On the other hand, he was dressed with the quiet elegance of wealth and taste, and he was neither young nor silly, being surely well into his thirties. Deep "crow's feet" were etched around his eyes. A man who laughed a lot or worried a lot. Either seemed to bode well for the pup.

Reaching her decision, she held the dog out to him.

He swept it up carelessly, and the puppy bit his finger. "What name shall I give the doorman?"

"Maybury," she said. "I'm Henrietta Maybury. And if such information will help him be kind to the pup, please tell him my father, Lord Overton, is with me. Sir, thank you for everything!" She fled back upstairs and made it back to her own box just as everyone else began spilling out of theirs.

"Where have you been?" Thomasina hissed at her. "I told Mama you were still in the passage, but you weren't. Did you meet someone?"

"Actually yes," Henrietta said, laughter bubbling up. "But not in the way you mean. I found a puppy and it is clearly neglected and hungry, so I've arranged to collect it from the doorman as we leave."

Thomasina blinked. "You're mad. Mama is still celebrating life without Spring."

"I think she secretly finds it a little dull without Spring."

"You mean *you* do."

"Yes, and so does Eliza. And the boys who will be home for summer soon. Besides, this little creature is nothing like Spring. It is quite timid and shows no signs of insanity."

"Yet, if it's as hungry as you say, it won't have the energy." Thomasina nodded toward their parents. "How are you planning to talk them into it?"

"Face to face, they're bound to love it. And if they don't..." She smiled. "You and Dunstan could always take it, just until I wear them down."

"Take what?" Dunstan demanded, moving closer to them in order to make way for the gentlemen who had just entered the box to pay their respects to Lady Overton. One of them was Lord Rudd, who'd become quite a persistent admirer of Henrietta's.

"Oh, Henrie has discovered a stray puppy in the theater of all unlikely places." Thomasina broke off as she recognized one of their guests, and lowered her voice once more. "Why, it's Lord Rudd again. I think you have made a conquest, Henrie."

"Fiddlesticks," said Henrie airily.

"It would be an excellent match. And quite a triumph, for so far he's avoided all the lures cast out to him."

"Well, I have no intention of luring him," Henrie stated.

Her sister frowned. "You're beginning to sound like Charlotte."

"Why is that bad?" Henri shot back.

"It isn't," Thomasina said wryly. "She never lured anyone in her life and yet she is a duchess."

Henrietta had once entered fully into her parents' plans to save the family fortune by settlements gained through their daughters' brilliant marriages. However, in the last few weeks, she had begun to find herself irritated by such talk and, even more unexpectedly, bored with the whirl of her first London season. It all seemed a trifle pointless when Charlotte's marriage and the generosity of her husband had restored the family finances already. Henrietta now had a respectable dowry to attract a husband, and yet somehow that had taken all the fun out of everything. How much better to be married for love rather than one's dowry.

She fanned herself a little too energetically.

"It is somewhat stuffy in here," Lord Rudd remarked, sitting in the vacant seat beside her. "How do you do, Miss Maybury?"

"My lord. Do you want the truth or the polite answer?"

He smiled faintly. "That bad?"

"Oh, London is so stifling in the summer, but I am glad to say we are leaving next week."

"For Brighton, perhaps?"

"No, for Audley Park."

"I am desolated," Rudd said in the somewhat intriguing way he had, so that you didn't quite know if he was serious or not. "For I have been commanded to Brighton by Prinny. I had hoped that I might at least have the pleasure of seeing you there."

"We might go for a day or two, for we're not so far away."

Rudd smiled. "I have rarely met a debutante with such little enthusiasm for the social scene."

"I bore easily," Henrietta said.

"Then I must strive to be much more interesting."

She laughed, for in truth, he was already more interesting than most. Although still in his twenties, his air was one of elegant world-weariness, which quite suited Henrietta's mood these days. He also had a bit of a reputation as a rake and had been disappointing hopeful mamas for years by failing to be enchanted enough by their lovely daughters to marry any of them. In short, he presented a challenge, although what she would do with the prize, she wasn't quite sure.

Neither of her older sisters had tamed a rake, although neither of their husbands, she suspected, had been precisely angelic either. So at least if she married Rudd, she would have that triumph. On the other hand, her imagination baulked at the prospect of being his wife. She could not quite envision their married life. Besides, how much fun would it actually be, being bored together at balls without even the diversion of flirtation left to them?

The future seemed just as dull at the present and she felt rather flat. Until her wandering gaze drifted again over the stunning lady in puce. A gentleman sat down beside her, causing Henrietta's heart to give a pleasant little lurch. It was *him* again. The man who had saved her, and who she had thought must be leaving the theatre. As though sensing her gaze, he turned from the puce lady and glanced over to her. A smile flitted across his face and he inclined his head as though telling her his task was complete and the pup was in the care of the doorman. She nodded her thanks with a quick smile in return.

"That is an odd connection for an ambitious young lady," Rudd remarked beside her.

"It isn't a connection at all," she retorted, "but a matter of common civility. The gentleman has done me a service."

"Hush, Miss Maybury," Rudd mocked. "A fashionable lady should never admit to such a service, for your knight is no gentleman."

Intrigued, she turned back to Rudd. "Then who is he?"

"Some banker's son," Rudd said with contempt. "An encroaching cit."

Henrietta was conscious of disappointment. It was snobbish, of course, but she did not wish to have been saved and helped by a cit. It lacked distinction. And while she could laugh at herself for such feelings, they had been bred into her and they remained.

"And the fabulous lady in puce?" she asked, deciding to be amused.

"I really have no idea. One doesn't *know* such people."

"Of course, one does not," she mocked Rudd, and inspired a fresh spark of interest in his jaded eyes.

All the same, when the interminable play finally finished and she stood up to leave, she pretended not to see the banker's bow and followed her family outside.

Sydney Cromarty, grandson of a successful and well-known banker, had indeed intended to leave the theater after depositing the skinny pup with a none-too-happy doorman. An innocent young debutante, however lovely, was really of no interest to him on any level. And while he had no objections to preventing her tumble downstairs, or transferring care of the cur on his way out, he had no reason and less intention to pursue her.

But something about her expression—far more than her mere youthful beauty—had attracted his attention while she sat in the box opposite. And nothing about her subsequent impulsive and slightly bizarre behavior for a young lady of fashion had lessened that interest. He was curious, and in a way that was quite safe, for she was far too young and naïve to inspire amorous pursuit. And so, he found himself returning to the box—which, in any case, he had paid for.

"I believe I will watch the end of the play," he said to Mrs. Jenkins. He had only invited them to secure the deal for his new ship and now that it was done, he had nothing more to do in London. Tomorrow or the day after, he would ride back to Sussex.

In the meantime, he discreetly observed the Maybury girl, and the somewhat possessive gentleman who sat by her side. Whoever he was, he clearly whispered poison in her ear, for she refused to look at him as she left.

Cromarty only smiled cynically. The girl's snobbery hurt him no more than anyone else's. He'd been immune through constant exposure since he was fourteen years old. And when he'd finally run away from school when he was sixteen, it had had nothing to do with his schoolmates and everything to do with him.

Still, he wished her well enough to linger in the shadows outside the theater as the carriages pulled up and swallowed the members of the ton, taking them back from the dangers of Covent Garden to more salubrious neighborhoods in Mayfair.

The Maybury girl emerged with another young lady who had been in her box—her sister perhaps, for they shared the same shade of shining chestnut hair. Henrietta darted to the various doormen until she received the pup whom she held up with delight for her sister to admire. The sister laughed and dragged her back to her parents. Cromarty realized he knew Lord Overton slightly. He was partial to decent French brandy and disliked to let a little thing like war get in his way.

Overton's voice said clearly, "Oh for the love of—"

"No, Henrie," Lady Overton said firmly and then, after the pup was brought closer to her and Henrietta wheedled, she threw up her arms and got into the carriage. Henrietta followed with the pup, though she paused to grin over her shoulder at her sister.

Cromarty turned and walked away.

He contemplated calling on his mistress to make up their quarrel in the most delicious ways he could imagine. But in the end, he had little enthusiasm for it. She had grown too capricious and her un-doubted pleasures were no longer worth the inconvenience. Their relationship would remain over. He looked forward instead to a good night's sleep at Claridge's Hotel, where he often stayed to avoid his old family home off Hanover Square. And then a swift return to Sussex and the sea.

I'm getting old and staid…

However, when he entered the hotel, it was to be greeted with the news that a gentleman called Mr. Godfrey awaited him in his rooms. Irritated that they had let the solicitor in at all, he scowled and hurried upstairs.

Godfrey, as usual, had helped himself to a glass of brandy as he waited. It wasn't the brandy Cromarty grudged him.

"What do *you* want?" Cromarty greeted him as he sprang to his feet.

"I was sent by your grandfather to impart important information," Godfrey said with dignity. "And issue an invitation."

"An invitation to go to the devil? I accepted long since. What is the rest of it?"

"Sir, I regret to inform you that your cousin, Jeremy, is dead."

Cromarty shrugged. "My grandfather is mistaking me for someone who cares. I never met the late Jeremy, and his death is of no importance to me."

"Actually, it is," Godfrey said sharply. "Of considerable moment, in fact. He was your grandfather's heir."

"I still can't care," Cromarty said, pouring himself a glass of brandy. "To Jeremy, whoever he was." He raised his glass and drank.

Godfrey pursed his lips at such flippancy. "He was the man whose death makes you your grandfather's heir."

That got his attention. He lowered the glass, frowning. "No. There is another cousin, isn't there? About to spawn, too, last I heard."

"Sadly, the child was a girl. Perhaps the disappointment aided Mr. Adrian's departure from this life a year ago. Even more sadly, you are now the nearest living male heir."

Cromarty stared at him. Then he laughed and poured himself another brandy. "No, I'm not. Tell him to get one of his by-blows legitimized if he has to, for I'm having nothing to do with any of 'em. Good night, Godfrey. Close the door on your way out."

CHAPTER TWO

Iғ Henrietta imagined that returning home to Audley Park would ease her restless discontent, she quickly found she was mistaken. The family had spent so little time here when she was growing up that it simply felt like another place to stay. A pleasant place admittedly, now that some of the necessary repairs and redecoration had been completed, largely thanks to Charlotte's husband the duke. But Henrietta, who had so longed to grow up, now found the constrictions placed on a young lady in London were not much relaxed in the country.

When Thomasina and Charlotte were at home, it was different. The three of them often went off together without supervision. But now that there were enough servants, she was told to take a maid to go wild strawberry picking, and not to go out of the grounds when she walked Minnie. Minnie—short for miniature—was the stray puppy adopted at Covent Garden, so named after closer acquaintance had proved her to be a female of the species.

Perhaps it was boredom that so often turned her thoughts toward the banker's son who had stopped her falling down the theater stairs. He was different, not at all part of her social circle, so it was probably inevitable he should intrigue her, though she could not account for the butterflies which soared in her stomach at the sight of him.

She had been very aware of those butterflies when she had glimpsed him again the day after the theater. She and Thomasina had been in a closed carriage with Minnie, on their way to the Green Park for a morning walk, and they had been forced to halt just in front of Claridge's while various trunks and bags were loaded onto a coach. And there, on the front steps, though keeping out of the way of the passing luggage, had stood her savior.

Her heart had given a funny little lurch, and the butterflies had taken flight. Unseen, she had watched him talk and laugh with another man as if he hadn't a care in the world. He had a wonderful, natural laugh that transformed his rather harsh face, adding impossibly to his attraction. It made her smile, breathlessly, even inside the carriage. Then a servant had brought his saddled horse, and he'd mounted unaided, reining in the restive, spirited animal with apparent ease. He'd stretched down to shake hands with his friend and ridden off without ever noticing her.

"Ah, at last!" Thomasina had exclaimed as they were able to move forward.

Henrietta had only peered backward out of the window to catch a last glimpse of her savior's retreating back. She couldn't understand her strange excitement but she had liked it.

It had come back to her over the next few days, too, in fainter and fainter echoes, whenever she'd thought of him. Probably because he was forbidden. After all, she might as well flirt with a footman as a banker. Not that she wished to flirt with either, or at least she didn't think she did. It just added to her general dissatisfaction.

On the third morning of their return to Audley Park, Henrietta simply lost patience with her constrictions and, aiding her young sister Eliza to evade her governess, she put the puppy on the leash and took them both for a long walk toward Seldon Manor. In the spring, they had often met the younger Laceys at the stream which formed the boundary between the two estates, and Henrietta was eager for distracting company. Eliza was a sweet child, if a mischievous one when her twin brother was home. Without him, she tended to wilt into isolated silence. This worried the whole family, though no one had any clear idea what to do about it.

"So, do you like your new governess?" Henrietta asked her as they walked in the sunshine.

"Miss Milsom. I'm beginning to. She doesn't shout. And she tells jokes she thinks no one understands."

Henrietta smiled. "But you do?"

"Do you think I should tell her?"

Henrietta considered. "I think you should smile if it's a funny joke. Or even laugh if it's *really* funny."

"You don't think she'd be angry?"

"I don't think anyone's angry if you laugh at their jokes. I must make a point of cultivating your Miss Milsom."

"Horry will like her, too."

Since the twins generally liked the same people, Henrietta didn't doubt it.

"Are you going to be married, as well?" Eliza asked after a long silence.

Henrietta paused to let Minnie sniff the gnarled old roots of a tree. "Not yet. One day, I suppose." She glanced at her sister. "Do you miss Tommie and Charlie?"

"Charlie said she would never marry. Everyone said that."

"Yes, but then she met his grace. Did Mama tell you, we're *all* going to stay with them in August? Unless they come here."

"Will Tommie come, too?"

"Yes, I think so."

Eliza nodded. "Can I hold the leash?"

Henrietta passed the leash, and when Eliza began to run with the pup, she ran, too.

THEY WERE SITTING on the bank of the stream eating the morsels of ham and bread supplied by Cook, when Matthew and Almeria Lacey rode up on horseback, greeting them with surprised delight.

"We heard you were home, but we did not expect to see you so soon," Almeria explained as they joined them on the bank. "Mama said you would need time to settle in before we called."

"Grown-ups always need time for everything," Eliza remarked.

"Are *we* not grown up?" Matthew teased.

"No," Eliza said, tearing off a tiny morsel of ham for Minnie.

Henrietta watched the pup jump for it. "I used to think when I was grown-up, I could do whatever I wished, but in fact, we're more hemmed in than ever. Or at least," she added with a quick glance at Matthew, "women are."

"Only because you choose to be. You may go where you like if you are just prepared to risk a few frowns."

Almeria laughed. "There would be rather more than a *few* frowns if Henrietta and I walked into the taproom of the Hart Inn, for instance!"

"Why the devil would you want to go there?" Matthew demanded.

"I don't suppose we would," Henrietta said, "but I would like the opportunity, just once, to see what we are missing."

"Go for tea and stick your head around the door," Matthew advised. "It will be quiet at that hour."

"Exactly!" Henrietta pounced. "I want to see it at eight or nine o'clock in the evening, when it's busy."

"Well, I can't think why."

"That's because as a man, you take it for granted you can go there whenever you like."

"Exactly," said Almeria.

"Well, I don't like," Matthew retorted. "I don't think I've been there above twice in my life."

"But if the notion took you, you *could* just walk in there," Henrietta said. "We could not."

"Yes, you could," Matthew disputed, looking somewhat harassed. "You'd just have to be a bit creative, but it's my belief you just don't want to be there. Otherwise, you of all people, Henrie, would have gone already."

"Don't be silly, Matthew," Almeria said. "It would cause a terrible scandal, and Lord Overton would be livid."

"Still," Matthew held out obstinately, "It's my belief she just doesn't want to."

Henrietta regarded him, a wild idea forming in her head and egging her on. "Then I *will* be creative and I will go."

"No, you won't," Matthew said with a derisive smile that was his undoing.

Henrietta smiled back. "Care to wager on that?"

THE HART EXPLOIT was just what Henrietta needed to raise her spirits. Some people, like her sister Charlotte, for example, seemed to fall into adventure without actually trying, but nothing truly interesting had happened to Henrietta since the family had come home from the Peninsula last year. Admittedly, only a few months ago, a London season had been the most exciting thing ever, but after her presentation at court and her first few balls, she had begun to wonder what it was all for. She had actually had more fun at Charlotte's ball in Lincolnshire. And the idea of "catching a husband" had grown both dull and vaguely distasteful. She now preferred the story of Charlotte's sister-in-law, Lady Cecily, who had been scandalously pursued and married by the sinister baron, despite all opposition.

Not that she was a romantic, she told herself, but the idea of being married to a polite and wealthy stranger just for the felicity of being allowed to run his house and bear his children—dear God!—had somehow become unappealing in the extreme. Not that she had forgotten her family duty, but her wager with Matthew Lacey would shake her up, remind her of her love of life.

Accordingly, after dinner, which was early at Audley Park, she raided her brother Richard's bedchamber for clothing. Eliza, who had followed her, watched in silence.

"What do you think?" Henrietta asked, standing in front of the glass in a pair of boots that were slightly too big.

"I think Richard will be mad as fire to see you wearing his favorite pantaloons,"

"Well, most of his clothes are with him at school. This is all there is. I suppose they are a little long, but you can't tell under the boots, can you?"

Eliza shook her head.

"And the coat is a little tight across the chest, but never mind. I do think I managed the cravat quite well. Do I look like a young man, Eliza?"

Eliza considered. "You don't look like Henrietta."

Henrietta laughed. "Then I shall be Henry for a change. Very well, let me take these off again for an hour. I'll plead a headache to Mama. Don't look so worried, Eliza, I'll be back well before morning and no one but you will know I've gone." She hesitated, searching her sister's worried face in the glass before turning toward her. "They won't ask you, Eliza. Just stay out of their way. If they do ask, then you must obviously tell the truth and I'll stand the scold when I get back."

It all seemed perfectly simple, and the first stages of her plan worked perfectly. She climbed down the ivy from her bedchamber window—a trick she had learned during one of their brief visits home when she was a child, and had practiced with Charlotte and Richard last winter. Feeling slightly guilty, she picked Richard's good hat off the flowerbed where it had fallen during her climb. Then, since it was still light, she made sure there was no one to observe her before she sauntered off toward the wood, practicing a male swagger as she went.

At the edge of the wood, Matthew was waiting for her on horseback, leading another slightly smaller mount. He grinned at her. "Good for you! I didn't really think you'd do it, you know."

He began to dismount to help her, but she stayed him with a quick gesture. "No, I'd best practice doing it myself, for it would look very odd if you helped me mount at the inn! Oh, will it look odd if I keep my hat on at the inn? I've tied my hair up tight under it, but I can't really take it off."

"Oh, just shove it to the back of your head in a rakish sort of way. No one there is going to care about etiquette or manners."

Henrietta mounted the rather large horse with only a little difficulty, and they set off through the wood. Sitting astride felt very odd at first, and she wondered how she would manage. However, once she got used to it, she felt balanced and proficient once more.

Riding across country was certainly quicker than going by road, but it was still a good hour's journey to the Hart. It was dusk by the time they got there.

"Did you bring a lantern?" Henrietta asked, wishing she'd thought of it before.

"Of course," Matthew scoffed, watching critically as she dismounted.

"Remember to call me Henrie," she murmured. "Just as my family do."

"It's not hard to remember," he said impatiently, handing over the reins to the waiting ostler. "Come on."

Her heart beating with wicked excitement, Henrietta strolled up to the front door with him. Inside was a hallway leading to a coffee room, a parlor, and the staircase to the bedchambers. It was a little-known fact beyond Henrietta's family, but her sister Charlotte had been married here to the Duke of Alvan. There was no real reason for such a venue or such urgency, and Henrietta had once thought it bizarre behavior on the part of the apparently proper duke. Now, she found she rather liked the spontaneity of it.

Matthew pushed open the door on the right, and the hum of voices beyond exploded. The smell of alcohol and tobacco smoke was so strong it almost blinded her.

"I told you, you wouldn't like it," Matthew murmured in clear amusement.

Henrietta grinned in a way she hoped was boyish. "It just took me by surprise. Lead on."

Inevitably, as strangers, they attracted a bit of attention, although a couple of farmers did nod in greeting to Matthew who, as the squire's son, must have been known to them. Henrietta concentrated on keeping her face stern and walking like a man.

She sat down on the hard bench beside Matthew with just a little relief. However, when a neat and pretty maid came over straight away, asking, "What can I get for you, young sirs?" she began to enjoy herself.

Shoving her hat to the back of her head at the rakish angle suggested by Matthew, she smiled at the maid in the lecherous manner she had observed in several men. The maid didn't blush—no doubt she had to deal with worse all the time—though she did blink rapidly before transferring her attention to Matthew.

"Two pints of ale, if you please," Matthew said hastily. "Oh, and brandy. Your *best* brandy."

"Right away, sir." The maid scurried off.

Matthew glanced at Henrietta in amusement. "Were you flirting with the innkeeper's daughter?"

"With any luck she won't look at me closely again!"

"What if she took a shine to you?"

"Oh, I'm much too lofty to do more than smile at such a person," Henrietta assured him, and he laughed out loud.

"You're game as a pebble, Henrie, I'll give you that."

"So, I've won our wager?"

"Not until we've drunk our ale and got out of here. But I'll tell you what, I've never had so much fun losing before."

The innkeeper's daughter presented them with ale, a bottle of brandy, and two glasses before hurrying on to her next customer. Remaining in character, Henrietta watched her go. After pausing to take the order of a couple of fishermen, almost in passing, she moved on to a lone figure lounging in the shadows at the back of the room. As he spoke to the girl, a not-infrequent memory popped into Henrietta's head—of the man who had saved her from falling down the theater stairs. She didn't know why she thought of him now, for she could not see this man's features clearly and there was little enough to remind her of *him*.

She looked away and somewhat gingerly lifted her mug of ale.

"Good health!" said Matthew and took a sizeable drink.

Henrietta imitated him and couldn't help her grimace as she swallowed. "Heavens, that's nasty."

"Yes, well, another reason ladies don't want to come to such places. Don't drink it all, now, and lay off the brandy, for God's sake, or you'll be drunk as a lord."

"I don't think I could drink it all if I wanted to," Henrietta said.

"The brandy's good, though. Definitely French."

"You mean it's smuggled?" Henrietta said, shocked.

"Of course it is. So is my father's and yours."

"Oh, no," Henrietta denied. "Not Papa's."

"Whatever you say." His surrender was so patronizing that she scowled at him, but he didn't seem to notice. His attention had moved on to a group of men who had just come in. They seemed to be talking among themselves while gazing at Matthew and Henrietta.

"Oh dear, do you think I'm rumbled?" Henrietta asked.

Matthew shrugged. "No reason to think so. But I'll drink up and we can be gone in ten minutes."

Although a mere ten minutes seemed rather tame—not even long enough to rest the horses properly—Henrietta began to see the point. Apart from the curious newcomers, another set of men at the next table seemed to have taken an interest in them, too—and it was they who caused the first trouble.

"Mind if we join you?" said one, a greasy looking individual with a leer in his eye, as he slid along the bench next to Henrietta.

"Actually, yes, we do mind," Matthew snapped, leaning around her to glare at the intruder.

"Think you're too good for us?" sneered the greasy man as his friends moved onto the stools opposite. "Well, *you* might be, young gent, but your companion sure ain't."

Matthew sprang to his feet in outrage. "Now listen here, you—"

"In any case," interrupted a man with a missing front tooth, "we wasn't talking to you."

The greasy man shifted closer yet to Henrietta and rubbed his shoulder and his thighs against hers. Revolted, she sprang to her feet, but he instantly yanked her back down by the arm. She shook him off furiously.

"Come, Henrie," Matthew said grimly. "We're leaving."

"Off you go," the greasy man invited. "Your friend here will have more fun with us, anyway."

Matthew, clearly expecting things only to get uglier, seized Henrietta's arm, and she stood with him. The men all laughed uproariously, rising to their feet in a seriously threatening manner that drew attention from the other patrons.

"Dad!" the innkeeper's daughter called over the counter.

But the man with the missing tooth drew back his fist to strike Matthew. In desperation, Henrietta tried to pull him the other way to escape, forgetting that the greasy man blocked her way.

In the sudden silence, a chair scraped back ominously, loudly enough to distract Matthew's immediate attacker. Even Henrietta glanced toward the sound and saw the solitary man she'd already noticed in the shadows. He stood and walked unhurriedly into the light until he stood beside Matthew.

The man without his front tooth dropped his raised fist. The stranger, who appeared to be their ally, looked around the other men until his gaze finally rested on the greasy one, who stumbled to his feet. In silence, the men melted away to a far distant table. Conversation started up again, buzzing in Henrietta's ears.

She barely noticed because she finally realized why her savior from the theater had sprung into her head when she had first seen the solitary man in the corner. They looked exactly alike. Apart from their dress, and this man's dark-stubbled jaw.

It's him. It has to be...

Slowly, his gaze moved to hers, and the butterflies soared all over again.

"The trouble is," he observed with lazy amusement. "You look nothing like a man."

"I do so!" Henrietta exclaimed.

His eyes laughed at her before they turned in Matthew's bewildered direction. "I suggest you send for whatever vehicle you arrived in. I'll wait with...your companion."

Matthew, clearly, had doubts about that, too, for he frowned in suspicion, clearly undecided what was best.

"I know him," Henrietta blurted.

Matthew's eyes widened, but at least, without further hesitation, he strode off to fetch the horses.

Silently, their savior turned on his heel.

"I thought you were waiting with me?" Henrietta flung at him.

"I can wait as well from over here," he replied and strolled back to the shadowy table from which he'd risen so recently.

Piqued, she sat down again. No one was paying her any attention at all now. As if the word, the protection of this banker's son was law.

A banker? In the theater, it had been conceivable if disappointing. Here, he looked nothing like a banker. Nothing of the respectable middling class clung to him at all. He might have been the banker's twin. *Perhaps that's it. Only what a coincidence that both should come to my rescue in such different ways!* Then again, it was quite a coincidence to come upon the same man here.

She pushed her barely touched mug of ale aside and drummed her fingers on the table. Where the devil was Matthew? In truth, she would rather help him with the horses than sit in here with every-one—except *him*—not looking at her. *His* gaze she could feel burning into her face. But she refused to be ashamed of her attire or her presence.

She stood abruptly and strode across to the door. The innkeeper's daughter stood aside for her.

The fresh night air felt delicious on her skin as she stepped outside and moved toward the stables at the other end of the yard. It was well-lit, so when the groan attracted her attention and she looked up, she saw Matthew's face quite clearly, even though his head lolled between the two men who dragged him between them.

"Leave him!" she shouted, running toward the men and the wait-ing horses.

But they didn't even slow down. They heaved him across the saddle of a man already mounted. One slapped the horse's rump and it took off at a gallop while the other two men leapt into their own saddles and whipped their horses into flight. Henrietta was left running after nothing.

"Oh, dear God," she whispered, tugging at her hair. "What the devil do I do now?"

Follow. She had to follow to at least discover where they were taking Matthew. He'd groaned, so at least they hadn't killed him. Yet. She spun around, running back to the stables.

"My horse!" she gasped to the ostler who was already leading out her borrowed mount. A shadow blocked the light from outside the door and the ostler's eyes went beyond her.

In fear, she jerked around, and saw her savior once more. Or his twin. "They took Matthew!" she blurted. "I think he's unconscious but I can't lose them."

He didn't ask questions, simply strode up to her and boosted her into the saddle before taking his own horse—already saddled—from the ostler. "Come, then. Which way did they go?"

Chapter Three

Since the road was quiet at this time of night, it was remarkably easy to discern and follow the bobbing lanterns of the men in front. In fact, Matthew's abductors slowed up after the initial gallop, clearly not expecting any hue and cry.

"It wasn't the men who bothered us before," Henrietta told her companion.

"Oh, no, they won't trouble you again. There was another group at the front of the room who seemed interested in you, too. They left just before your friend. They were strangers at the inn."

"I don't understand why they would take him with them just to rob him," Henrietta said worriedly.

"Who the devil is he?"

"Matthew Lacey from Seldon Manor."

"The squire's son? Why are you gallivanting in men's clothes with the squire's son?"

"For a wager, of course. We are old friends."

"Not sure he's a very *good* friend."

"It was my idea," she said defensively.

A hiss of laughter escaped him. "Oh, I know *that*." He considered. "There was some sort of ransom racket going on around here not so long ago."

"They caught most of them and scared the rest away," Henrietta said impatiently. "I can't imagine they would come back or inspire anyone to imitation. Sir?"

"Hmm."

"What do you plan to do when you catch them up? Are they afraid of you, too?"

He glanced at her. "I imagine we'll find that out."

"Why are the others afraid of you?" she asked, because she really wanted to know.

"Because I look mean and fierce," he replied flippantly.

"You don't look at all as you did in London. You *are* the same man, aren't you? Not his twin?"

He didn't answer that with more than a crooked smile.

"Thank you for giving Minnie to the doorman," she offered. "I have her with me at Audley Park."

"It didn't put me out in the slightest."

"A friend told me you were a banker."

"I'm sure he did."

"Then you're not?"

He shrugged. "I'm a sea captain. With trade interests."

She frowned. "Then where does the banking come in to it?"

"It's my grandfather's profession, my father's, too, before he died. What a curious girl you are. They've gone right at the crossroads."

"Where does that lead?"

"I have absolutely no idea. This is your country, not mine."

"The trouble is, we were never here much, until this last year, and I don't really know it as I should. But I've been thinking. There were four of them, and there is really only one of us… Unless you have a pistol?" she added hopefully. "If so, I can shoot one of them for you."

"Thank you, I appreciate the generous offer." He paused, examining the road sign pointing where the men had taken Matthew. "Corzone House," he read. "Does that mean anything to you?"

She shook her head. "To my knowledge, I've never met or heard of anyone who lives there. But our acquaintance in Sussex is quite small."

"Is that why you are bored?"

"What makes you think I'm bored?"

"Because it's either that or idiocy that took you to the Hart dressed as a very unconvincing boy."

"I thought I looked excellent as a boy!"

"I never said you did not look good," he said wryly. "I said you were unconvincing."

She eyed him uncertainly, wondering, somewhat ridiculously in the circumstances, if there were a compliment in there. "Anyway, the Hart is a respectable house. Everyone says so. My sisters have taken tea there and even stayed the night."

"Not in the taproom, I'll wager."

This was indisputable. She let her shoulders droop as they wished. "It was an impulse. I thought it would be fun, and it was right up until the end. I certainly never meant anyone to kidnap poor Matthew!"

"No, that does seem very odd behavior." He reached out, grasping her horse's bridle. "Slow down. We don't want them to hear us."

"But shouldn't we rescue him before they take him into the house?"

"Then we might never know why they took him."

"But they won't let us in after him!"

"Oh, there are always ways in," he said vaguely. He glanced at her. "As there are ways out. I don't suppose, for example, you left your own home by the front door tonight."

She brightened. "That is true. I hope the house is covered in ivy, for in this weather, there is bound to be an open window."

She thought his lips twitched, but by then, they had reached a turn in the drive and heard human voices mixed with the snorts of horses which were a little too close for comfort. They reined in and he dismounted silently. Without appearing to look at her—in fact, he seemed to be peering around the curve of the drive—he reached up and lifted her down. His hands were firm on her waist, the strength of his arms obvious. She remembered them catching her as she tumbled down the stairs. She had felt stupidly safe then, too.

There was nothing safe about this situation. From close into the hedge beside him, she edged forward until she could see round to the house itself. Well-lit both inside and out, it was a small, classical dwelling. Henrietta was pleased to note it had a decent covering of ivy in several places.

The men were dragging the struggling figure of Matthew between them up to the entrance. Outraged and terrified for him, Henrietta started forward, but her companion caught her arm, holding her still.

At the top of the front steps, an elderly butler awaited Matthew and his escort.

"Good God, I know *that* Friday face," her companion murmured, releasing her arm. He seemed to be trying not to laugh. "You'll be pleased to know we won't need the ivy after all." Leading his horse, he walked openly around the curve of the drive toward the house.

All Henrietta could do was trot after him with her own mare. They tied the horses to the rail on the terrace, without anyone appearing to notice their arrival. The captain walked up the steps and pulled the bell, while Henrietta could only follow, with bewildered dread but fierce determination in her heart.

The captain spared her a reassuring smile. Then the door opened and the same butler stood there. His eyes widened with alarm, even as his mouth dropped open.

"Evening, Tranter," the captain said, brushing past the astonished butler. Henrietta scuttled after him. "Take us up to her ladyship!"

Who would, presumably, deal harshly with the violent criminals in her house. Cheered, Henrietta pushed her hat to the back of her head and looked about her. Although well-lit and elegant, the entrance hall gave unmistakable signs of recent neglect. It smelled musty and a few cobwebs hung about the corners.

The butler, Tranter, turned toward a doorway on the left. "Please step in here, sir, and I shall inform her ladyship—"

"Imbeciles!" The shouted insult came from a woman in one of the rooms to the right.

And it was in that direction her companion immediately strode. "No need, Tranter. We'll find our own way."

Thoroughly intrigued now, Henrietta hurried after him, listening with some satisfaction to the continuation of the lady's scold. "How old is this boy? Nineteen? Twenty? Does he look *anything* like the mature and dangerous man I sent *four* of you to bring to me?"

Henrietta stopped dead in the doorway, her pleasure evaporating. The lady, whoever she was, had *caused* this. The captain, however, didn't miss a step as he strolled past Henrietta into the room, finally attracting the attention of all inside.

The lady and the four ruffians gawped at him. One of the men moved instinctively toward him, allowing Henrietta a glimpse of Matthew who sat slumped on the floor, his head in his hand. There was blood on his fingers, on his cravat.

With a cry, Henrietta launched herself across the room and threw herself down beside her old friend. "Matthew!"

He raised his head, staring at her from slightly unfocused eyes. "Henrie?"

Henrietta took his hand and glared at the lady who merely cast her a curious glance before returning to the captain.

"You could have sent a note," he said mildly. "A civil invitation."

"Would you have come?" she drawled.

He spread his hands. "Here I am. Although flattered that you sent four men to bring me, you must have given them a very bizarre description."

"He were the only toff in the place!" exclaimed the nearest ruffian.

The lady waved one careless hand toward Matthew. She was quite beautiful, all golden hair and white, perfect skin. It was impossible to guess her age. She could have been twenty-three or thirty-five. "And how threatening does he look to you, fool?"

"He could be," Henrietta raged. "If he were not set upon by four men at once! Shame on all of you for cowardly scoundrels!"

The lady regarded her with aloof fascination. "My dear, who *is* this? *What* is this?"

"I believe you've lost the right to a formal introduction," the captain said, strolling across the room. "You may regard her as a severely ruffled feather."

Henrietta kept her furious gaze on the lady. "I require water, salve, and bandages for his wound. And you had better not have killed him."

A brief amusement flitted through the lady's cold eyes. "He does not look dead to me." She turned her head to the uncomfortably waiting butler, who left. More impatiently, she dismissed the four incompetent ruffians who fell over themselves to get out the door first.

The captain, meanwhile, appeared to be helping himself to a glass of brandy from the decanter on a slightly dusty cabinet. Henrietta's hackles rose afresh. He was already far too comfortable in this situation, with this woman he clearly knew very well, and now he was drinking her brandy.

"You always travel with the comforts of home," he observed, walking back toward Henrietta and Matthew. "Is this establishment a recent acquisition or have you merely borrowed it in the owner's absence?" To Henrietta's surprise, he crouched down beside her and shoved the brandy glass into Matthew's hand. "Drink this, it will make you feel more human."

"You needn't make me sound like a flim-flammer," the lady snapped. "Of course, the house is mine. If you must know, it was my dowry. A trumpery thing, but finally useful."

"For what?" the captain asked, watching Matthew's face as he obediently sipped the brandy.

"For finding you, of course!"

The captain glanced up at her. "Should I be flattered? Again?"

"No," the lady said crossly. "You have something of mine and I need it returned before you disappear back to sea or whatever else it is you get up to."

He rose to his feet as Tranter came back into the room bearing a bowl of water and a small chest under his arm. Henrietta thanked the butler and took them from him. At least Matthew was looking a little better. The frightening pallor of his face had warmed slightly and his gaze seemed steadier.

Although she had little experience dealing with wounds—her mother and later Charlotte had always taken care of such things—she had received a lady's education which included the proper care for sick and injured members of the household. In normal circumstances, of course, one would have servants to direct, but she was not about to trust Matthew to any of *this* lady's people.

"Sorry, Matthew, I don't want to hurt you," she murmured, and set about cleaning him up. Concentrating on her task, she nevertheless kept her ears open.

"You're not even wearing it," the lady said angrily. It was an odd anger. Henrietta couldn't tell if was mere irritation for the upset of her plan, or if she was genuinely hurt. But the nature of their relationship began to dawn on her with considerable distaste.

From the corner of her eye, she saw him walk close up to her, saw the lady's breast heave in brief agitation before her cool, mocking manner returned.

"I'll send it to you," he said. "Why is it so urgent?"

"Edward is ill," the lady said carelessly. "Wants everything brought to him so he can make his will all over again."

The captain curled his lip. "You gave me Edward's ring? And they say *I* am vulgar?"

"Don't try to be self-righteous," she said with contempt. "It doesn't suit you."

"Who the devil are these people?" Matthew asked Henrietta, low-voiced. "And what on earth do they want with me?"

"Nothing," Henrietta said ruefully. "Her stupid servants—or hired bravos, whatever they are—took you in mistake for *him*. No one has any idea how they made such a mistake. But I have to say that *he* has been quite helpful in finding you."

"You know him already." Matthew frowned with the effort of remembrance. His head must have ached like the very devil.

"Not really. I met him once. He was at the theater the night I found Minnie, and he saved me from falling head-first down the stairs. I don't think this will have to be stitched, Matthew. It seems to have stopped bleeding. Let me just dress it and bandage it for now."

"Where is it?" the lady was asking the captain. "In London? Or in Sussex?"

"I'll send it to you," he repeated. "You'll have it the day after to-morrow."

"I suppose that will have to do. Pour us some brandy, Sydney, and I'll get them to make up a room for the night."

So, his name was Sydney. Henrietta couldn't make up her mind if it suited him or not.

After a moment, he walked to the decanter once more. "Don't bother. I won't stay. I'll be taking my friends home."

"There's two of them," the lady said carelessly, as if they weren't present and listening. "Can't they take each other home?"

"No." He sloshed brandy into two glasses. "Thanks to your people, I doubt he can take himself to the front door." Unexpectedly, he glanced at Henrietta. "A spot of brandy, ma'am, to keep out the cold? Or shall I prevail upon our hostess for some other refreshment?"

"No, thank you," Henrietta said coldly, winding the bandage about Matthew's head.

"There you are," Sydney told the lady, depositing one glass into her waiting, elegant hand. Carelessly, he clinked the side of his own glass against it and tossed the contents down his throat.

"I suppose they can stay as well," the lady said grudgingly.

Sydney laughed. "My dear, you are priceless. Can you think of any reason why they would?" He threw his glass down on the table and walked up to Matthew, holding down his hand to him. "Come, my friend, time to stand up."

Henrietta took the glass from him.

Matthew took Sydney's hand and pulled himself up. "Not so bad," he pronounced in apparent surprise.

"Can you ride?" Sydney asked.

"Yes, I think so."

"Drat, there are only two horses," Henrietta exclaimed in sudden dismay.

"Well, you're only a slip of a girl," the lady drawled, "and weigh as little as the ruffled feather he called you. I'm sure the gentlemen will think of something. I'm sure you'll excuse me if I retire at this point. I've had a disturbed night."

"*She's* had a disturbed night," Matthew said wrathfully as she made her perfect exit. "She'll have a damned sight more when the magistrates are after her and her bullies!"

"I wouldn't bother," Sydney advised. "She's very well connected."

"So am I," Matthew fumed. "My father is the magistrate!"

"Yes, but you are hamstrung by other considerations," Sydney pointed out with a glance at Henrietta. He actually closed one eye in the subtlest of winks, and quite inappropriate laughter caught at her breath.

"Damn it, so I am," Matthew agreed, following the captain to the door. "I'm sorry, Henrietta, I don't know what I was thinking letting you commit this folly!"

"*Letting* me?" Henrietta said at once. "I seem to remember you only came along to protect me. Or at least win the wager."

"Well, I've made a mess of both," Matthew said ruefully.

"But only think of the fun you're having," Sydney pointed out, leading the way across the hall to the front door.

"Well, it has been fun for us," Henrietta said, surprised to discover this was true, now that her anxiety had abated. "For Matthew, not so much."

"I could live without the headache," Matthew agreed, stepping past the captain into the fresh air. "But only think how frustrating, Henrie, we can never talk about this!"

Henrietta walked down the steps behind him. "Well, I shall have to tell Eliza, and Charlotte will love the story, but no, I don't think we should tell our parents. Or Almeria."

"We may have to tell them something," Matthew said grimly, "if your absence is discovered. After all, we've already been gone far longer than we intended."

"You might have to marry him," Sydney said, untying Henrietta's horse.

"She might have to marry *you*," Matthew retorted.

"Sadly, I am unmarriageable, or I would consider it an honor as well as a pleasure."

"Why are you unmarriageable?" Matthew demanded. "Leaving aside our late hostess."

Sydney held the stirrup for him, signifying he should mount. "You are guessing, wrongly as it happens. Besides, you are not so naive as to imagine such relationships are impediments to genteel marriage."

Matthew landed in the saddle. "What is then?"

"Birth."

Matthew stared at him. "You mean, you're not a gentleman?"

"Matthew!" Henrietta exclaimed.

But the captain only laughed. "Do you want to go back to the lady of the house? I assure you, her lineage is impeccable."

Matthew flushed. "I didn't mean that, and of course I'm grateful, whoever the devil you are. I was only concerned for Miss Maybury."

"Well, stop bandying my name about," Henrietta advised, holding up her hand, "and take me up in front so that I can guide the horse."

"I'm perfectly capable of guiding him myself!" Matthew exclaimed.

"No, you're not. You've been hit on the head and not half an hour ago you couldn't even focus on my face."

"Well, I can now," Matthew retorted, making it clear it gave him no pleasure.

Henrietta smiled at him. "You are a gudgeon," she said affectionately.

Matthew's eyes narrowed, and she knew she had said precisely the wrong thing.

However, before she could make it right, Sydney made a noise of impatience, seized her around the waist, and swung her up into his saddle instead. "We don't have time for this. You have parents to placate, and I have the morning tide to catch." He leapt up behind her and gathered up the reins, presumably in case she imagined she had any chance of guiding *his* horse. "Matthew, this is your country. Since you're injured, I suggest we go first to your house. How long from here?"

"Under two hours to Seldon—maybe an hour and a half if we take the shortcuts. But then it's another hour to Audley Park."

"And your horse is still at the Hart," Henrietta remembered.

"I'll deal with the horse," Sydney said. "I expect you fell off it when you hurt your head, so it will be no surprise to your family when a stranger brings back the horse tomorrow morning."

"You're very good at this," Henrietta said admiringly.

He spared her a glance, reminding her how close he was. His arms enclosed her, his chest brushed against her back as he reined the horse around to face the drive. "Thank you. I'm adapting. Lead on, Matthew, fast as you're comfortable with, but for God's sake, say if you feel sick or dizzy. It can happen after a blow to the head, and the last thing any of us need is for you to be injured further."

Chapter Four

Making use of the lanterns to light their way, they reached Seldon Manor in good time and without mishap. Henrietta was very aware of her uncharacteristic silence during the journey, but she had a lot to think about. To begin with, she worried about Matthew's head wound and if he was truly well enough to ride. And then, she felt very strange, both oppressed and excited by riding with Sydney so close behind her.

Not that there was anything remotely amorous about his attitude, for there wasn't. Apart from inevitable and accidental contact, he never touched her, and he also was silent and somewhat remote during the ride.

"We're on the Seldon estate now," she observed as she finally recognized the landmark river and gentle slopes, and the manor house standing clear and sharp under the moonlight. "We should be able to get right up to the drive without disturbing anyone…unless I've been discovered missing and Eliza has had to give us away."

But as they approached the drive, all was quiet and most of the house lights were out.

Matthew waited for them to catch up. "I think we must have got away with it," he said with a quick grin. "No more wagers, Henrie."

"Best pay up then," she teased. "Or it will be double or quits."

"Hoyden," Matthew accused and stretched out his hand to Sydney. "I'm sorry for being ungracious. I truly do appreciate your intervention and your escort home. And for what it's worth, I do trust you to look after Miss Maybury. You've certainly done better than I so far!"

Sydney shook his hand, with a lopsided smile.

"Be good, brat," Matthew said to her.

"Brat yourself," she returned with a quick smile. "And Matthew? Perhaps ask the doctor to take a look at your head?"

"Perhaps," he agreed. "Good night."

For a few moments, they watched him ride along the side of the house to the stables, then the captain wheeled the horse around. "This way to Audley Park, I believe."

Once clear of the house, they rode fast for the first time, as though both horse and captain were quite familiar with the route. It was exhilarating, but also alarming, especially in wooded areas, and Henrietta found herself shrinking closer to her companion as though for protection. She pulled herself away at once, grasping the pommel with both hands instead.

"I won't let you fall," he promised.

"It's the horse falling that worries me," she said breathlessly. She cast a glance over her shoulder. "You've spent all night on our business, and I have not even thanked you."

He slowed the horse as the wood thickened ahead. "I beg you will not. I believe I have enjoyed it."

"You are just being kind," she said, and his gaze dropped quickly to her face.

"I'm not known for it."

"Then you should be." She straightened, staring between the horse's ears, and took a deep breath. "That night in the theater, when my family was leaving, I pretended not to see you. Someone told me who you were. I'm sorry, that was unforgivably rude."

"Oh, ladies give men the cold shoulder all the time."

"Yes, but not in *this* way," she objected. "And not after such a service. I wish I hadn't."

He didn't say anything for a moment. Then something touched the top of her head, like a kiss, and her whole body flushed.

"You're very sweet."

"I wasn't sweet at all," she said gruffly, "so why *did* you help us?"

"Boredom and curiosity."

She could understand both of those so well that she merely nodded, her mind flitting on to other questions. "Are you hurt that the lady wants her ring back?" She heard his intake of breath and glanced over her shoulder. "I'm sorry, that was indelicate, wasn't it? And obviously none of my business. It's just that I wasn't sure you noticed *she* seemed hurt that you were not wearing her gift."

He regarded her. "Are you trying to mend my entirely irregular and adulterous relationship?"

"Put like that, it doesn't sound quite so romantic," she allowed. "But I do like people to be happy."

"You are thinking about married couples, which is not the same thing at all."

"I expect it's not so different," she argued. "Except, I suppose, liaisons are easier to get out of. One cannot end a distasteful marriage. Or at least, not without a great deal of trouble and scandal."

"Are you thinking of entering such a marriage?" he inquired.

"Hardly. Only...it never entered my head until recently that any marriage was distasteful. It was merely the duty of a lady of birth, and stupidly, I was eager to make a better one than my sisters. Only then, Charlotte married the Duke of Alvan, and I don't think anyone can better that."

"There's always a royal duke or a foreign prince."

"You're making fun of me."

"I think you were making fun of yourself."

She smiled. "I was. Apart from poor Matthew's head, I had a lot more fun tonight than I've had all this season. I don't think I want to be married at all."

"How old are you? Nineteen? Twenty?"

"Eighteen," she confessed.

"Dear God," he uttered for no obvious reason, causing her to twist around again to look at him in surprise. His smile was twisted. "You are a bit of a handful, aren't you? You have plenty of time to meet and marry some poor devil and lead him a merry dance. He'll love every minute of it, too."

She thought about that for a moment. It didn't sound so bad, but she couldn't quite picture it. "What about you? Will you marry the lady if her husband dies?"

"God, no."

"Don't you love her?"

He stared down at her. "No. There is no love on either side. And if there were, she would not marry out of her own class. Not many would. Why are we talking about marriage? Are you contemplating the evils of being forced to marry young Matthew?"

She laughed. "Oh, that wouldn't be evil, precisely, since we're friends. But we are quite unsuited. And he's too young."

"Says the mature lady of eighteen summers."

"I miss travelling," she confided. "I didn't think I would, because being at home and going to balls was different."

"Where have you travelled?" he asked curiously, and she told him something about the family's adventures in America and Russia, Portugal and Spain.

"I appreciate it all so much more now," she added. "Since most people are trapped at home by the war. Sailing must be risky for you."

"It can be a little hair-raising."

"I expect that's why you do it," she said shrewdly. "How did you go from banking to sailing?"

"I ran away from school. But that is a story for another day."

To her surprise, they were already approaching Audley Park. Over the house, the sky was already lightening.

"It's almost dawn," she observed. "What time do you sail?"

"About seven."

She frowned. "Where from?"

"Close by," he said vaguely.

"Are you going somewhere exciting?"

"Oh no. Mostly short journeys, around the coast and so on. How is the best way to approach the house?"

"Follow the edge of the wood around to the back of the house and I can run from there."

He obeyed and at last reined in his horse. The house was still, shuttered and dark. So far as she could tell, there was no panic caused by the discovery of her absence.

She twisted in the saddle, strangely sad that the adventure was over, instead of relieved as she should have been.

"Thank you for *everything*, Captain Sydney," she said warmly.

A smile curved his lips and lightened his rather hard eyes. "Call me Sydney. Or Captain. But not both together. Sydney's my Christian name."

"That doesn't seem very proper," she said. "What is your sur-name?"

"Cromarty. But don't hold it against me. One thing before you go... Don't take risks as you did tonight. That could have been you instead of Matthew."

She opened her mouth to say something trite about even the lady's servants not being stupid enough to mistake her for the captain, but seeing the seriousness in his eyes, she bit her lip and only nodded. "It was foolish," she agreed humbly, although she spoiled it with an irrepressible smile. "But I did enjoy it!"

He laughed. "Go away, hoyden." His hands closed around her waist, lifting her so that she could swing her leg over the saddle, and then he let her slip gently to the ground.

Suddenly and rather stupidly shy, she stretched up her hand.

"Goodbye, Captain. And thank you."

"Goodbye, my sweet." His tone was teasing as he took her hand, bent from the saddle, and kissed her fingers. He released her. "Good luck."

Suddenly breathless, she smiled just a little tremulously and fled across the garden toward the house. The fingers he had kissed were tingling. She stroked them with her thumb as she ran.

CAPTAIN CROMARTY WATCHED her with an odd pain behind his enjoyment. She was sweet and fun and innocent, and very much not the type of woman he admired. And yet, he liked to look at her in those shocking boy's clothes as much as he had in her fashionable gown at the theater. When she reached the wall of the house, she really did jump up and begin climbing up the ivy, using footholds in the stone as well, as agile as a monkey and a hundred times as brave.

He waited until she all but fell through the open window on the first floor. His breath hissed out in laughter. Thank God she was not for him. He wheeled his horse around and rode hard for the Hart.

He arrived under a beautiful, golden sunrise, looking forward to two hours' sleep before he went on board. But inside the inn, he was confronted by a bizarre repetition of the first evening he had seen Henrietta Maybury.

Mrs. Villin, the innkeeper's wife, emerged from her kitchen. "Morning, Captain! There's a gentleman waiting in your bedchamber."

"For the love of… What the devil did you let him in for?"

"He's a gentleman, sir!" Mrs. Villin said, shocked.

"Exactly. I'll only kick him out again!"

Mrs. Villin sniffed. "That's your privilege, sir, not mine."

He narrowed his eyes. "You do remember I asked for a *private* bedchamber?"

But Mrs. Villin could not be intimidated. It was one of the reasons he liked her. "You'll understand when you see him."

Cursing beneath his breath, he strode up the stairs, eager to throw out the damned lawyer so that he could sleep.

All but kicking open his bedchamber door, he marched in. "Out, Godfrey, I won't be har—"

He broke off as a gentleman rose from the chair by the window. Not Godfrey but a much older and much haughtier gentleman. Ramrod straight and perfectly dressed, the pouches of age under his eyes and jowls did not diminish the fierce gleam in his eyes. His pure white hair did not seem to have thinned but merely receded at the temples. A distinguished man, still, in his own world.

Cromarty had only seen him once in his life before, and that from a distance, beyond his father's grave. He had never had any desire to see him again and nothing had occurred to change that.

Cromarty threw his hat on the bed. "Forgive my rudeness, my lord, but I must ask you to bespeak your own chamber. For I am about to sleep in this one."

"Yes, they said you were insolent."

Cromarty lifted his brow. "This from the man trespassing in another's private chamber."

"Trespassing!" The old gentleman waved his cane in disparagement. "I'm your grandfather!"

When Cromarty had been a boy, he had longed for this moment. Older and wiser, now, he still took it. "No, you're not," he said deliberately.

The old man smiled thinly. "Waited a long time to throw that in my face, eh?"

Cromarty shrugged. "When I was a child, I thought it mattered because it hurt my father. It never hurt me."

"Godfrey told you, you're now my heir."

"How can I be when my father was not your son? When you believe *I* was not *his* son and my mother some whore desperate to get her hands on the family silver?"

The old man flushed slightly. "I was angry. I said things I did not mean. Everyone makes mistakes in their lives."

"You had many years to acknowledge your mistakes. There is no point in doing so to me."

"I came to his burial," the old man uttered, turning away.

Cromarty curled his lips. "That must have meant a lot to him."

"Damnation, you bear almighty grudges, man!"

Cromarty laughed. "Sir, the only grudge I bear you is that you prevent me from sleeping. I sail in less than three hours."

"Sail? From here? Then it's true, you're a damned smuggler. That will have to stop."

Cromarty lifted one eyebrow. "Then who would supply your fine cognac?"

The old man turned a worrying shade of purple as he tried not to rise to that bait. Eventually, somewhat to his grandson's surprise, he succeeded. With an attempt at coolness, he asked, "Why do you bother? At five-and-thirty, are you not a little old for schoolboy pranks?"

"Have to earn a crust," Cromarty murmured, yawning rudely as he sat down on the bed.

"Liar. I'm well aware the extent of the "crusts" you earn from perfectly legitimate enterprises!"

"I have my share of the family firm," Cromarty said carelessly. "And believe it or not, despite disappointing my own father in my initial choice of trade, I learned a lot from him. He had an eye for investments and stocks, you know. Took to it like a duck to water. In short, you might call me a "warm" man, in terms of wealth. I don't need yours. I don't want yours. And I certainly don't want to move in your world, being toadied by the very imbeciles who once shunned my father and me. Let your damned title die out. I don't care."

"*I* care!" bellowed the old man.

Cromarty stretched out on the bed and closed his eyes. He wished he could sleep, but his grandfather's heavy breathing distracted him.

"I hear Lady Carew doesn't shun you," the old man said slyly.

Cromarty opened one eye. "But she don't invite me to parties, and we only bow distantly in public."

The old man glared at him from across the room. Cromarty closed his eye again.

"Come to Steynings," the old man said abruptly.

"My ship is waiting for me."

"Come to Steynings, within two weeks. I have something of your father's you should have."

In spite of himself, he found he was squeezing his eyes shut. "No."

"I'm an old man and I'm stubborn. I acknowledge mistakes. I want to make it right."

"You can't," Cromarty said simply. "It's too late."

There was silence, and then movement within the room. "Is it?"

Footsteps crossed the floor and the door closed. Cromarty's eyes sprang open and he punched the pillow. *Damn the old bastard. How am I to sleep now?*

CHAPTER FIVE

AMAZINGLY ENOUGH, HENRIETTA'S extended adventure went unnoticed by any except Eliza, whom she found asleep on her bed when she lit the candle. Hastily, she undressed and donned her nightrail and a dressing gown before shoving Richard's clothes to the back of her wardrobe to be returned later.

She hesitated over whether or not to wake Eliza, who, in her dressing gown, lay over rather than under the covers. She was trying to pull the sheet gently out from under her when the child woke up and threw her arms around Henrietta's neck.

Surprised and rather touched, Henrietta hugged her back.

"I thought you'd gone," Eliza whispered. "You were so long."

"I was longer than I intended, but of course I came home in the end. Do you want to sleep here or in your own chamber?"

"I'll go back now," Eliza said.

Henrietta lit the way for her, tucked her up in bed, and blew out her candle before returning to her own room and falling, finally, into bed.

OVER THE NEXT few days, Henrietta thought a lot about Captain Cromarty. She had never met anyone like him before, so it was not surprising that he would pop into her head at odd times, remembering amusing things he'd said, the smile in his eyes, or the total confidence with which he had faced both threatening men and the beautiful lady who had been responsible for Matthew's mistaken abduction.

She wondered a lot about his odd life, this son of a banker, turned sea captain who seemed to know rather too much about smuggled brandy. He spoke like a gentleman, had seemed as much at home at the theater as in the Hart taproom. He was not the sort of man she would ever have been introduced to in the normal course of her life. Her father might talk business—or brandy—with him in his study, but he would never be invited to her mother's drawing room.

And yet, he intrigued her more than any man she had yet encountered. In itself, that was a curiosity, but one she rather liked.

Socially, not a great deal was happening in the neighborhood, so Lady Overton decided to hold an informal dinner party, inviting Lord Verne, the sinister baron himself, for the first time. Now that he was married to Lady Cecily, the daughter of a duke and Charlotte's sister-in-law, he was considered respectable enough to be in the house.

"I could take the invitation over to Finmarsh House," Henrietta offered at breakfast when her mother had voiced her decision. "Cecily will love to meet Minnie. Eliza could come with me, perhaps."

"And Miss Milsom," her mother said brightly, smiling at the governess. "Do you want the carriage?"

"It would be quicker to ride," Henrietta said. "Do you ride, Miss Milsom?"

The governess's rather severe face brightened, making her suddenly appear much younger. "Oh yes."

"Well, be sure to take one of the grooms," Lady Overton commanded.

Lord Overton, who was rifling the post beside his plate, cast a card of invitation toward his wife. "What do you think of that, my dear? Old Silford is holding a ball over at Steynings, and invites us."

"Good lord, how unusual. I thought he would be in mourning.

Did one of his grandsons not die unexpectedly?"

"Tragic thing. I expect his name and the title will die out now," Lord Overton said.

"Well, we must go. An invitation to Steynings is too rare to miss. And we are invited to spend the night since it is too far to travel home afterward. There, Henrie, a ball to enliven your spirits!"

"My spirits are not low," Henrietta protested.

"Here's a letter from Rudd," Lord Overton said, tossing that, too, toward his wife. "Wants us to go to Brighton to some soiree of the Prince Regent's. He says an invitation will be forthcoming."

"Oh, good. I wonder if Rudd means to offer for Henrietta?"

There was a time when the prospect of a proposal from such an eligible gentleman would have filled Henrietta and the entire household with excitement. She thought back to the massive upheaval when they were sure the Duke of Alvan was coming to offer for Thomasina. Henrietta had been more pleased by that prospect than by receiving her own proposal.

She supposed it was different now the family was no longer in financial difficulties. There seemed no great triumph or happiness in receiving Rudd's addresses. In fact, she rather hoped he would not speak, for she didn't want to answer. She didn't want to think about him at all.

So, she finished breakfast, went to change into her riding habit, and collected the letter from her mother to Lady Cecily.

Although it was her first visit to Finmarsh House, Henrietta had no difficulty finding the way. Since coming home last year—and indeed on their infrequent visits before that—she and her siblings had made a point of sneaking onto the sinister baron's estate in the hope of a glimpse of this terrifying personage. In fact, their one sighting had been in Finsborough, and that only the back of his head. Until last month, when he had attended the Alvans' ball.

This sighting had been much more satisfactory, and Henrietta looked forward to seeing him again. His wife, the Duke of Alvan's sister, was already a favorite of all the family. In fact, on first meeting her, Henrietta had found her everything she herself wished to be—beautiful, graceful, witty, and supremely comfortable in any company.

They were taken up to a drawing room on the first floor, where Lady Cecily, more properly Lady Verne, sat surrounded by samples of curtains and chair coverings.

"How wonderful," she greeted them warmly, coming to kiss Henrietta's and Eliza's cheeks. She even shook hands with the governess, whom she had never met before, and sent for refreshments.

"I thought the house would be much darker and scarier than this," Eliza said in clear disappointment.

"Well, it was," Cecily said. "But we are making it brighter and more welcoming, for although it may be more interesting as it was, it is not quite so comfortable to live that way! Goodness, Henrie, who is this?" she added, becoming aware at last of Minnie who clung to Henrietta's skirts.

Enticed, the puppy pranced toward her and made friends, and soon everyone, even Miss Milsom, was sitting on the floor and playing with her.

"Oh. I nearly forgot the main purpose of our visit!" Henrietta exclaimed at last, extracting her mother's note from where she had tucked it inside her riding habit. "Which is to invite you and Lord Verne to dinner on Friday. The Laceys are invited, too, and the Walshes. But it won't be a large party."

"It sounds delightful," Cecily assured her. "Verne will be up shortly, but he's closeted with his estate people for the next half-hour. You will stay for luncheon?"

After a rather amusing interlude helping Cecily decide upon her fabrics, they decided it was too beautiful a day to stay indoors and went outside to walk in the gardens. After the deaths of the previous Lord and Lady Verne, who had kept the gardens very formal and neat, the sinister baron had let them run wild. Cecily had tamed them without making them in any way artificial, and they were currently a riot of color and sweet summer scents.

Minnie was delighted, sniffing everything and tugging at her leash to get at the next delicious smell. After a little, she pulled with more force. Amused, Henrietta gave in, half-running with the pup along the paths, and around a most beautiful red-rose bush until she saw a male figure approaching the house. At first, with the sun in her eyes, she thought it was Lord Verne, escaped from his estate meetings. But then her heart gave a funny little lurch, for this man walked with more of an unconscious swagger that was quite familiar.

Any doubt was removed by Minnie who lurched at him, her little paws scrabbling on the spot in her desperation to get to him. Henrietta let herself be dragged a few more steps until she could see his face, but all his attention appeared to be on the puppy who was wagging her tail off and trying to lick his boots. He dropped into a crouch, and Henrietta slackened the lead to let her jump onto his knee. His large hands caught Minnie as she tried to lick his face, ruffling her fur in a careless caress.

Henrietta was too stunned to think of anything to say. And when he lifted his gaze to her face, her mouth dried.

"Does she remember me?" he asked. "Or is she like this with everyone?"

"I'd say she remembers you. She dragged me across the garden to get to you. Are you a friend of Lord Verne's?"

He rose to his feet. She had forgotten how tall he was, how imposing. "We've known each other a few years. Are you?"

"My sister is married to Lady Verne's brother."

His lips quirked. "The tangled web of the aristocracy. Were you found out?"

It took her a moment to think what he meant. Then she smiled. "No, I got away with it. So did Matthew, although his father read him a very mean lecture about getting in such a state at the tavern that he fell off his horse. Poor Matthew had to bite his tongue and bear it."

Cromarty grinned, causing butterflies to rise in her stomach.

"How was your trip?" she asked. "I hope you got to your ship in time."

"Profitable, and yes, I did. Who needs sleep when one can rescue damsels in disguise?"

She didn't know if he was teasing or flirting—heady thought—so she was almost glad to be interrupted by Eliza's childish exclamation. *"There* she is!"

Almost guiltily, she turned to face her sister, Miss Milsom, and Lady Cecily.

"Captain Cromarty," Cecily said in some surprise.

The captain bowed. Although dressed informally in a worn, brown coat, carrying a wide-brimmed hat, he performed the courtesy with the same grace as in the theater.

"Are you here to see Verne?" Cecily asked, offering her hand.

Although the captain shook hands with her, Henrietta could have sworn he was surprised. "If he is available."

"Go up. I think his guests have gone, but he's probably still in the library."

"Thank you." He bowed to the rest of the company and sauntered on up the path to the house.

"You know him," Henrietta observed as she walked with Cecily in the other direction.

"Verne introduced us. They are old friends. More to the point, how do *you* know him?"

Henrietta considered. Cecily had no real evidence that she had known him before running into him here. Then again, their first meeting was respectable enough to share. "We met at the theater. He helped me rescue Minnie. I confess, I was surprised to find him here."

"So was I." Cecily glanced at Henrietta. "You do know he's not exactly a *respectable* person?"

Henrietta lifted her chin. "Because his father was a banker?"

"No, because he's a smuggler!" Cecily frowned suddenly. "I didn't know his father was a banker."

CROMARTY, THROWN AND yet not at all unhappy to have discovered Henrietta there, wandered up to the house, but didn't walk round to the front door. Instead, he followed the garden path to the library's French windows, through which he could see Verne writing busily at his desk.

Cromarty tapped on the window, then opened it and strolled inside.

Verne glanced across, then his eyebrows flew up and he tossed down his pen, spattering ink across the desk. "Good Lord. To what do I owe the honor? There's no trouble, I hope."

"None that I heard of. I was just passing, thought I'd drop in and see how your rehabilitation was going."

Verne rose and went to the decanter. "Why? Considering one of your own?"

"Hardly. In any case, mine is immutable. Your lady was remarkably welcoming, especially considering she has guests."

"Does she? Well, Cecily accepts people for who they are, not what the world says they are. I should know." He came back, dropped a glass into Cromarty's hand, and clinked his own off it. "Your health."

"And yours."

They both drank, and Verne waved him to a seat by the window.

"So, are you?" Cromarty asked, sitting down.

"Rehabilitated?" Verne gave a slightly contemptuous shrug. "In part. Apparently, the world cannot believe the Duke of Alvan would marry his sister to a murdering arsonist, so most are prepared to give me the benefit of the doubt."

"Do you care?" Cromarty asked.

"For Cecily's sake."

Cromarty searched the face of the young man he'd known since fishing him out of the sea when he was sixteen. And made a discovery. "You're happy."

A tinge of color crept into Verne's cheeks. "I seem to like being married. You should try it."

"You mean give up the sea and marry some prim banker's daughter? No, thank you."

"There's always Lily at the Hart."

"Lily is too good for me. Besides, she makes me uncomfortable."

"Really?" Verne sounded amused. "Why?"

Cromarty shrugged. "She sees too much. It's as if she reads your soul in your face."

"You have a point. I suspect she gave both Cecily and me a little push toward each other. Which is odd when you consider how ill-suited the rest of the world thought us."

"Her parents say they run a lucky house," Cromarty said disparagingly.

"I don't know about that." Verne laughed suddenly. "Though my friend Alvan first met his wife there, too, so who knows? Will you stay for luncheon?"

Cromarty blinked. "Good God, no. You'll be ostracized again before you know it. No, it's time I was off. Thanks for the wine."

"Pleasure."

"I'll be gone for a few days."

Verne understood him immediately, for it was he who'd first involved Cromarty in smuggling spies into France with British manufactured goods—and bringing them home again to England with information, fine cognac, and wine. "I'll keep an eye on things."

Cromarty dropped his glass on the desk and turned away, just as the door opened and Lady Verne came in with Henrietta and her other guests. It was odd, but the library seemed to light up.

He wasn't normally on visiting terms with Verne. He could count the number of times he had been inside the house on one hand. He fully expected Verne to announce that the captain was just leaving. It was what Susannah Carew did whenever they were interrupted by her "quality" callers.

But Verne merely said cheerfully, "Good afternoon, ladies. Have you come to root us out for luncheon?"

"If you wish to come," Cecily said. "Since it's such a beautiful day, we thought we would take it into the garden."

"Why not?" Verne said. "I don't suppose you know Captain Cromarty? Cromarty, Miss Maybury, Miss Eliza Maybury, and Miss…" He paused at the dowdier lady who looked like a poor relation. "I'm sorry, ma'am, I'm forgetful with names!"

"Miss Milsom," Henrietta said. "She's Eliza's new governess."

Cromarty bowed to everyone once more. "I'll leave you to enjoy your al fresco." He was sure disappointment flickered across Henrietta's face, and he couldn't resist a quick grin and a conspiratorial wink as he turned and sauntered out of the open French doors.

By the time he'd caught up with his horse, munching happily on one of Verne's hedges, he'd decided to ride directly to London.

On the road, it struck him that he, who had never run away from anything in his life, was actually fleeing from a slip of a girl. It was such a novel idea that instead of dismissing it out of hand as he should, he allowed himself to dwell upon her.

In truth, he didn't know why she had got under his skin. She was lovely to look at, of course, with a seductive figure she seemed utterly unaware of. But such charms had never been enough before to inspire him with more than a temporary lust. Perhaps that was the problem. He could not have her, and was not yet such a cad that he would seduce a gently-born innocent.

But that was to trivialize her, and he strongly suspected she was not trivial at all. At the tender age of eighteen, she had already thrown off the paltry obsession of most debutantes, namely the catching of an eligible husband. And yet, what else was open to a well-born girl? Her main purpose in life was to attract a husband that would benefit her family's wealth and influence. Once, he was sure that had been enough for her. By the time he had met her, she was already discontented. Marriage as a goal was no longer enough for her.

Perhaps that was it. He had a fellow feeling for her. He, too, grew quickly bored with his various goals in life—education, sailing, banking, free-trading. Verne, certainly, had imbued him with a new sense of purpose by involving him in the secret aiding of his country in the war with France. And he was the kind of man who thrived on excitement. But somewhere, he had been increasingly aware of an empty gap in his life, a spreading space that needed to be filled, though with what he had no idea.

Henrietta felt that, too, with more cause, hence her escapade to the Hart in boy's clothes. But for women of her class, there was little alternative. Somehow, he didn't like to think of her devoting all her energies to an unknown and unappreciative husband, several children, and genteel charitable works. Surely it would eventually dull the light of fun in her eyes, the vital energy of her restless soul.

Now, you are growing poetic, imbecile, he castigated himself. *She is little more than a child, and she will conform in the end and be content. Like her sisters. Like Verne.*

Forcing his mind away from her, he concentrated hard on dull things like numbers and investments and sailing times, and in this way, finally arrived in London after dark, heartily bored.

The family house in which he'd grown up was just to the unfashionable side of Hanover Square. His sister and her husband, mill owner Neville Miller, lived there, too, which one reason he tended to avoid it these days. He didn't much care for Neville for one thing. For another, he'd begun to feel he was intruding in their home, even though it was he who owned it. Fortunately, they had gone north for a month.

The house was large, comfortable, and well-run, mostly by old retainers of his late maternal grandparents. They were used to him turning up at odd hours of the day and night and rarely batted an eyelid, whatever his dress. He asked for supper to be brought to his office, where he sat down and poured himself a large brandy while the servants lit the lamp on the desk and the candles in the wall sconces.

He rifled through his post without a great deal of interest. He recognized a note addressed to him in Susannah Carew's hand and tossed it to one side with vague irritation. Why should the woman have turned so clingy? He'd sent her back her damned ring which he had only taken to please her in the first place. How utterly *paltry*—not to say illegal—of her to have given him her husband's property.

He piled up his business correspondence in order of importance, keeping it separate from his few social invitations. Among the latter, he was surprised to receive a card of invitation to a ball.

He tossed it aside without reading it properly. Then something made him pick it up again. It was from the Earl of Silford and his sister Lady Manson, inviting him to a ball at Steynings.

"What the…"

It seemed the old man was not giving up. Instead, he was providing the opportunity for him to come to a social occasion and rub shoulders with all the august people he was supposed to be missing. Presumably, he was to be so impressed by their superior company that he would immediately accede to his grandfather's wishes and behave as his heir. Well, he wouldn't do that either.

THE FOLLOWING EVENING, after a full day "shuffling papers" as he called this dull side of his work, he was changing his clothes to join a friend and partner for dinner, when he was brought news of visitors.

He took the card from Stephen, his elderly footman. "Mr. and Mrs. Cromarty," he read ominously. "Who the devil are they?"

"Quality, sir," Stephen replied without expression. "Possibly family."

"God, I hope not." Cromarty sighed. "Very well, where did you put them?"

"In the drawing room, sir."

Cromarty pulled on his boot and stood. Only honored callers were ever admitted to the drawing room. In this case, he suspected snobbery had got the better of Stephen's normally excellent perception.

From the drawing room doorway, he was afforded an excellent view of his visitors, and there were three of them, not two. A small, balding man in spectacles sat on the sofa with his head almost buried in a book, while a large lady of similar middle years was walking about the room, examining the candlesticks and the porcelain which had been his mother's obsession. The third visitor, a young, fair man, sprawled in the winged armchair, oozing discontent from every line of his face and body. Clearly, he would rather have been anywhere but here—which at least gave him and Cromarty something in common.

"Good afternoon," Cromarty said, entering the room before they could become aware of his scrutiny. He bowed civilly to the lady while both men rose to their feet, reluctantly in the case of the younger man.

"Mr. Cromarty!" the lady exclaimed, advancing with her hand held out, like a ship in full sail. "How charming to meet at last. Forgive us calling so late, but we only just discovered your direction and just had to come straight to meet you."

"Why?" Cromarty asked discouragingly. He took the lady's hand very briefly, bowing over it with cold disinterest.

The lady laughed, a somehow alien sound that grated on his nerves. "Why? Because we are your cousins!"

Cromarty would have uttered that they had always been cousins and it made no conceivable difference to him, but the older gentleman suddenly spoke in a quiet, apologetic manner.

"I'm Lord Silford's cousin Gareth, the son of his youngest uncle. This is my wife Augusta, and my eldest son Charles."

"How do you do," Cromarty said, prevented from rudeness by the embarrassed and somehow gentle eyes of the older man. "I'd offer you refreshment, but I'm already late for an appointment. If your business is urgent, perhaps I could call on you, sir, at some mutually agreeable time?"

Augusta laughed again. "Oh, bless you, Cousin, we have not called upon business but upon family matters. To come to the point, you will have received his lordship's invitation to the ball at Steynings?"

She left a tiny pause for him to reply. When he didn't, she charged on. "Gareth, who is the kindest of souls, insisted we come and offer you support."

Cromarty blinked. "Support for what?"

"Well, you will know no one. The whole world of Steynings and the invited company will be new to you. Gareth is eager to offer his help and counsel. And it would be so delightful to travel down to Steynings together. It will be so much more comfortable for you."

Augusta Cromarty's idea of comfort was clearly very different from his own. "I'm sure you're right," he said, again prevented from sharpness by the resigned agony of embarrassment in Gareth's eyes. "And I appreciate the thoughtful offer. However, it is quite unnecessary since I am not going to Steynings."

The lady's mouth fell open. Even the bored Charles regarded him in surprise.

"Not going?" the lady repeated faintly. "But Steynings! Silford! The ball… Perhaps I should not say so, but it is in your honor, Cousin, now that you are his heir."

Cromarty shrugged. "Then he should know better. I told him I would not come."

"I expect balls aren't your thing," Gareth said kindly and received glances of contempt from both his wife and son.

"Ah!" Augusta exclaimed. "You are worried that you cannot dance, that you will not know how to behave. You must come to us and learn. My daughter Selina will make an excellent practice partner. She has been dying to meet you. Shall we say tomorrow afternoon? And, of course, you will stay for dinner, and then you will see how things are done in our world."

"Sadly, that won't be possible," Cromarty said, allowing a hint of impatience into his voice. "Or even necessary. I am very glad to make the acquaintance of my cousins, but I leave town tomorrow. I must beg you to excuse me."

It was much like herding rowdy sailors out of whatever tavern they had lost track of time in. Good-naturedly ushering the leader—in this case, Augusta—without actually touching her, the rest would follow. And so, it proved. He didn't even trouble to call for Stephen but showed them out the door himself.

"Bless you, my boy," Gareth mumbled, and it struck Cromarty that he might actually be a clergyman, though no one had said so.

Beside him on the step, Augusta looked a trifle bewildered as though she couldn't quite understand how she had got there. Charles, sauntering out after them, cast Cromarty a look of contempt, although he bowed with perfect grace. A bit of a dandy, he favored a bright yellow-striped waistcoat and a cravat of intricate folds that made it positively frothy.

Cromarty laughed and closed the door. He didn't know whether they had been sent by his grandfather or whether word about him being Silford's heir was getting out, but either way, he didn't like it.

Chapter Six

THE DINNER PARTY at Audley Park was pronounced a great success by all who attended.

"I must say, I was so pleasantly surprised in Lord Verne," Mrs. Walsh, the vicar's wife, confided as she finally donned her pelisse and bonnet for the journey home. "I had expected a much rougher, ill-mannered man."

"Presumably holding some black mass under the dining table with his abducted virgins," Henrietta muttered to Miss Milsom who sniggered before she remembered to turn her disapproving face in Henrietta's direction. Interestingly, her eyes laughed while her pursed mouth scolded. Henrietta decided she liked the governess.

"But one would not really expect Lady Cecily to marry a rough, ill-mannered man," Lady Overton pointed out.

"A most charming young woman," Mrs. Walsh approved. "So amusing, and yet never straying outside the bounds of what is pleasing. I have to say, if I were invited to Finmarsh House, I now would have no hesitation in accepting."

"Come along, my dear," the vicar said patiently. "No point in planning your next engagement before we have left this one!"

"Well, that went off very well," Lady Overton said with relief, having finally waved off the Walshes and seen the front door closed on the darkening sky. "Mrs. Lacey will now be planning an evening party in order to invite the Vernes! Oh, don't rush off, Miss Milsom. Lady

Verne and I were talking, and we have a proposition for you. Would you like another pupil? With a commensurate increase in salary, of course." Still talking, she led the way back to the drawing room. "Lord Verne's niece—his ward—lives with her grandmother and has no one to teach her. Apparently, now that he is married, she is coming to live with him more permanently and he would like to bring her over here each day to have lessons with Eliza."

"Is she a pleasant child?" Henrietta asked doubtfully, for she knew Cecily did not care for the grandmother, Mrs. Longstone.

"Cecily likes her. She's a couple of years younger than Eliza."

"I think it will be good for Eliza," Miss Milsom pronounced. "It might stop her missing her brother so excessively if she has a friend of her own."

"We should try it," Henrietta agreed. "But if Eliza doesn't like her, it won't answer."

The plan her mother formed, which Henrietta didn't much like, was that young Jane should be brought to stay at Audley Park while the Vernes and the Overtons were away at Steynings for the ball. Henrietta would rather have been at home so that Eliza didn't feel surrounded by strangers with no family present, but Miss Milsom assured her she would keep a close eye on them, and Eliza herself seemed as excited as she was nervous to meet a new friend.

The day before Jane was expected and the adults were to travel to Steynings, Henrietta induced Miss Milsom and Eliza to accompany her to the market at Finsborough, in search of new ribbons for her bonnet and other fripperies.

Eliza, having pronounced the scarlet silk her favorite, quickly lost interest in ribbons and wandered around the other stalls with Miss Milsom, leaving Henrietta pondering between the scarlet, which Mama would almost certainly dislike, and the more decorous pale blue.

The woman whose stall it was kindly produced a hand mirror, and

Henrietta tried both colors beside her face and under her chin.

"Why don't you take a length of both?" the woman suggested.

"I shouldn't," said another voice entirely. "One startles and the other is insipid. Try this."

Her heart bumped as she turned to face Captain Cromarty, who looked almost respectable in town clothes. Only his smart Hessian boots were muddied, which made her think he had been travelling by land, and he wore no hat.

"Captain," she managed.

"Miss Maybury," he returned with a hint of gentle mockery, although whether aimed at her or himself was hard to distinguish.

"And what do you know of ribbon, sir?" she challenged, smiling because her heart lit up every time she saw him.

"Nothing," he confessed. "But I am a good judge of color and beauty."

"Who on earth told you that?" she teased.

"Oh, many ladies of my acquaintance."

"Are you being outrageous?"

"Oh no, many of my acquaintances are quite innocent."

He held up a reel of sunshine-yellow silk to the stall owner who cut a good length. The captain then held it to her cheek, and placed his finger under her chin to tilt her face back to the mirror. Her skin tingled and flushed under his touch, so that she had difficulty concentrating on her appearance.

"That's how I think of you," he said softly. "Like summer sunshine."

She didn't know if it was the effect of his presence or the yellow ribbon, but as she stared at her suddenly vital reflection, she knew she looked at her best.

"I'll take all three," she said in a rush, thinking of giving the scarlet to Eliza and the blue to Miss Milsom who badly needed something to brighten her dress. She cast a quick glance up at Captain Cromarty as his hands fell away. "Thank you for your assistance."

"My pleasure." His eyes danced. "Might I help you with anything else?"

Not used to being so overwhelmed, she lifted her chin. "Sir, are you flirting with me?"

In her experience, such a direct question generally resulted in embarrassed denial and swift retreat. The captain, however, only smiled in a way that deprived her of breath. "Yes, I believe I am. Do you mind?"

"I don't know," she managed, honestly, brushing past him to pay for her ribbon. "I think you flirt too easily for it to mean much."

"Ouch," he said after a short pause, while he took the parcel from the stall owner. "That took the wind out of my sails."

"Might I help you with anything else?" she quoted sweetly.

He laughed with what sounded like pure amusement. "I like you, Henrietta. I hope you will always put me in my place."

"It will be my pleasure, though I doubt you will stay there."

"I like to be unpredictable."

"You are certainly that."

"Then may I invite you for luncheon?"

Again, he took her by complete surprise. She stared up at him, wondering if she dared. Even with Eliza and Miss Milsom. Especially with Eliza and Miss Milsom. Her breath caught. Oh yes, she dared.

But before she could speak, he did so. "I'm sorry. That was unfair. Of course, I may not. Your company is too beguiling, but sadly, I must forego it. I'm glad I met you." And with a quick smile, he bowed and walked away across the square toward the tavern.

Baffled, Henrietta wondered what had happened. Had he saved her or rejected her? It was probably best if she never found out.

ALTHOUGH THEY DID not travel together, Henrietta was glad the Vernes and the Laceys were to be at Steynings, too. After her months in London, large parties were hardly a novelty to her, or anything to cause her anxiety, but the things that had once made such events exciting—gowns and jewels and flattering gentlemen—had palled somewhat, and she preferred simply friendly company. Now she would have the Vernes and Matthew to get up to mischief with.

"What has made the old gentleman hold such an event?" she asked Cecily when they met in Finsborough only an hour after she had encountered Captain Cromarty. "My father says it's quite out of character. Especially while he's in mourning for a grandson."

"The rumor is, he is introducing his new heir, who is guaranteed to put other noses out of joint. There is a cousin, a clergyman, who imagined he would inherit. Which, apparently, he cared nothing for, unlike his wife and his large, hopeful progeny. So, the world and his wife will almost certainly be at Steynings in the hope of catching a quarrel between the new heir and the over-presumptuous cousins. There is that to look forward to."

Henrietta wrinkled her nose. "I think I'd rather stay here and wait for my brothers to come home and fight."

"But there will be dancing," Cecily pointed out. "And I know you love to dance!"

ALMOST AS SOON as the carriage stopped on the impressive front terrace of Steynings, Lord Rudd strolled across to greet them. He had been in Brighton with the Prince Regent. "But I was so desperate to get away," he drawled, "even this turgid affair seemed preferable. And then I heard you would be present, Miss Maybury, and I could not resist. Ah, here comes Lady Manson, our hostess."

Lady Manson was the Earl of Silford's sister and acting as his hostess for the ball. "I used to be so good at large parties," she confided to Lady Overton, "But in recent years, I have quite got out of the way of it, so you must say if anything is not just as you like. Mrs. Granger here is the housekeeper. She will show you to your rooms and make sure all is satisfactory."

Behind her back, Rudd caught Henrietta's gaze and rolled his eyes. Henrietta smiled only perfunctorily, for in truth, she rather liked the wittering lady.

Steynings itself was a large and impressive country mansion, second only to Mooreton Hall in Henrietta's opinion, though far newer and built on more classical lines. Inside, everywhere was well decorated and furnished, although in the somewhat old-fashioned style of the previous century. Henrietta's bedchamber was comfortable, with plenty of space to hang her evening gowns.

Almost as soon as they arrived, it was time to prepare for dinner. Since Henrietta still did not have a maid of her own, she managed as best she could, dressing her own hair and choosing jewelry until her mother bustled in with her maid. While her stays were tied and her gown donned, she listened patiently to her mother's instructions.

"Lord Rudd has distinguished you with his attentions, so there is no harm in a little modest encouragement. Just be careful never to step beyond the line of what is pleasing, for he has a bit of a reputation as a rake, you know. Don't make things too easy for him."

"I don't even know what you mean by that," Henrietta said. "So, I doubt I will."

Released from the maid's ministrations, she stood and bore her mother's critical survey from head to toe.

Lady Overton nodded. "You will do." She hesitated, then dismissed the maid. "He is different with you, Henrie. Several people have remarked upon it. He would be a good match for you."

"But you no longer need the money, do you?"

"Not desperately, as at the beginning of the year. You bring a decent dowry with your hand, and Rudd will make a decent settlement upon you. Your father will see to that. A match with Rudd will be quite a feather in your cap, for any number of females have cast out lures to him in the past, and he has never taken the bait. To use your father's vulgar phrases," she added hastily, "which I beg *you* will not."

Henrietta glanced at her reflection in the glass. "I think Charlotte was right all along. The whole business of the marriage mart is vulgar. And yet, we look down our noses at those of lesser birth who do things differently."

"No, they don't," her mother argued. "It is all a question of degree and the taste with which the matter is managed. You know perfectly well we would not tie you to a man you did not like."

"But what if I liked a very different man?" She cast around in her mind for someone quite ineligible and came up, inevitably, with Captain Cromarty. "A merchant sea captain, perhaps, or a banker's son, someone who worked in the city. If he was my choice, would you let me marry him?"

"Of course not," her mother said, scandalized. "Stop being ridiculous. You will never even meet such a man! Come, it is time to go down."

Henrietta smiled wryly and followed her mother.

It was a large party who had gathered in the gallery, too many for everyone to be introduced to everyone else, although Lord Silford and Lady Manson welcomed all their guests as they appeared. As Henrietta and her family passed through the throng, Lord Rudd glanced over from a group of friends and bowed, but didn't immediately excuse himself to join them. Henrietta was relieved and hoped her mother was wrong about his intentions.

Her mother paused to greet Lord and Lady Verne, and her father moved on to speak to some old friends he recognized. Presented with a glass of ratafia, Henrietta gazed around the elegant throng.

"We could easily be in London," she observed. "Everyone looks familiar, even if I have never met them."

"An invitation to Steynings is rare enough," Cecily replied. "Even without the incentive of meeting the new heir, who is to be produced, presumably, from behind a screen at some point in the evening. I was disappointed not to see him standing with the earl as we came in."

"Perhaps he is mingling with the guests already," Henrietta suggested, pleased to have a puzzle to solve. "Which of the gentlemen could he be? Is there anyone here you don't know?"

"I don't know any of 'em," Verne said sardonically, leaning his shoulder against the wall.

Henrietta swept her gaze around the gallery for likely candidates, and found a young, blond, arrogant-looking man whose expression was so discontented, he appeared to pout like a child about to burst into tears. "What about him?"

"Oh, excellent guess," Cecily approved, following her gaze. "He is in fact family, but his nose has been put out of joint by the discovery of this missing heir. It is his father who is next in line for the earldom." Cecily broke off to exchange nods with a passing lady who made Henrietta's heart lurch unpleasantly.

The lady who had kidnapped Matthew in mistake for Captain Cromarty. A little more formally attired, perhaps, but otherwise she looked exactly the same. From her fashionably riotous golden hair to her shimmering gown, so fine it should have torn at one touch of her beringed fingers, she was quite unmistakable.

With relief, Henrietta remembered that she did not look anything like the hoyden dressed as a boy who had turned up to demand Matthew's release that day. Hastily, she adopted her most aloof smile and tried to look as if she had never seen the lady in her life before. Thank goodness Lady Overton was engrossed in conversation with another matron and was paying little attention.

The lady, having exchanged bows with Cecily, let her gaze linger a little too long on Lord Verne. She smiled.

"My husband, Lord Verne," Cecily introduced him. To Henrietta, she sounded reluctant, despite the perfect civility of her tone. "Verne, Lady Carew."

The lady offered her languid hand, and Verne took it. "My lady."

As he released her, she made to pass on, her disinterested glance barely acknowledging Henrietta. But before Henrietta could breathe a sigh of relief, that bored, blue gaze came back to her with a hint of puzzlement.

Lady Carew smiled. "Why, my little feather. How do you do?"

Ready to sink, Henrietta inclined her head. "How do *you* do?"

As Lady Carew passed on, Henrietta looked wildly around for the Laceys. She needed to warn Matthew. However, he was not in her line of vision, and she could hardly charge up and down the gallery looking for him.

Instead, she murmured to Cecily. "Who *is* Lady Carew?"

"Sir Edward Carew's wife, and not someone your mother would encourage you to be intimate with. Not before your marriage at least." Cecily brought her too-perceptive gaze back to Henrietta. "But you seem to know her already."

"I bumped into her once," Henrietta admitted vaguely. "But I didn't know her name."

At that moment, everyone began to move toward the dining room. Lord Rudd materialized beside her, offering his arm. "I believe we are seated together."

"What a coincidence," Henrietta murmured, her mind still on Lady Carew as she laid her fingers on Rudd's sleeve.

"Not really. I arranged it that way."

"I don't believe you," Henrietta said baldly.

A light of amused challenge gleamed in his eyes. "You don't believe I am capable of such arrangement?"

"Oh, I'm sure you are more than capable. I merely see no reason why you would bother."

He regarded her thoughtfully. "I cannot quite work out whether that is maidenly modesty or a set-down."

Henrietta smiled sweetly, and he laughed.

Only after they had sat down did she catch sight of Matthew, about to walk past behind her. Pretending to readjust her gown, she rose and exchanged smiles with him.

"That woman is here," she breathed. "From Corzone House."

His eyes widened, his gaze immediately darting around the table. Henrietta, her duty done, sat back down.

Rudd regarded her with sleepy curiosity. "Surely not your favored suitor?"

Henrietta laughed. "Hardly! We are old friends and neighbors. You probably know his sister, Miss Lacey."

"I can't think of her."

Since Rudd had never been anything other than good company, dinner, which was excellent in terms of both quantity and quality, passed quite pleasantly. Henrietta conversed as much with the gentleman on her other side, but in any case, no one could have accused Rudd of trying to monopolize her. Either her mother was wrong about his intentions, Henrietta concluded, or it was a clever way of piquing her interest. It would probably have worked, too, when she had first gone to London, a naïve and rather silly young girl. A lot seemed to have changed in the last few months.

"I hope you will save the first dance for me," Rudd said as the ladies began to depart in Lady Manson's wake. "Better still, the waltz, since I believe there is to be one."

"You may hope," Henrietta said lightly. "But I cannot promise."

Something predatory that she didn't quite like flickered in his eyes as she left him to join her mother. Fortunately, Matthew again caught up with her at the stairs. "Second dance is a waltz," he muttered. "We can talk best, then."

Henrietta nodded. It was an excellent idea and had the added benefit of keeping Lord Rudd at bay.

She changed into her ball gown and patiently allowed her mother to swap jewelry around and let the maid re-pin her hair. She barely heard her mother's latest advice and instruction, for a certain sense of unreality seemed to have gripped her, along with a restless impatience she was at a loss to account for.

I think I would rather be home with Eliza. The unprecedented wish took her by surprise, but even then, she knew it wasn't quite true. Something would still be missing.

Obediently, she rose and accompanied her parents downstairs to the ballroom which had been built onto the back of the house. The air was oppressively warm, both because of the heat of the summer evening and the number of candles illuminating the Grecian style ballroom. It was also packed with people, not only those who had dined at the house, but many other guests, too.

Most were talking about the absence of the earl's guest of honor, the promised heir. Some said it was only rumor that had made such a promise, not his lordship. Others were of the opinion that the lout— why lout, Henrietta wondered?—had let him down. Others, again, looked forward to his dramatic entry at some point in the evening.

For the first country dance, she stood up with the young man she had sat beside at dinner. Unfortunately, she had forgotten his name, and felt unable to ask, but at least it was an enjoyable experience, and she returned to her mother much more happily to rest and drink a glass of iced lemonade.

Matthew joined her almost immediately with all the informality of an old family friend. With equal informality, Henrietta felt able to more or less ignore him while she looked around the ballroom. Her gaze was caught by the blond, disgruntled looking young man who stood in line for the earldom, scowling across the floor. Quite suddenly, he looked around and caught her staring. Immediately, she looked away, but the damage was done. From the corner of her eye, she saw him seize Lady Mason's arm and almost drag her in Henrietta's direction.

"Might I present my cousin to you, Lady Overton?" said the flustered Lady Manson. "I believe he wishes to solicit your charming daughter for the waltz."

Matthew's head shot up. "Sorry, she's already promised to *me* for the waltz," he said abruptly. Everyone stared at him for his rudeness until he reddened up to his hair. "Well, she is," he said defiantly. "Though I apologize for my rude interruption."

"Be fair, Matthew," Lady Overton said coldly. "You haven't actually asked her."

"Then *I* do so now," the discontented young man said, looking more pleased by the conflict than anything else. "Miss Maybury—"

"We agreed after dinner," Matthew interrupted once more.

Henrietta's mother looked as if she was about to give Matthew the set-down of his life, when Lord Rudd suddenly materialized between them.

"The matter is easily resolved, ma'am," he said smoothly. "In fact, Miss Maybury promised the waltz to me *during* dinner."

The blond, young man glared at Rudd as more serious competition, presumably, than Matthew. Henrietta, overwhelmed by the ridiculousness of the situation, began to laugh.

"Henrietta," her mother scolded.

Other people were looking across at them with amusement. Henrietta realized she was in danger of becoming a laughing stock and wondered if she cared. And then fingers lightly clasped her gloved hand and raised it.

She spun around to face the one person she had been sure she wouldn't see there.

"Run," he advised.

CHAPTER SEVEN

CAPTAIN CROMARTY HAD no intention of going anywhere near Steynings, certainly not within the fortnight stipulated by his grandfather, let alone to attend the ball by which the old earl intended to force his hand.

And yet, he found himself in evening dress, riding over the land to which he was now heir. It seemed to be good land, and yet it could have been made better. There were also a few too many unattended repairs to cottages and barns, a few too many pinched and discontented faces among the villagers he passed.

I could do no better. I know nothing about farming or land management.

He told himself he was going in order to show his grandfather the contempt his lordship's friends had for him, even when acknowledged by the earl himself. There may even have been an element of truth to that. But mostly, it was sheer curiosity, the same curiosity that had compelled him to visit Verne, as well as to see the patrimony he was ignoring. And the mischief which never quite left him wanted to see if he could gain entry to the ball at which he was, apparently, the guest of honor.

And so, he left his horse with a servant and, among a crowd of wealthy, fashionable guests, he simply sauntered into the massive pile he had seen previously only from a distance. No one asked for his card of invitation, which was still in London. He followed the crowd into the overheated ballroom and propped his shoulder against a faux-

Grecian pillar while he looked about.

His grandfather stood nearby, beside a woman who resembled him closely enough to be his sister. They were welcoming the new arrivals, although a country dance was already in progress.

Without approaching the earl, Cromarty strolled further into the room. No one paid him much attention, but he surveyed them, recognizing a good number of them from business and even from school.

He spotted Henrietta almost at once, and allowed himself a moment to watch her grace and her smiling, happy countenance. He should have known she would be there. Perhaps he had guessed it. Perhaps she was the real reason he had come. For she had been haunting him more than ever since he had run into her at Finsborough. Since he had flirted with her. He'd no real idea what had possessed him that day, except she was lovely and fun, and he'd wanted to beguile her and make her smile…

Restlessly, he moved on, picking out Lord and Lady Verne, Augusta Cromarty and Susannah Carew, among others. He discovered his cousin Gareth watching a card game in one of the ante-rooms. Rudd was there, too. Cromarty left as the music stopped and continued his circling of the room. Still, it seemed, no one had noticed him, let alone reported his presence to Lord Silford.

Henrietta now stood beside her mother, her cheeks pleasantly rosy as she drank a cooling glass of lemonade. Young Matthew Lacey was beside her. Cromarty leaned against another pillar and forced himself to look away. There was something about that girl…

Inevitably, his bored gaze returned to her as the orchestra struck up for a waltz. Idly, he wondered what she would say if he asked her. Would she pretend neither to see nor hear, as in the theater that first evening, once she had discovered he was not of her class? Or would friendship win?

Either way, he had no intention of forcing her to make such a choice, for the same reasons he had withdrawn from his luncheon invitation. He would never force his company on anyone by any means, and he could never use a person's innate politeness to compel them to accept it. He could never bring any kind of harm on Henrietta.

Besides, he had not come to dance, let alone embarrass the only person there he seemed to care about.

In any case, she seemed to be spoiled for choice. His cousin Charles Cromarty and Matthew appeared to be arguing over the honor when Rudd joined them as if his very presence settled the matter. Those standing nearby cast looks of scandalized amusement at the scene. Lady Overton was frowning at Henrietta as though it were her fault, while Henrietta herself laughed and looked as if she would simply walk away from the whole parcel of them.

That she didn't bothered Cromarty, until he realized she didn't have a choice. She couldn't leave her mother's side without permission and an escort. Well, he could supply the latter and cared nothing for the former. And he had no objection to putting Rudd's or Cousin Charles's contemptuous noses out of joint.

He walked up and took Henrietta's hand. She swung on him with alarm, and then with pure relief that translated into a blinding smile. He could barely breathe.

Somehow, he managed to advise sardonically, "Run," before he glanced at Lady Overton. "With your permission, ma'am."

To avoid fuss and unwanted attention, of course, she was obliged to smile and nod – although her expression was glacial. Under the noses of the furious Charles and the narrow-eyed Rudd, Cromarty stole off with his prize.

"How very clever of you," Henrietta said breathlessly. "And I am most definitely grateful! I should have taken Matthew's arm at the outset, but I didn't think fast enough. It is so frightfully hot in here."

"It is," Cromarty agreed. "Now, where would you like to go? To

Lady Verne, perhaps?"

She looked up at him in surprise. "Why, don't you want to dance?"

It would be as close as he ever came to holding her in his arms.

Her expression changed to one of contrition. "Or don't you dance?"

"I have done," he said gravely. "And I am quite at your disposal. Only think of your reputation."

"I have thought of nothing else for months," she said with odd grimness, all but tugging him toward the dancers.

"Apart from visiting the Hart in disguise," he reminded her, as he encircled her waist with his arm and swung her into the dance.

"Oh, I have to tell you, that lady—your Lady Carew—is here!"

"I know. I saw her."

"Really? Wouldn't you rather dance with her? There is only to be one waltz, I believe."

"Yes. No. And I am happy to have the honor. Although you are now in the unenviable position of explaining me to your parents."

"Oh, I shall tell them you helped me with Minnie at the theater. Providing Matthew doesn't come up with some silly whopper in the meantime. I am delighted to see you, of course, but what are you doing here? It surely is nothing to do with Lord Steynings's brandy."

A laugh escaped him. "No, not exactly. I wandered in to see if I could and no one stopped me."

Her eyes sparkled. "You see, this is what my wager with Matthew was all about. Men can do more or less as they like. While I cannot even decide for myself who I wish or don't wish to dance with! But won't Lord Silford's people throw you out when he realizes no one knows you?"

"No, I don't believe he will."

"I suppose it would look bad for him," she said.

"My aim is to see how long it is before he notices me."

"You might make it through the whole ball, for there must be lots of people here he doesn't know personally. He did not know me, for example, before dinner. And lots more people have come since then."

He only smiled. She made him want to smile all the time. Graceful, soft, and yielding in his hold, she was utter, innocent pleasure. At least, the innocence lay on her side, not on his.

"Why do you dance with me?" he asked abruptly. "Are you still apologizing for the theater?"

Her eyebrows flew up. "I'd forgotten about that." She smiled. "You are too generous to bear a grudge."

He scowled. "No, I'm not. You would not credit the size of some of the grudges I bear."

"Then I must not be important enough to count," she said.

"Or it's the other way round."

"But that would be silly," she objected. "Who could bear a grudge about something that was not important to them?"

He searched her face, absently swinging her around to avoid an oncoming couple. "That is a very good point."

"Is it?" she asked.

"I'm beginning to think you have wisdom beyond your years while mine is considerably less."

A faint frown tugged at her brow. "I don't know why you would think so, but if you tell me your trouble, I'll be happy to give you my opinion and help if I can."

"Why should you imagine I have troubles?"

"A man with such massive grudges? Of course you have."

He smiled. "Perhaps I will tell you one day."

"What is wrong with *this* day?"

"It's a party. You're meant to be enjoying yourself."

"I am," she said, and immediately flushed slightly. "I like dancing with you. You waltz more naturally than any other partner I've had."

"I thought I was being restrained. The English waltz is so stuffy. One day, I'll show you how they waltz in Europe."

"Truly? I would like that. Where in Europe have you danced? In wartime!"

"That too, I will tell you—"

"—one day," she finished. "You have so much to say and do on that day, what on earth is there left for now?"

"You are an impudent baggage and I'm very tempted to show you."

She laughed. "I dare you."

If her eyes had not danced in that particular way, he would never have done it. But she was the embodiment of every desire and sweetness and fun all rolled into one. He was reckless, and the French doors at either end of the ballroom had been flung open to cool the room. He danced her straight out the one at the top. Finding the terrace empty, he bent his head and held her close into him, still dancing.

She gasped, her eyes wide and sparkling, her tremulous lips parting in astonishment. She had pretty lips, rosy and shapely.

"Still daring me?" he asked, low.

"Yes," she whispered.

And he closed the distance, taking her mouth with slow, tender sensuality. She tasted divine. Her shy response almost undid him. Her feet stumbled. He had to force his own to keep dancing, his arms to loosen and hold her more decorously as he raised his head and danced her back through the French door at the bottom of the ballroom.

"Still having fun?" he flung at her, suddenly angry, not with her but with himself.

She smiled, a dazzling, happy smile that almost had him dragging her back outside. "Yes," she whispered.

Dear God, what have I done?

NO ONE HAD ever kissed Henrietta like that. Nor had she ever been as close to any man that she felt all the contours of his body. Unbearably sweet and wildly exciting, the experience overwhelmed her so completely that if he had not been holding her, she doubted she could have remained upright. For the first time in her life, her feet stumbled in the waltz as he danced her back into the room.

The whole interlude could have lasted only seconds, and yet she knew her life had changed forever. He had seemed angry, or perhaps just afraid that she would be. And so, she'd smiled with her heart in her eyes, for there had never been such intense happiness as this and she wanted him to know it.

"Oh, Henrie, Henrie, what am I to do about you?" he murmured ruefully.

"Why, am I in trouble?" She cast a quick glance around the ball-room. "Is my mother glaring daggers at me and everyone staring at us?"

"No," he admitted. "If anyone noticed our brief departure, it will be considered a merely eccentric taking of the air."

"But it wasn't."

"Yes, my sweet, it was."

The kiss had so shattered her, it had never entered her head that it could mean nothing to him. Hurt pierced her sudden happiness, letting some of her foolish certainties seep away.

He seemed to tear his gaze from hers. "Live for the moment, Henrietta. You are too young to make plans."

"I have not asked you to marry me," she retorted.

His lips twisted. "Well, if you were ever foolish enough to want to, no one would allow it."

He was right, of course. But he liked her. She knew he did. It was there in his eyes along with the pain he was so good at hiding. And so, she would take his advice and live for the moment. Which didn't mean she couldn't ask questions.

"I expect you have loved many women."

His eyes gleamed, as she'd known they would, at the utter impropriety of her question. "Being so old? There have been women, yes, but I doubt anyone would dignify such relationships with such a word as love."

"Like Lady—" she began and then, catching the expression in his eyes, broke off.

"And you, Miss Maybury?" he inquired, with a hint of mockery. "Have you found no one to love among your many suitors? Or was your heart given long ago to some poor stable boy who worshipped you?"

"I think the stable boys all worshipped Thomasina. She was older and prettier."

A hiss of laughter escaped him. "You have an answer to everything except the question I asked."

She considered. "I would not have liked you to kiss me if I'd loved anyone else."

The smile in his eyes died slowly. "You have no understanding, for example, with Lord Rudd?"

"Of course not." But he had brought reality back. The reality where she would be expected to marry Lord Rudd or someone very like him. Not share adventures and exciting kisses with a banker turned smuggler. Or was it the other way about? "I'm living for the moment."

His smile caught at her breath all over again. "That's my girl. And now, I fear, our dance is ending."

Did he share her disappointment? It was hard to tell. He was a man too used to keeping his own secrets.

"Then you must return me to Mama to receive all my scolds."

The music came to a close. The warmth of his arm at her back vanished as he bowed and she curtseyed. And then she placed her hand delicately upon his sleeve and they walked across the room to her mother.

Matthew still stood beside her, scowling, but Lady Overton herself was deep in conversation with Lady Manson, who appeared to be an old acquaintance. She glanced up and nodded distantly as Cromarty bowed to her.

He bowed again to Henrietta, with a subtle wink that made her smile. After which he cast a quick grin and a flick of his eyebrows at Matthew and sauntered off. At least it smoothed Matthew's frown.

"You made me look a bit of a dolt," Matthew accused her. "There was I holding out for our dance and you swanned off with *him*!"

"It was simplest and stopped the argument," she countered. "Mama would never have ruled in your favor anyhow. Nor in Captain Cromarty's," she added fairly. A quick glance showed her the blond man approaching once again, but she let her gaze drift over him before she rose to her feet, all but dragging Matthew with her. "Matthew is taking me for a turn around the ballroom," she said hastily when her mother glanced up. "Shall we bring you some lemonade? Or a glass of wine? Lady Manson?"

Both ladies declined, and she and Matthew started off, tracing the quieter path around the outside of the room.

"What did you tell Mama about him?" she demanded.

"Nothing. She never asked me."

"Then he's just the man who rescued Minnie," she said in relief. "But Lady Carew is another matter. I don't believe she is at all discreet, for she called me her 'little feather'."

"No one will know what she means," Matthew said comfortingly. He frowned. "Not sure I do."

"Yes, but I would avoid her, for God alone knows what she might call *you*."

"I doubt a woman like her would even notice a man like me."

"I think she notices all men."

"Well, she certainly notices the captain, for I saw her watching you dance with him. Oh, Henrie, I have to tell—"

"That blond man is still watching me as if I'm his dinner. What is the matter with him? Apparently, he's related to the earl, too."

"He is. Charles Cromarty."

Her eyes flew up to Matthew's face. *"Cromarty!"*

"Exactly. If I ever knew, I'd forgotten that Cromarty is Silford's family name."

Henrietta's head had begun to whirl. "I never knew… So, he didn't sneak in. He must have been invited all along. Oh, Matthew, you don't suppose Captain Cromarty is the missing heir?"

Matthew gave a snort of laughter. "No wonder Silford's been so mysterious about him. His heir's in trade, and a smuggler to boot. Look, there he goes, let's ask him."

Between the sets forming for the next country dance, she glimpsed the captain's tall, straight back strolling toward the entrance. The old earl still sat in the vicinity, surrounded by people. But by chance they shifted position, a few drifting off, allowing, for the moment, a clear space between Lord Silford and Captain Cromarty.

The captain cast a quick glance across the space and paused, for the earl had seen him. Instinct made Henrietta halt, dragging Matthew back when he would have single-mindedly pursued his quarry. For an instant, Silford and Cromarty stared at each other while those with the earl glanced in puzzlement from one to the other.

Then Cromarty laughed, bowed, and strode off, kissing his fingers to the earl as he went.

"He came," the earl said, clearly triumphant. "I *knew* he would come."

CHAPTER EIGHT

CAPTAIN CROMARTY LEAPT up the few curved steps from the ballroom and strode along the marble passage that led to the front hall. He was in a hurry to escape, now, for any number of reasons, so his heart sank when he realized the lady walking toward him on the arm of some fashionable fribble was Lady Carew.

He kept walking while sparing her no more than a curt bow.

"Leaving so soon, sir?" she drawled, forcing him to halt from mere common courtesy.

"I have matters to attend to."

"I would have thought there were also matters here to attend."

"Then you would be wrong."

She released the fribble's arm. "Run along, Maury, and let me have a private word with this gentleman."

"Maury" looked somewhat put-out, but he minced haughtily off without demur.

"What is it, Susannah?" Cromarty asked with undisguised impatience.

"I merely think that since you made the effort to come, you should stay a while longer." She smiled. "Grow used to your patrimony."

Patrimony," he said contemptuously. "It means nothing to me."

"Then why are you here?"

"Curiosity. Mischief. Now both satisfied."

She tapped her fan against his chest. "Wretch. I had hoped you might have come to see me."

He blinked. "Why would I do that? I took my congé with good grace."

"Edward is ill. I think he might die."

His straying gaze returned to her. He frowned. "I'm sorry."

"Don't be. I'm not. He is an old man and it's his time. And then, Sydney, it could be our time."

He blinked. "To die? I've no intention of that."

"Of course not, you fool! Our time to be happy. Together."

She didn't fool him for a moment. Before tonight, she had barely acknowledged him in front of her friends. And now, having somehow discovered his heritage, he was suddenly worthy of marriage. She probably considered the timing of Sir Edward Carew's imminent death convenient.

He smiled. "That boat has sailed, my dear, long since. Goodbye, Susannah." And with a nod, he strode on without once glancing back.

It was clearly not quite so easy to escape as he had imagined. For he had just taken the reins of his horse from the stable hand when he became aware of another figure standing in front of him. The torchlight played across blond hair and a handsome, discontented face. His cousin Gareth's son, Charles.

"Did you come incognito, to look over your inheritance?" Charles sneered.

"Hardly incognito," Sydney said mildly.

"Not staying?" Charles taunted. "He had the best guest chamber prepared for you."

"You have it," Sydney offered, continuing to walk forward so that Charles had to step aside or be buffeted by the horse. "I have my own."

"At some sleazy inn?" Charles mocked, leaving Sydney to wonder if he knew about the Hart. Certainly, the old man had tracked him there.

"No. On board my ship. Give my regards to your parents."

"Of course." Charles's full lips curled, though he turned and walked beside Sydney. "Where do you sail from? Southampton?"

"Not this time." Sydney mounted and settled in the saddle, reining in his impatient horse a moment longer. "Good night, Cousin." He loosened the reins and let the horse take off at a gallop.

CHARLES CROMARTY STARED after him, his resentment bitter and angry.

"It makes no difference, you know," said a voice behind him. "Whatever either of you wants, whatever Silford himself wants, the title and Steynings will go to him."

Charles turned to see Lord Rudd also watching the unconventional departure of the heir.

"It makes a mockery of everyone," Charles muttered. He knew he should keep his mouth shut on such issues. He was barely acquainted with Rudd but was slightly in awe of him for being everything he wished to be—titled, wealthy, suave, and confident.

"It does," Rudd agreed unexpectedly. "It's none of my business, of course, but it goes against the grain to see such a fine property and an even finer name descend to the gutter. God knows which of his doxies he'll install as his countess. I shudder to think of the children."

Charles smiled sourly. "Well, the Maybury chit seemed quite taken with him."

"That will never happen," Rudd said with certainty. "What is your interest in the girl?"

Charles smiled lasciviously.

"I see." Rudd pursed his lips. "You know her father is Lord Overton? You can't ruin her with impunity."

"Who said ruin? Doesn't she come with a fortune?"

Rudd shrugged. "Barely. There are wealthier women to be had. Besides, you should know this one is mine."

Charles flushed. "I meant no disrespect," he muttered.

"I shall take that as read, since it seems we might be able to do each other a favor…"

LORD RUDD DID not ask her to dance again, which was a relief in many ways, although she did find herself beside him as they made their way from the ballroom at three o'clock in the morning.

"Miss Maybury," he greeted her. "Did you enjoy the ball?"

"Very much," she said absently. "Did you?"

"As much as to be expected. One tires of such events, especially in country houses where one cannot escape."

"Yes, you can," Henrietta said. "You just need a little imagination."

"Like your late waltz partner? I see you *did* pursue the acquaintance. You must not let him encroach."

Henrietta smiled. "I never let anyone encroach. The gentleman you refer to merely did me a service."

He smiled faintly, although his eyes seemed to reflect flint. "As I have not?"

"Lord, I don't know. I don't count up such things. Do you?"

He lowered his voice. "You are learning a shrewish tongue, Miss Maybury. Be sure it does not grow sharp enough to cut you."

And with that, he fell back and they became separated.

The encounter made her uncomfortable. His rudeness she did not mind—she had brothers, after all, and was used to it—although it was surprising in a man supposedly trying to fix his interest with her. But more than that, she had the indefinable feeling that she had been threatened.

THE EXCITING EVENTS of the ball, in particular Captain Cromarty's astounding kiss, prevented Henrietta from sleeping late the following day. She did not even *want* to sleep. Awake, she could remember their dance, every nuance of their conversation, the feel of his strong arms and his hard body, the wild yet tender kiss she could still imagine on her lips.

It was too much to bear indoors, and so she dressed, wrapped a shawl around her shoulders, and slipped out of the house to walk. In fact, if she could just lose the sight of the house, she meant to run.

Of course, she had no idea where Captain Cromarty was, if he was staying nearby—or even in the house!—or if he had vanished back to sea, or elsewhere. But it did enter her head somewhat wistfully that he might find her as she walked. She even skirted the edge of the nearby wood so that they would not be seen. But it was a dog that broke cover and came to a halt, staring at her.

"Good morning to you, too," she greeted it, holding out her hand, which the dog sniffed with a wag of his tail. He came closer to have his long, silky ears tickled.

"Ah, that's where the wretched animal went," said a bluff, gentleman's voice, and she looked up in surprise to see her host, the Earl of Silford. "Good morning, young lady. You are abroad bright and early. I hope you were not uncomfortable?"

"Oh, goodness, no, I was *extremely* comfortable," she assured him with a curtsey. "But I seem to wake up at the same time every day without regard to when I went to sleep. And it is such a beautiful morning."

"It is indeed. The best part of the day. I hate to miss it." He cast a closer glance at her. "You're Overton's girl, aren't you? You'll forgive an old man who is forgetful of names and barely remembers faces."

Henrietta smiled. "Of course. I confess I am the same, especially at large parties where one meets so many new people at once. But yes, I am Henrietta Maybury."

"I hope you enjoyed the ball." Lord Silford began to walk, and Henrietta fell into step beside him, while the dog followed, its nose in the undergrowth.

"Very much, sir," Henrietta replied. "I love to dance!"

"I hear you danced with my grandson."

She cast him a quick glance.

His sharp old eyes were not unkind. In fact, she thought them rather sad. "I only bring it up because you appear to be the only lady he did dance with. And if my great-nephew is to be believed, he more or less abducted you from under the noses of everyone including your mother."

Henrietta laughed a little nervously. "Well, it was not quite like that. I had got into a bit of an embarrassing scrape where three gentlemen seemed to believe I had promised the waltz to them. Captain Cromarty merely cut through the argument and rescued me."

"To be honest, I am surprised he obtained an introduction to a young lady of your family."

"Well, it was a somewhat *unconventional* introduction. We met at the theatre one night when he was kind enough to help me catch a stray pup who had wandered inside and got lost."

"Then your parents do not know him?"

She flushed. "Not exactly. You must think me a hoyden. But I assure it was all chance and Captain Cromarty has always behaved with perfect propriety." Apart from the kiss.

"Propriety," he repeated, a sardonic smile playing on his lips. He refocused on her face. "Be easy, child, I make no judgements on you or him. In truth, you must know him better than I. You might say we are…estranged."

"I'm sorry. I believe you would like him."

"I'm beginning to think I might, too." He gazed at the dog trotting ahead, but she doubted he saw it. "The estrangement is my fault," he said abruptly. "I cast off my youngest son for disappointing me, waited for him to learn sense and come back and apologize. He never did. Broke my heart, to be truthful. And now his son, my heir, hates me."

Henrietta regarded him thoughtfully. It struck her he had said more than he meant to. She remembered the captain's pause as his gaze met his grandfather's at the ball, his defiant gesture as he'd walked away. "I don't think he hates you. I think he *wants* to."

In surprise, he searched her face. "You are rather more than a silly flibbertigibbet, aren't you, Miss Maybury?"

"I hope so," she said, startled.

"Then tell me this. Do you think he will come back to Steynings? Take his rightful place as my heir?"

"I don't know," Henrietta said honestly. "You will have to give him time."

"I'm not sure that's a commodity I have in great supply."

"I think you have enough."

A gleam of amusement entered his eyes. "Someone has taught you to say the right thing."

She laughed. "Not very well! I am usually in trouble for saying the *wrong* thing!"

"You shouldn't be. You are refreshing and intriguing. I'll wager my grandson thinks so, too."

She looked away, wishing it were true.

"Did he come to see you? Or Steynings and me?" he asked.

She frowned at this interesting question. "He can't have known I would be here."

"Perhaps," the old man said neutrally. He glanced up at the sky, which had clouded over since Henrietta had come out. "I think that's a drop of rain. Shall we go back and have breakfast?"

HENRIETTA'S TÊTE-À-TÊTE WITH their aged host did not escape Lord Rudd's attention. Observing them walking together from his bed-chamber window, he drew his own conclusions. He could no longer afford to let the grass grow under his feet. He had to make up his mind, either to walk away from the girl or tame her. Indolence urged the former...but his lust for the latter was always going to win. He had been pursuing her too long. More than a silly, naïve chit so recently out of the schoolroom deserved.

By the time he descended to the breakfast room, neither she nor Lord Silford were there. Lady Carew, however, was the company he really sought. And she, yawning delicately behind her hand over a tiny piece of nibbled toast, was barely tolerating the company of Maurice Ashworth at her side and Mrs. Gareth Cromarty across the table from her. Apart from them, the breakfast room was sparse, save for a group of jovial, sporting types at the head of the table who he suspected were still drunk.

"Rudd," Lady Carew greeted him with some relief. "Do join me."

"Gladly," he replied, setting his full plate on the table and taking the vacant seat next to her.

To his relief and everyone else's, Mrs. Cromarty retired to rout her poor husband out of Silford's library.

"In fact," Rudd admitted, "I'm glad of the chance of a word." Providentially, at this point, Ashworth was hailed away by the sporting young men at the end of the table, so Rudd needed only to lower his voice to be sure of privacy. "You must be delighted by the discovery of Silford's heir."

She smiled beguilingly. "You could have knocked me down with a feather. I thought he was nobody."

He will be again. But to some degree, her plans must differ from his own and Charles Cromarty's. Rudd smiled back. "How fortunate that you were there ahead of the pack. Although if my eyes did not deceive me, I believe you have competition."

"I?" she said incredulously. She laughed. "You mean the little Maybury girl? Naïve and sillier than most."

"Naïve, I allow. She is but eighteen years old. However, I have never found her silly."

"That is because you have never seen her in the middle of the night dressed in boy's clothes that do nothing to disguise her sex, in the company of...well, we shall leave that."

He regarded her with considerable interest. "I confess you have surprised me. But I can use it—if you do not spread the information around. I take it you have not, so far?"

Lady Carew shrugged. "I'd no idea who she was until I saw her here. She does not interest me."

"She should," Rudd said frankly. "For she stands in your way."

Lady Carew's eyes flashed pure venom although it wasn't clear whether the poison was aimed at him or at Henrietta.

He said, "I am prepared to take her out of your way."

Her smile was no longer pleasant. "Taken a fancy to the chit your-self, Rudd?"

"Yes, as it happens, so I won't have her name blackened. But some evidence of your continuing relationship with Cromarty might prove helpful to my cause."

"And in return, you marry the chit. Do you really think that will stop him?"

"Oh, yes," Rudd said softly.

Her eyes gleamed.

"You needn't perform a play for her," Rudd went on. "A letter in his hand, perhaps, with the date altered if necessary. I leave the evidence up to you so long as it proves his faithlessness. And once she sends him about his business, if you cannot pick up the pieces, you are not half the woman I take you to be."

"Oh, I'm twice the woman you think me, Rudd."

"Good," he said, addressing himself to his breakfast at last. "How *is* poor Carew?"

CHAPTER NINE

ON THEIR RETURN from Steynings, Henrietta could not throw off her restlessness or her impatience to see Captain Cromarty again. Something had changed with his kiss, releasing a longing she hadn't known was in her. So, when Eliza announced that her brothers finished school at the end of the week, she jumped at the chance.

"Oh, you are quite right," Lady Overton exclaimed. "I always relied on Charlotte to bring them home. And Nurse has gone to her sister in Portsmouth." She frowned. "I suppose your father or I could go…or Miss Milsom!"

"The boys have never met Miss Milsom," Henrietta pointed out. "It would be strange, especially for Horry, to be met by a stranger. But I could go, and Miss Milsom, perhaps, could accompany me."

"And then who would teach Eliza? And Jane Verne who is coming to stay for the weekend again."

"They will be delighted to have no lessons for a day," Henrietta said wryly. "The other option is that you and I go together."

"I'll speak to Miss Milsom."

The upshot was that Henrietta and Miss Milsom set off in the travelling coach early on Friday morning. Unfortunately, the governess did not appear to be at her best. Her eyes watered and her nose ran constantly, and as the morning went on, she began to look really ill.

"If I'd known, I wouldn't have dragged you out on such an outing," Henrietta said contritely.

"I'm happy to help," Miss Milsom said wanly. "I'm eager to meet your brothers. Eliza has told me so much about them."

And in fact, she did seem to perk up once they had collected the boys, who seemed to bring a whirlwind of noise and fun with them.

For once, none of the three brothers asked to sit with John Coachman, since they wanted to meet Miss Milsom properly. So, they all squashed inside, with Horry on the floor, to ask questions and share amusing stories about school. Their activities seemed to have very little to do with learning.

Miss Milsom took it all in her stride, even Horatio's slightly anxious questioning since, as Eliza's twin, he was afraid of her being thrust under the thumb of some harsh person with no understanding. Fortunately, although he clearly still reserved judgement, Miss Milsom appeared to pass most of his tests.

Despite the governess's cold, the journey was somewhat riotous and full of chatter and laughter. Henrietta was delighted to see her brothers again and wondered if she was too old to run wild with them at Audley Park. At Easter, she had had no desire to, being so concerned with the novelty of being a young lady about to embark on her first season. Four months later, it seemed, everything had changed. It wasn't that she wished to revert to childhood, not really. But she had missed the fun and found life in London far more constricting.

And then there was Captain Cromarty.

"There, ahead to the right," Richard said. "That's the road up to the Hart Inn. We had to go there once when it was too foggy to go on, and the whole inn was deserted. We stayed the night."

"Really?" Miss Milsom marveled.

"Actually, they did," Henrietta told her. "My sister Charlotte was with them and there was nothing else for them to do!"

"It was a great adventure," George enthused. "We met the Duke of Alvan who has bang-up horses, and he had to fight armed robbers!"

"I don't know so much about *that* side of things," Henrietta said uneasily. "But they do seem to have had quite an adventure!"

"Can we go again?" Horatio demanded. "Come on, Henrie, we'll show you around, and Miss Milsom, too."

Henrietta hadn't actually thought of this before, since the Hart was slightly off their path. But, of course, she had an ulterior motive for agreeing to go. Captain Cromarty was frequently there, and she had not seen him since the Steynings ball. Against the scheme was her late visit there with Matthew a couple of weeks ago. But even if the staff had perceived her as a girl dressed as a boy, they were surely unlikely to associate such a person with Lord Overton's fashionably dressed daughter.

Miss Milsom looked at her somewhat doubtfully.

"Contrary to what they have just told you, it is actually a respectable house," Henrietta reassured her. She made her decision. "I suppose we could have an early tea there and still be home for dinner."

George and Horatio cheered while Richard, almost grown up at the age of fifteen, merely grinned at her. Just in time, George yelled the new instructions out the window at John, and the coach turned onto the Hart road just a little too fast.

Only minutes later, they pulled into the courtyard of the inn. Richard remembered his manners without prompting, and courteously handed out Miss Milsom and Henrietta. The innkeeper came out to meet them, greeting John like an old friend and beaming when the coachman introduced him to Henrietta.

"Welcome, Miss! Come in, come in and my wife will attend you. The private parlor is free, but the coffee room is quiet also."

"The coffee room is fine," she said, aware once more of her ulterior motive. If Captain Cromarty was here, he might not see them in the private parlor.

"Oh dear, it's cold in here, is it not?" Miss Milsom said as they were shown into the coffee room.

"Do you think so?" Henrietta said in surprise, throwing off her bonnet. "Come, sit in the window seat and let the sun warm you!"

Obediently, the governess sat in the beam of sunshine, but it seemed to Henrietta that her cheeks were rather hectically flushed for someone feeling the cold. When she touched Miss Milsom's face, her skin was hot and tight.

"Oh dear, you really are not well," Henrietta said anxiously. "We shall go as soon as we've had tea and get you home to bed."

"Oh, I shall be right as rain in a few moments…"

But this optimism was clearly misplaced. Miss Milsom swayed dizzily when she stood up and her stomach threatened to relieve itself of the tea she had just drunk.

"I think you must have influenza," Henrietta said anxiously. "Elsie the chambermaid is down with it. Do your bones ache, too?"

"A little," Miss Milsom admitted.

"Then maybe we shouldn't bump you around in the coach just yet. It's another couple of hours to Audley Park by coach… Richard, are the inn rooms comfortable?"

"Yes, clean sheets and feather beds," Richard assured her, swallowing the last of his bread and butter and reaching for a slice of cake. "Maybe you should lie down for a little, Miss Milsom."

"Let me speak to Mrs. Villin."

The innkeeper's wife immediately sent her daughter for a hot posset and insisted on helping the governess upstairs to bed. Henrietta loosened her gown and helped her into bed.

"Maybe she'll be better after an hour's rest," Mrs. Villin said as they watched her eyes close.

"Maybe," Henrietta said doubtfully. "I think she must have been hiding this for days. I should never have let her come."

"Well, we'll see how she is. You go back down and finish your tea."

As she rounded the half-landing, she caught sight of the wrong

Cromarty.

The blond, petulant Charles, who had once asked her to waltz, walked across the entrance hall and was bowed by Mr. Villin, the innkeeper, into the private parlor where an unseen man greeted him.

Henrietta, who had ducked back out of sight, continued her descent of the stairs rather more rapidly, rejoining her brothers in the coffee room. "Who arrived while I was upstairs?" she demanded.

"Dull looking fellow in a coat he was too fat for," George replied at once. "And an old tricorn hat. His horse was an old nag. And then a very bang-up gentleman with a grumpy face. Showy chestnut," he added in case anyone was interested in the horseflesh.

"I wonder who the dull fellow is?"

The boys shrugged. "He asked for a Mr. Cromarty and then demanded the parlor," Richard added.

"*Mr.* Cromarty?" Henrietta asked anxiously. "Not Captain?"

"No, Mister."

The innkeeper's pretty daughter, whose name was Lily, came in then to see if they desired anything else. Since she seemed friendly enough, Henrietta asked her bluntly who was with Mr. Cromarty in the parlor.

Lily smiled. "Mr. Pollard, Miss. Exciseman. He checks up on us all the time. Never finds anything."

"And *Captain* Cromarty," Henrietta said in a rush. "Is he here?"

"The captain?" A frown flickered across Lily's smooth brow and she looked at Henrietta more closely. "No, he isn't here."

Although the disappointment was sharp, it mingled with relief because she just knew his cousin Charles meant him ill.

"Do you know the captain?" Lily asked.

"A little," Henrietta replied, trying not to blush.

"And the gentleman with Mr. Pollard. Would he be a relation of the captain?"

"A cousin, I believe."

Lily nodded thoughtfully and turned to go.

"Lily?"

The girl turned back, "Yes, Miss?"

"I don't believe he means the captain well."

Again, Lily's eyes searched hers. She was a very pretty girl, a strand of golden hair escaping her white cap. More than that, there was something very deep and beautiful about her eyes. Something almost *over*-perceptive. And yet, if she recognized Henrietta from her evening in the taproom, she gave no sign.

"Thank you, Miss," she said and went out.

What did that mean? That she would somehow warn the captain? A twinge of sadness, flecked with something very like jealousy, twisted through Henrietta. Lily Villin, innkeeper's daughter, was more part of his world than she. It shouldn't matter, but it did.

She and her brothers took a turn about the inn yard, and George inevitably dragged them off to the stables to look at the horses. The ostler, whose name was Jem, was very good natured about it. He let them look at the showy chestnut and the old nag, as well as their own horses. They saw the inn's spare team for travelers and the Villins' own ponies. And another horse Henrietta thought she recognized blew down her neck.

"It's as if he knows you," George said, impressed.

"Perhaps he does," Henrietta said vaguely. "Boys, I'm going to check on Miss Milsom and then we must decide what's to be done."

Miss Milsom was so sound asleep that Henrietta didn't want to wake her. Her skin still felt a little less feverish to the touch.

"Best thing for her, sleep," Mrs. Villin said comfortably. "Poor lady. You leave her here with us, Miss, and your man can come back for her tomorrow or the day after."

"Oh, no, I couldn't leave her," Henrietta said, genuinely shocked at the idea she should abandon a dependent of her family to the care of strangers. "Though perhaps I should send the boys home."

The boys, however, were dead against this plan and all for staying together for the night at the Hart.

"Who knows what will happen?" George said enthusiastically.

"But Mama and Papa are looking forward—"

"What a whopper, Henrie," Richard said cheerfully. "You know perfectly well they won't notice."

"Of course they will! They love to have you home," she said.

"Yes, but they don't really mind when we're not," Horatio said shrewdly.

"Eliza does."

Horatio looked somber for a moment while his brothers nodded. "I wish you'd brought her with you."

"There wouldn't have been room in the carriage. It's squashed enough as it is."

Horatio sighed. Then his head jerked up again. "But you said she has a friend staying. The sinister baron's niece! She won't miss us too much before tomorrow, and we won't have the chance to stay here again after we're home. Come on, Henrie, let's stay."

Henrietta glanced up at the inn, then over toward the sea. "I suppose we could send John back with the news, and he could come back for us tomorrow."

The decision made, John was dispatched with the coach. Henrietta made sure there was fresh water by Miss Milsom's bed, and then she and the boys went for a walk down to the sea.

Lily came running out after them, a seaman's eyeglass in her hand. "Are you going to look at the ships?" she asked, offering it to Henrietta.

"If there are any to see. Thank you."

Richard took the glass from his sister. "Wonderful!" he enthused, trying it out while George and Horatio jumped up and down in front to annoy him.

Lily laughed, although her gaze lingered on Henrietta, almost as if she were trying to tell her something without speaking the words.

"Are your guests gone from the parlor?" Henrietta murmured.

"Yes. One is heading back to London, he says. The other returns to his work."

Searching for contraband. After meeting with a man who meant Captain Cromarty ill.

Henrietta had to catch her breath. "Is there a ship we should look for especially?"

"*The Siren* is pretty. Comes in close sometimes. But you can wave to any ship you see." Lily smiled and went back inside.

Have I just been asked by an innkeeper's daughter to warn smuggling vessels away from the coast?

No, she was reading too much meaning into a casual conversation. No lowly person would ever suggest *any* task to a lady of her standing, let alone one that went against the law. Henrietta was of the opinion that wealthy people at least should pay what they owed without cheating duty. And she knew, besides, that some smugglers were in league with France for their own ends.

Not Captain Cromarty.

But she didn't know that. She just wanted it to be true.

As they followed the path down the side of the cliff to the sea, she had to hold on to her bonnet, for despite the blue sky and sunshine, the wind had sprung up. The boys took turns with Lily's glass, looking out to the water and back at the inn and at the birds perched along the rocks.

"There's a man hiding over there," Horatio said, nodding over to the left.

"It's a large seagull," Richard assured him.

"Below the seagulls! I can tell the difference!"

"Actually," Richard said, having snatched the glass from his little brother and looked for himself. "He's right. There *is* a man, there. With his back to us."

"What's he doing?" asked George, peering in the same direction.

The breeze blew his hair right back from his head.

"Nothing. He's just sitting there," Richard replied.

"Is it the exciseman?" Henrietta blurted.

"Can't see his face, but I don't think so. He's wearing a floppy hat, not a tricorne."

As they walked on, Henrietta could see over the rocks to a little cove, where two small rowing boats were tied to a boulder. Glancing up, she found the watcher no longer visible. Perhaps Horatio was right about him hiding.

The path led down to a tiny, pebbly beach. They sat on the rocks, and the boys dangled their feet in the little pools left by the tide. When they grew tired of that, the boys scrambled over the rocks, exploring. Henrietta, hampered by her skirts, regretfully let them go without her, but they were back quickly enough, tense with suppressed excitement.

"We climbed over the rocks on the other side of that beach, too, and there are several men hiding up there," Richard said. "They must be excisemen waiting for smugglers."

Henrietta took the glass from him and peered though it out to sea. To her relief, there were no ships anywhere near the shore. But then, it was broad daylight. The watchers must have gone into hiding early so that any smuggler look-outs wouldn't see them.

"Maybe we could take the boats out and row around the coast," Richard said eagerly.

"They aren't our boats," Henrietta replied. "And there's no one to ask. Besides, they might belong to the excisemen."

"We don't know that," George argued. "And it wouldn't be for long. I'll get hungry soon, anyway."

"No," Henrietta said firmly. She raised the glass again. A small ship she hadn't even noticed earlier was now sailing toward the land, aided by the gusting wind and the tide. She handed the glass to Richard who, being closest in age, was most likely to disobey her. "There's a ship sailing toward the shore. Can you see what it's called?"

"Not from this angle…"

"I'll bet it's smugglers!" George exclaimed, and Horatio grinned with delight.

Henrietta had the horrible feeling he was right. It was none of her business, of course, if smugglers sailed into a trap and were caught. Not unless the smuggler was Captain Cromarty. She owed him.

"Perhaps," she said casually, "I could come and look at these boats of yours."

Having done it before, the boys were able to show her the easiest way over the rocks. Every few steps, Richard paused and pointed the glass toward the ship. "It's still coming…it's changing course, slightly…*The Siren*. It's called *The Siren*. Isn't that the name Lily said?"

Henrietta paused on the rocks, straightening while her stomach twisted. "Yes…"

"What's so pretty about it?" George demanded.

"Why don't we wave to it?" Henrietta said. From there, she was sure the hiding excisemen would be able to see them, but surely waving at passing ships was an innocent enough pastime?

She and the younger boys both waved merrily while Richard watched the progress of the ship.

"It's still coming closer," he reported.

"Maybe it can't go back with the tide and the wind as they are," Henrietta said worriedly.

"No, it doesn't need to come this close," Richard insisted. "Perhaps they just haven't seen us waving. Or perhaps they don't care because they're not smugglers!"

Henrietta turned and looked at the men on the rocks. One held a rifle at his side, pointing upward. Further up the rocks, another rifle pointed straight at the ship.

If Captain Cromarty died, Charles's father would be Silford's heir. Had he arranged an *assassination*? Even if he hadn't, this was suddenly far too dangerous.

"Still coming," Richard said. "There's activity on the ship... I think they're lowering a long boat."

There was no other decision possible for Henrietta.

"Richard, you have to take the boys back to the inn and look after them. Tell Lily what we've seen."

"What?" Richard lowered the glass, staring after her as she began to scramble over the rocks unaided, without a care for her dress. "Where the devil are *you* going?"

"Please just do it!" she called back. "And take care of Miss Milsom! Hopefully, I'll join you for dinner!" With that, she jumped from the rock on to the next pebbly beach.

By this time, the sea had reached both boats. To her relief, neither appeared to be leaking. It was simple to release the rope and climb in, using one of the oars to push the boat off.

She hadn't rowed since she was a child and one of her father's assistants had taught her along with Richard and George. That had been on a lake in Italy, not the sea.

Her body seemed to remember the movements, but it was much harder work against the wind and the tide. It took all of her strength and attention to force the boat in the right direction, so it was several minutes before she realized the boys were following in the other boat.

"Oh, dear God! Go back!" she yelled furiously, afraid to let go of the oars. Why could they *never* do as she told them? Well, she had never done what Thomasina or Charlotte had bidden her, unless there was no option. But that had been over trivia, not *lives*.

She was having increasing difficulty controlling the oars. Her one hope seemed to be the small boat from *The Siren*, speeding toward her...or was it trying to run her down?

CHAPTER TEN

CAPTAIN CROMARTY'S SHIP had been skulking for an hour, looking for any movement on the cliff that might spell danger to his cargo or his crew. It wouldn't be the first time he had landed goods in broad daylight, but it wasn't something he cared to do too often. He wouldn't even be thinking about it now if didn't need to sail to France with the turn of the tide, and if he hadn't seen the boats waiting on the beach. This meant his comrades on shore were ready to distribute and it was therefore safe. Probably. Or that they'd left the boats there on the off-chance and forgotten about them.

As they sailed closer, his eyeglass picked out movement on the other beach—a woman and three boys, playing. From their attitude, they were of no interest to him and his business would be nothing to them.

He gave the order to lower the boat and load it up.

"They're waving at us, Captain," one of his men reported. "But it don't look like the warning waves to me."

Cromarty only grunted and impatiently ushered his two oarsmen down the ladder into the boat. It was only as he climbed down himself that he saw the woman rowing the boat out from the shore.

"What the devil is she doing?" he said, irritated. "She's going to get in our way."

In any case, such a silly little boat would struggle in these currents, especially with the wind whipping up. As he took his place and the boat was cast off, his men began to row, and he raised the glass to his eye once more.

His heart lurched once and he adjusted the focus. He couldn't breathe. Henrietta Maybury was rowing toward him, being tossed about on the waves, and shouting over her shoulder at another tiny boat following her. Not excisemen but a youth and two children.

"Get alongside," he ordered, leaping to his feet. "We'll take her on with us."

He had never been so frightened in his life as in those few minutes as the waves all but upended her boat, and his men had to balance between getting close to her and ramming her. She was shouting something to him as he leaned out and hauled the side of her boat against his. He only caught, "back!" and "excisemen". But still she clung to the oars as if she actually meant to row back to shore.

"Come here!" he yelled, too furious yet to admit admiration for her bravery. "Leave the oars or you'll die!"

She glanced behind her again at the boys, but at least she stumbled to the side, reaching up so that he could grasp her hands and then grab her under the arms and haul her up. Her boat took a wave that knocked it right over, just as he swung her inside his boat and hard against him. She was soaking wet and shivering, her hair blown out of its pins and plastered against her face. She had never looked so beautiful. From sheer relief, he covered her gasping mouth with his for the barest instant.

"My brothers," she sobbed. "They were supposed to go back to the inn but they followed me."

"We'll get them," he assured her, sitting her down on the bench and reaching for the blanket beneath. By the time he'd draped it around her, holding her against him for warmth, they were alongside the other little boat. The oldest boy, who might have been fifteen or sixteen, cooperated fully, helping his younger brothers into Cromarty's grip before accepting the help of his oarsman.

"Back to *The Siren*," Cromarty ordered.

Henrietta, who had been hugging and scolding her brothers at once, jerked her head up. "Oh, no! Miss Milsom!"

He blinked. "Miss Milsom? The governess? Don't tell me she's out here, too?"

"No, no, she's back at the inn but she is ill with influenza or something similar and…"

"The Villins will take care of her," he interrupted impatiently. "What the devil are you all doing?"

"We saw your cousin at the Hart with an exciseman," Henrietta said unexpectedly. "And then we saw the men hiding on the cliffs. They're armed, and I was afraid they had some order or bribe to kill you. We tried to wave, as Lily said, but—"

"Lily?" he broke in, frowning. "Never mind, go on."

"I told the boys to go back and decided to row out to meet you and warn you. I'd no idea the sea would be so rough."

"It's these currents. Especially at high tide." He touched her cheek, which was all that was visible now outside the blanket, and her gaze flew up to his. "It was very brave of you. Thank you. But you should not have risked this for me."

She held his gaze, her own consciously brave. "Why should I not?"

"You know." He stood. "Can you manage to climb on board?"

She looked up at the rope ladder up the side of the ship they were almost bumping against. It seemed a long way up. "I'll try."

"I'll be right behind you. I won't let you fall."

She jerked around. "The boys!"

"Cutter and Haines will do the same for them," he assured her, holding onto the ladder to keep them steady.

She made no further fuss but clambered onto the ladder with his help and began to climb.

His men knew better than to express any surprise let alone disrespect to anyone boarding the ship, so Henrietta was helped onto the deck with rough courtesy, and the boys treated with perfect good nature.

"As soon as the boat is secured, get under way for France," he ordered his capable lieutenant.

"*France?*" Henrietta repeated, spinning to face him in clear startlement. "We can't go to France!"

"Sadly, we must."

"But Miss Milsom! Our parents!"

"They already know we won't be home tonight," Richard pointed out, his eyes shining at this new adventure. "This is wonderful, sir! Are you really a smuggler?"

"Free trader," Cromarty said flippantly.

"And we're actually going to France? Into enemy territory? This is better than anything!"

Henrietta groaned. "How did I not foresee this?"

Amused, Cromarty led the whole family down to his cabin—a spacious apartment furnished with a large bed, a desk, a bookcase, and a cupboard, which he immediately opened. He took out a few pairs of trousers, a small pile of shirts and stockings, and his two spare coats.

"I'll have to scrounge a couple more coats. And you'll have to roll up all the sleeves and legs, but at least you'll be dry."

Henrietta looked from the clothing on the bed to his face, as though she suspected him of alluding to their encounter at the Hart. Which in fact was true.

He grinned at her. "You're not going to make a fuss, are you?"

"Of course not," she said with a glare. "Thank you. Boys, you change first," she added, following him from the cabin into the narrow passage. "Sir, I am grateful, but…are we truly going to France?"

He wondered what he suspected him of, but in the gloom of the passage he could see no accusation in her eyes.

"French waters. You won't set foot on French soil, and with any luck, neither will I."

"But you already have a cargo of French brandy," she argued, "or whatever was in the boat with us, which you would have landed today in England."

"I have a different cargo for France."

"Why do you do this?" she asked abruptly. "You have no need. Even without Lord Silford, you have no need."

"Brandy won't smuggle itself, you know. Treat the ship as home as long as you are here. Except if I tell you to do something, you must do it at once. So must your brothers. All our lives could depend upon it."

He knew she still stared after him as he ran up the ladder. He didn't blame her. After lecturing her on risk, he was taking her and her brothers into enemy territory.

If there had been another way, he would have done it, but he had to land his passenger tonight.

BY THE TIME Henrietta emerged from the cabin, a thick cloak wrapped around her baggy male attire, she thought she had grown used to the rolling of the ship under her feet. But she had to cling to the handrail of the ladder as she climbed onto the deck in search of her brothers.

They were having a wonderful time, rushing from place to place on the deck, exchanging jokes with any seamen they encountered, and then rushing back to Captain Cromarty, who lounged by the wheel, looking more amused than irritated.

"Henrie, this is *much* better than the Royal Navy ship!" George exclaimed.

"I'm not sure His Majesty would be pleased to have his frigate compared so unfavorably to a—this vessel," Henrietta finished hurriedly.

The captain straightened, smiling sardonically at her avoidance of the term "smuggling vessel". "It's a good little trading ship. She was my first investment."

"I would like to hear the story of your life, some time."

His lips twisted. "I don't think you would."

She wrinkled her nose. "Suitably edited, of course, to remove any tales of blood and violence."

"Where's the fun in that?" George demanded.

"I'm not a pirate, you know," Cromarty said in clear amusement. "Free traders do a lot more sneaking than fighting."

"Sneaking," Horatio repeated doubtfully. "Is that fun?"

"It can be like a battle of wits. Or it can be floundering about in the dark."

The boys' eyes gleamed. "Dodging the excisemen and the revenue cutters?"

"That kind of thing," Cromarty said vaguely. "But I would like to point out that most of my trading is *not* free and *does* pay duty."

"Then why do you do this?" Henrietta asked.

He shrugged, looking out to sea, "Because it is fun. And because I get to be at sea a lot without going very far. It gives me—" He broke off. After a barely noticeable instant, he waved his arm to encompass the ship and the surrounding sea. "It gives me this."

It hadn't been what he was going to say but she let it go.

He said, "And your father was a diplomat and you travelled in Royal Navy ships."

"But we weren't allowed to run around in case we got in the seamen's way," Richard said, wrinkling his nose. "So, all our voyages were dull!"

"Will your father go abroad again?" the captain asked.

"If he's asked, I suppose he will," Richard said. "But I don't know that we'd all go with him again. The estate went to the devil because we were never there, and we nearly went under. Which is when he came up with the notion of marrying off the girls."

"Richard!" Henrietta objected.

"Well, he did," Richard said defiantly. "And you all went along with it, even Charlotte."

"Yes, well, Charlotte didn't like it at all, if you want the truth. She only went along with it because no one expected her to marry well, and Tommie and I thought it was a wonderful idea to be great wealthy ladies and save the family at the same time." She gave a deprecating smile. "We were naive. We thought we would fall in love with only the handsomest and wealthiest of gentlemen. But it was Charlotte who married the duke and saved the family."

"Then there is no pressure on you," Cromarty said without emphasis.

"Only the usual."

"In the London clubs, they're betting on Rudd."

Her mouth fell open. "I think I should be outraged by that. But I shall have the last laugh when they lose their money."

She didn't look at him as she spoke, but she felt his eyes burning her face. She felt at once breathless, exhilarated, and contented, as if an unknown hope was seeping up from her toes like some reasonless bout of happiness.

"I believe dinner is ready," he said. "It will be informal and not what you're used to, but you are cordially invited to join me in the cabin."

Dinner was lively and amusing. Cromarty seemed to take the boys' curiosity and bluntness in stride. He never spoke down to them or appeared remotely irritated, simply answered their questions in as much or as little detail as he thought fit. He teased them and asked them questions in return, entering into the spirit of their humor and the things that were important in their lives.

Content with the laughter and with learning more snippets of the captain's life, Henrietta smiled a lot but contributed little. He remarked upon this fact after the boys had settled down to play cards in the cabin and she accompanied him on deck to watch the sun set.

"You were quiet during dinner," he said, leaning on the rail.

"It is difficult to get a word in when my brothers are in full flood."

"Then you are not uncomfortable in this situation?"

She smiled, nodding at the brilliant pinks and golds in the sky and their muted reflection in the rolling sea. "How can one be uncomfortable surrounded by this? I know I should be worried—about Miss Milsom, about the boys being here, about tomorrow and the future—but I don't seem to be." She laid her hands on the rail beside him. "I like being here. With you."

"Why?"

She smiled, because only he would ask such a thing. "I don't know. It just feels...*right*." She glanced up and met his fixed gaze. Perhaps it was the light, but there seemed a wealth of pain behind the exciting heat in his eyes. "You make me happy."

"Henrietta," he began with a hint of warning that she couldn't bear.

"Don't," she interrupted. "I don't want you to pretend anything. I know I'm nothing but an amusement to you—to say nothing of the trouble I bring!"

His hand covered hers. "You talk a lot of nonsense, you know."

"I know."

In silence now, they watched the brilliant sunset fade into the grey of dusk. And quite close now, was the silhouette of land.

"France," he said. "And now I need my wits about me."

She suspected he had for the entire voyage, keeping pretty constant watch and making sudden course changes to avoid ships. But she left him to it, returning to the boys in the cabin.

Horatio had fallen asleep on the floor. Henrietta covered him with a blanket and told the others they were approaching France. Of course, Richard and George immediately wanted to rush on deck, but she warned them to be calm and to obey the captain.

Henrietta sat on the bench under the sloping window, watching her little brother sleep and thinking of her other siblings and other very different voyages. But her thoughts kept coming back to Captain Cromarty. Inevitably, she crept back on deck to see what was happening.

The rumble of the anchor sounded as she emerged on deck, and she saw they were in a wide, sheltered cove, surrounded by jagged rocks.

"Your pardon, Miss," someone murmured behind her, and she immediately stood aside.

A complete stranger touched his hat to her and walked across the deck to the captain. He was not dressed like a seaman, more like a lower order of merchant, with a large bag hanging from either shoulder and another strapped to his back.

The small boat—or did they call it a long boat?—was being lowered into the sea. The same two oarsmen who had helped to rescue Henrietta and the boys stood by to climb down.

Catching sight of her, Captain Cromarty stopped talking to his men in a low voice and came toward her, collecting one of the better dressed seamen on his way.

"This is Kettle, my lieutenant," he said. "While I'm gone, he is in charge, and whatever decision he makes, you must abide by it without fuss."

"What sort of decision?" she asked suspiciously, and a breath of laughter escaped him.

"Concerning the ship and where and when it goes," he said. "Such matters are already agreed between us."

"You're going ashore," she accused. "You said you would not."

"I don't plan to. I'm just landing my cargo."

"What cargo?" she asked, looking around the empty deck.

"Be good, my sweet," he said carelessly and strolled back to the oarsmen who were starting to climb down to the boat. The stranger followed, with the captain behind, and then the gate was closed.

"*He* is the cargo?" Henrietta murmured. "Who is he?"

Kettle smiled faintly but did not answer. If he knew, clearly, he felt it was not his secret to tell.

Richard materialized beside her. "He wouldn't let me go with him," he complained.

"I expect he wanted experienced men for the task," she said consolingly. "Do you still have the eyeglass?"

Richard produced it, having a quick look himself before he passed it to her. She watched the progress of the boat, trying not to linger too much on the captain. Not that she could see his face, let alone his expression in the dark. The moon was new and didn't supply a great deal of light. She thought they must have eyes like cats to navigate the rocks and reach the beach.

As they drew closer to the shore, she raised the glass to the cliffs. There was definite movement there, several figures moving along the ridge.

"There are men up there," she said anxiously to Kettle, who was watching through his own glass.

"I see them."

"Does *he*?" she asked.

"I imagine so."

"Are they friends?"

"I would doubt it," Kettle replied with a hint of grimness. "They look like soldiers."

"Then why does he keep going?" she demanded, distressed. "Why doesn't he just come back? As he did to avoid the excisemen in England…"

"This is more important."

Her heart in her mouth, she watched them pull the boat ashore. The stranger leapt out, pausing only to shake hands with Cromarty and salute the seamen and then he was loping across the beach, away from the direction of the soldiers now spilling down the cliff toward the boat.

"Hurry, hurry," Henrietta urged uselessly. But instead of simply pushing the boat off again, the seamen strode to meet the soldiers. Worse, Cromarty leapt out to join them and she saw they all had pistols.

CHAPTER ELEVEN

S HE SAW THE flash as one of the French soldiers fired first. In terror, she could not at first answer the boys' impatient questions. And then, a barrage of gun shots followed the first. One of the French soldiers fell. Helplessly, she watched as the rest dived into a melee of hand-to-hand fighting. Shouts drifted back to her on the wind.

She knew what they were doing. They were giving their precious cargo time to get away. Even though they could die. *He* could die…

"Can't we *do* something?" she whispered.

"Just be ready," Kettle replied.

Which is when she also understood Cromarty's final words to her. The ship would leave, if necessary, without the men on shore.

One of the crew in the rigging called down softly. "Frigate to starboard."

And Cromarty's lieutenant hastily doused the only lantern on deck. "Come on," he muttered.

But a little higher on the cliff, a soldier was taking aim at the figure she took to be the captain. Something like a whimper left her lips. Another shout went up ashore. The captain suddenly ducked and something—perhaps a thrown knife—struck the aiming soldier in silence, so that he fell like a boulder down the side of the cliff.

Someone shouted an order. She was sure it was Cromarty's voice, and the men began to separate. The oarsmen, presumably backed toward the boat, while the captain kept the remaining French soldiers covered with his pistol. When the boat was pushing off, he leapt backward into it. As the men began to row, he still kept his pistol aimed at the soldiers.

When one of the Frenchmen moved toward the path, he fired and the soldier leapt back. Cromarty dropped the pistol and another appeared in his hand.

"Oh bravo!" exclaimed Richard, who had seized Mr. Kettle's glass while that gentleman began issuing urgent orders concerning the anchor and the sails. "And he says he's not a pirate!"

Henrietta gave a shaky laugh.

Presumably reckoning that Cromarty's pistol was out of range, the French began scrambling to reload their own weapons, and Henrietta, who had begun to relax into hope, found herself biting her lip in fear once more.

"They're clear," Kettle said heavily. "They're clear." And in fact, when the first soldier fired, he seemed to hit nothing. Mr. Kettle seemed more concerned about the lurking frigate, which Henrietta couldn't even see. She supposed it was on the other side of the headland.

Cromarty and his men swarmed on deck.

"Soon as you're ready, Kettle," the captain said cheerfully, and went to help hoist the boat.

The anchor was already raised. A sail unfurled, the wheel was spun around, and the ship began to roll, turning, creaking, and plunging in the waves.

Henrietta didn't know whether to laugh or cry as Cromarty strode toward her, grinning. He flung a casual arm around her waist and another around Richard's, herding George in front of them to the ladder.

"Frigate's not moving, sir!" one of the seamen shouted. "Don't think it knows we're here."

"Then let's make sure it stays that way. Full sail for home!"

Cromarty released her, so that she could follow the boys down to the cabin. But to her disappointment, he did not come, too.

"By Jove," George declared. "I think that was as good as Alvan at the Hart! How the devil do you know him, Henrie?"

"Didn't I tell you? He's the man who helped me rescue Minnie when I found her at the theater."

Richard frowned. "Yes, but that doesn't really explain how you knew it was him the excisemen were after."

"Not that we're complaining," George put in, "because we're not."

Henrietta hesitated. "Well, Eliza will tell Horry anyway. So, I might as well tell you, too, but you're not to say a word to Mama or Papa. Or Thomasina! I had a wager with Matthew Lacey." And so, she told them an edited version of her first adventure at the Hart and how the captain had helped her rescue Matthew from the strange lady. "All while I was dressed in your best suit," she added apologetically to Richard.

"It doesn't fit me any more anyway," he said carelessly. "But honestly, Matthew must be a bit of numbskull, for you don't look anything like a man!"

"Yes, I do," Henrietta protested, throwing off the cloak so that she could swagger about in Cromarty's ill-fitting garb, a process that entertained her brothers so much that Horatio woke up, and she was called upon for a repeat performance.

She was still in full swing when she realized Captain Cromarty stood just inside the door, arms folded as he watched her display.

She froze, flushing to the roots of her hair. "It isn't meant to be you," she said.

"Thus, assuring me that it is! I shall endeavor to walk with rather less flamboyance."

"But you don't at all," she assured him.

"She just exaggerates everyone's tiniest mannerisms until they're unrecognizable," Richard said. "She does a very funny version of

Papa."

"No, I don't," she said hastily, making a grab for the cloak again. As she did so, she saw that his jaw was bruised and his lip cut. "Are you badly hurt?"

"Devil a bit," he said, striding to the washing bowl where he poured some fresh water and washed his hands and face without embarrassment. His knuckles were grazed and there was a dark shadow of stubble on his face. "We seem to be safe for now. So you can relax. We should be back on English shores by morning."

"What if the excisemen are still there?" Richard asked.

Cromarty's lips twisted into a sardonic smile. "They're more likely to be looking for my cousin and recompense for the false information that had them sitting on a cliff most of the day and night."

"But they probably saw us warning you and going back to *The Siren* with you," Henrietta argued.

"Exactly. At no point did you look anything like a smuggler's d—" He broke off and corrected himself. "…like a smuggler's lady friend. They'll assume you some silly chit who was rescued by a passing ship. And if I'm wrong, and they are still waiting, I'll just land you somewhere else."

"Thank you," Henrietta said, trying to be grateful about the end of the adventure. She watched him pat dry his face and hands without wincing. "Would you like your cabin back? The boys and I can easily—"

"No, I'll be on deck," he interrupted. "The cabin is yours, and I suggest you sleep if you want to pretend to your parents that you spent the night at the Hart."

"Anything else would worry them," Richard insisted.

"I'm sure they have plenty of worry with all of you as it is."

"Actually, they don't," George said. "Because most of our adventures happen without them, and if we tell them, they don't believe us."

"I certainly doubt they'll believe this one," Henrietta said forcefully. "And I sincerely hope no one else does, either."

Cromarty laughed and threw the towel on the washstand. "My lips are sealed. Forgive the intrusion." He bowed. "Good night."

When he had gone, she ordered the boys into the large bed. Then she lay down across the bottom with a blanket over her. Despite the boys' protestations, it wasn't long before she heard the peaceful sounds of their slumber. Her own heart was beating too loudly to let her sleep.

Eventually, she gave up and rose. Swapping the blanket for the cloak, she felt her way out of the cabin and up the ladder toward the muted lights on deck. Cromarty was sprawled on a bench with one hand on the wheel and one knee under his chin while he exchanged friendly insults with the two men who appeared to be on watch.

He straightened when he saw her approach. "Miss Maybury," he said politely. "Is anything wrong?"

"Only that you are calling me Miss Maybury again. I couldn't sleep. May I join you or would you rather be alone?"

"Never," he said gallantly, inviting her to sit with one easy gesture. "It's really a matter of keeping watch and making sure these imbeciles stay awake, too. Are your brothers asleep?"

She nodded, sitting on the space beside him. It brought them very close together, but he didn't appear to mind.

After a few moments of silence, he said with resignation, "Out with it. What do you want to ask me now?"

She couldn't resist casting him a mischievous smile, but she was perfectly serious as she asked, "Who is he? Your cargo whom you landed tonight?"

"I'm not allowed to say."

"He's a spy, isn't he?"

His lips quirked, but he didn't answer.

"I thought so," she said with satisfaction.

He stirred. "You don't ask me if he's a British spy I smuggled into France, or a French spy I'm returning because his work is done."

"I don't need to ask that," she said scornfully.

He looked down at her enigmatically. "Yes, you do. You're far too trusting and you don't know me, Henrietta."

"I know that much. Why do you want me to think badly of you?"

He sighed. "Because it would be more natural. And easier for both of us."

Her heart beat faster at the implications of this. Greatly daring, she raised her hand and touched his unbruised cheek. Immediately, he reached up as though he would pluck it away, yet when he touched her, it was a caress.

She raised her face to his in open invitation. When he only gazed down into her eyes, she caught her breath and pressed her lips to his.

"Oh, Henrietta," he said hoarsely. "You should not kiss a man like me."

"Why not?" she whispered.

"Because I'll never resist kissing you back."

He touched her trembling lips with his fingertips, parting them, and then he bent his head and kissed her with a slow, sensual passion that melted her bones. His arm was around her, beneath the cloak, warm and strong and irresistible. She gave herself up to him in wonder until she gasped for breath. He raised his head, but only for an instant, while his glittering eyes devoured her. And then he smiled and kissed her again.

Although she was disappointed when he ended the kiss, she had the impression it was even harder for him. His arm trembled for a moment before he drew her head onto his shoulder and took a deep, ragged breath.

"It's the sea and the stars and the excitement," he told her. "You'll forgive me eventually."

"There is nothing to forgive. It was I who kissed you first." She gazed up at the clear sky. "Do you navigate by the stars?"

"Of course, when I have to."

"What is that one?" She pointed. "It's brighter than all the others."

"The North Star."

The time drifted by in a mixture of conversation and silence and the sweet warmth of his arm holding her still against his side. Despite her awareness and the tingle of desire deep in her belly, he did not kiss her again. Instead, they watched dawn break together and shared a mug of tea one of his men brought. Cromarty made no effort to free her, seemed not a whit embarrassed by their pose. Neither was the seaman, which led her to the rather troubling conclusion that it was not such an unusual situation for him.

It didn't matter. The night and the new dawn breaking over the southern English coast were magical. She knew he cared for her, that she was special to him. And she knew now beyond a doubt that she loved him.

At last, he stood, stretching prodigiously. "Come. It's time you woke your brothers and changed back into your own clothes. I can't have you distracting me while I find a safe place to land you."

"And your brandy."

"And my brandy," he agreed, holding out his hand. "Come."

She went with him, following him down the dark ladder. At the bottom, she missed her footing and he caught her, almost like on the theater staircase on their first encounter. But this time, he did not let her go. He pressed her back against the ladder and covered her mouth with his. As she flung her arms around his neck, his hand slid inside her too-big, borrowed coat, and closed over her breast.

Her world caught fire. In that moment, there was nothing she would not have done. She was won.

With a groan, he tore his mouth free and pulled her upright, all but shoving her through the cabin door. Dizzy and disoriented, she stared in surprise at her sleeping brothers. They looked positively angelic in the rising sunlight that spilled through the big window over the bed.

WITH NO SIGN of any danger threatening from any of the little coves and beaches near the Hart, Captain Cromarty decided he would take Henrietta and her brothers ashore in one boat and check out the lie of the land before risking his cargo.

Henrietta found him brisk and businesslike, which contrasted unfavorably with the sweetness of the night and the hot, passionate interlude outside the cabin. But, this was daylight, the return to reality, to her family and respectability. And so, although her heart sang whenever she glanced at his face or took his hand to disembark, she only smiled with her usual friendliness.

"May we sail with you again, Captain?" Richard asked.

"Oh, I'm sure we'll meet again," Cromarty said easily, as though his mind was somewhere else entirely. "For discretion's sake," he added, swinging Henrietta off the boat, over the edge of the water to the dry beach, "you should escort your sister back up to the inn without my presence."

"What will you do?" Henrietta asked, feeling suddenly cold without his touch.

He grinned. "Land some brandy, but don't tell."

"I mean after that."

"I'm not sure yet. I might go and visit my cousin Charles."

"Or your grandfather?" she suggested.

He frowned, staring at her with a strange bleakness that broke her heart. "That bird won't fly," he said abruptly. "I can't limit myself to a nobleman's constricting life."

"And yet you will be an earl."

"Will he?" Richard said, astonished.

"Wishing it otherwise doesn't change that and never will," Henrietta pointed out. "Perhaps you should consider the advantages, instead of all those imagined constraints." She held out her hand. "Goodbye,

Captain. You know where to find us."

He took her hand, bowing over it. At the last moment, as though he couldn't help it, he pressed a quick kiss to her fingers and released her to shake hands with each of the boys. It took an effort to leave him, for she had the uneasy feeling he was saying goodbye for good, but she forced herself to smile and to herd the boys up the path with her toward the inn.

On the way, they decided to say nothing to Miss Milsom of their adventure, if she did not know they'd been gone.

"After all, she is employed by Papa, and would probably feel compelled to tell them," Henrietta said. "If we cannot avoid telling her, then I shall own up to Mama."

"We'd be better blaming it on me," Richard pointed out. "Then Papa will put it down to my high spirits and you will avoid awkward questions. In fact, you'll probably get praise for trying to rescue us at personal cost."

"Yes, but that wouldn't be remotely true, would it?"

"No." Richard hesitated, then, "You like Captain Cromarty."

"Yes. Of course I like him." She glanced behind her. "Come on, Horry! We'll get breakfast at the Hart."

Lily was sweeping the front step as they walked across the inn yard, but at sight of them, she dropped her broom with a clatter and hurried to meet them. "Oh, thank God! What on earth happened to you? Where have you been?"

"With Captain Cromarty," Horatio confided with a shining grin. "But don't tell anyone."

Instead of looking shocked, Lily only smiled. "Your secret's safe with me, young sir." Her gaze seemed a little more anxious as she scanned Henrietta's no-doubt-exhausted face, but she said only, "You'll be ready for breakfast. My mother's already cooking it."

"Did you happen to look in on poor Miss Milsom?" Henrietta asked, walking into the inn.

"Yes, I did. She just slept. But she seems better this morning."

"I'll just go up and see her. Boys, go and wash your hands before breakfast."

She discovered Miss Milsom sitting up in bed, drinking tea and eating a slice of toast. She looked very pale still, but her eyes were much brighter and healthier.

"Good morning, ma'am," Henrietta greeted her. "I'm so glad to see you looking better. How do you feel?"

"A little washed out, to be truthful. But I must apologize for yesterday. I just could not keep my eyes open and then I was convinced I was only having a half-hour nap while I slept away the whole day and the night, too!" She looked more closely at Henrietta. "But my dear Miss Maybury, *you* seem unwell now! You are quite pale and your eyes are shadowed."

Henrietta laughed. "You mean I look hagged? No, I assure you I'm quite well. I just did not sleep well." *Or at all.* "We're just going to have breakfast downstairs and then we'll decide if you are up to travelling today. No arguments, if you please! Mama will expect me to look after your health." Rather than abandoning the poor governess to warn a smuggler who was perfectly able to take care of himself.

A smuggler who, in his own way, was aiding his country. And would one day be Earl of Silford whether he acknowledged it or not.

CHAPTER TWELVE

THE COFFEE ROOM at White's Club was quiet at this time of the morning, so Charles Cromarty was able to converse with Lord Rudd in privacy.

"I'm not surprised you botched it," Rudd said contemptuously. "What on earth made you do anything at the Hart? They were bound to warn him!"

"Because I knew I would find him there," Charles argued. "*You* told me I would. And I could hardly bribe enough men all along the south coast! Besides, it was a brilliant idea. He would not only be dead as a common smuggler but his reputation tainted by smuggling links to Bonaparte. It was perfect."

"Except it didn't happen."

"He was there," Charles insisted. "He just didn't come in close enough."

"Well, it's inconvenient. I was hoping to have him dead and discredited before I go back to Brighton. Now I must rely on the fair Lady Carew, who, as you might imagine, has a slightly different agenda to you and I."

"But I can still rely on your help?" Charles said anxiously.

"For anything that benefits us both. What do you expect me to do? Hold him up for you to shoot?"

Charles flushed. "Hardly. If I can follow his movements, there will undoubtedly be other opportunities. All I ask—"

"Rather sooner than you imagine," Rudd interrupted, drawling.

Charles followed his gaze to the coffee room door and saw none other than his cousin Sydney Cromarty stride in. His stomach lurched unpleasantly and he found himself shamefully glad of Rudd's presence. On the other hand, the chances of him looking this way were remote.

Sydney nodded to a gentleman drinking coffee alone near the door. Then his eyes fell on Charles and Rudd and he walked straight toward them.

Oh damn.... Charles looked pointedly up at the elegant, curved ceiling.

"Good God," Rudd drawled, "Are they accepting dashed bankers as members here, now? I might be forced to find another club."

"There is no need for panic," Sydney mocked them quite blatantly. "I am not a member, but no one objected in the slightest to my coming in search of you."

"I don't care to be bearded in my club," Rudd said disdainfully.

Sydney didn't look at him. "I wasn't talking to you. Cousin Charles, a word, if you please."

It went against the grain to jump to the bidding of the man whose existence he so detested. Besides which, fear still held him paralyzed. How much did Sydney know? Anything at all?

"You can have nothing to say to me that others may not hear," Charles said grandly.

Sydney laughed. "Very well, then. Don't send the revenue men after me. You'll only come to grief. Consider it a friendly warning. Not a familial one, because you should know I have no sense of family at all. Good morning, gentlemen."

Somehow, he managed to make the word *gentlemen* sound like an insult. Then he strolled away, exchanging nods once more with the fellow by the door.

"Insufferable!" Charles burst out. "How dare he threaten me in my own club?"

"There, I cannot disagree with you," Rudd said. "Get the matter done, old chap."

HENRIETTA COULD NOT work up a great deal of enthusiasm for the removal to Brighton for a week. For one thing, she had not given up hope that Captain Cromarty might look for her at Audley Park. For another, although Miss Milsom seemed quite recovered, she did not like the idea of leaving all the children—plus Jane Verne during the days—in the governess's sole care. And, frankly, the prospect of more parties, even one at the Pavilion on the Prince Regent's own invitation, did not excite her as it would once have done.

She wondered if she were growing like Charlotte, who had never cared for large parties. But then Charlie, giving her first ball as Duchess of Alvan, had seemed perfectly happy once her nerves had calmed. It was, Henrietta thought, a matter of moderation. Parties were fun only when they were not *constant*.

However, it was not an argument that weighed with her parents. They were delighted that Lord Rudd had bestirred himself to obtain the Regent's invitation and clearly hoped an offer of marriage would be forthcoming during or shortly after their trip. Which was another reason Henrietta did not wish to go. Although having no wish to disoblige her parents, she knew she could never bring herself to marry Rudd.

She tried to tell her mother this as they strolled together to the circulating library in search of the latest novels. Fortunately, Lady Overton was not one of those parents who disapproved of such frivolous reading matter.

"I wish you were not so set on Rudd making me an offer," Henrietta confided. "Because I do not believe I can accept him."

Her mother's eyebrows flew up. "Why ever not? He is a perfect gentleman, and you like his company."

"Not enough to marry him, and in any case, I like him less now."

"Why?" Her mother peered at her. "Has someone else taken your fancy?"

"No, no," she said hastily, crossing her gloved fingers as though that could truly make up for a lie. "But I find him…of a more coercive disposition than I had imagined."

"In what way?" her mother demanded, frowning.

"Oh, just something he said at Steynings. I can't remember precisely, but it did frighten me a little. I think it was because I did not choose him for the waltz."

"Well, you didn't have a lot of choice in the matter since that other gentleman all but carried you off." She thought about it. "If that man truly was Silford's heir, he would in fact be the better match, but he has shown no interest in you since. If you have no affection for anyone else, Rudd is still your best option."

"But Mama—"

"A strong man makes a good husband," her mother insisted. "And you are too keen to have your own way. You will like a firm husband in the end, far more than some milksop who bows to your every whim."

"I don't have whims," Henrietta objected, without strict regard for the truth.

However, as they wandered around the library, she began to wonder if her feelings for Captain Cromarty were indeed nothing more than a whim. He was different enough to catch her eye, dashing enough to fascinate. But what did she really know of his character? Apart from his disregard of the law. And that he bore a long grudge against his grandfather. And that he was a womanizer.

The beautiful and somehow decadent Lady Carew swam into her mind, corrupting her view. The innocent joy of those hours spent with Cromarty on his ship began to make her uncomfortable. She had behaved like a hussy, a trollop, like all his other women, and she was only lucky he had not taken full advantage of her. Exactly what this entailed, she wasn't quite sure, but she had been so beguiled and enchanted, she would have surrendered to anything. To see her own and his behavior in this light appalled her, and she no longer knew if she yearned or feared to meet him again.

She grabbed a novel at random, and just as they were leaving the library, she and her mother ran into none other than Lady Carew. It was as if she had conjured the woman from her own guilt.

Henrietta and her mother both bowed, as did Lady Carew, although after a moment, she offered a languid hand. "How nice to see you in Brighton. The company has been quite excruciatingly dull until now. I'll send you cards for my soiree. I've discovered the most heavenly tenor whom you must hear." And she drifted on to greet the next acquaintance.

Henrietta and her mother exchanged glances of complete understanding. Lady Carew would forget.

IN FACT, SHE didn't. The invitation to Lady Carew' soiree arrived the following morning, together with a brief, scrawled note apologizing for the lack of notice. The event was tomorrow, the evening after the Prince Regent's party.

"We have no real need to go," Henrietta said. "I imagine we have another invitation for that evening which we have already accepted."

"Actually, we don't," Lady Overton said without much regret. "We shall have to go. Oh, don't worry, the world and his wife will be there. She may live on the edge of scandal but she has never quite crossed over."

ALTHOUGH HER FATHER had warned her about the Prince Regent's palace, known as the Marine Pavilion, the sheer opulence still took her by surprise. As did the excessive warmth, for there were fires lit even in the height of summer.

The prince had once been young, handsome, and charming. Now, Henrietta found him middle-aged, fat, and rather lecherous.

Lord Rudd stood beside him as they were presented. "Close friends of mine, sir," he told the prince. "Though, of course, you will know Lord and Lady Overton already."

"Indeed, indeed. Charmed to renew your acquaintance once again. Still glad to be home on English soil, eh, Overton?"

"Indeed, your highness. Allow me to present my daughter, Miss Henrietta Maybury."

"Enchanted, my dear," said the prince, retaining her hand too long and bowing so close that she could smell his breath. "Utterly enchanted." He patted her hand between both of his in a not quite avuncular manner. "We shall talk more later. Welcome to my little haven!"

To each his own, Henrietta allowed, but to her, the prince's haven was nothing less than oppressive.

"What do you think, Miss Maybury?" Lord Rudd asked only a few minutes later, presenting her with a glass of lemonade.

"Honestly? I hate it. It's too opulent and I can hardly breathe."

"Yes, it's pretty unpleasant," he agreed. "Prinny never had any taste."

Henrietta blinked. "Do you tell him that?"

"Good God, no. Being his friend is valuable to me. It shall be our secret." He stayed conversing for several minutes on other topics before excusing himself with a bow to her and to Lady Overton.

Henrietta was almost sorry to see him go, not because she enjoyed his company but because at least he was a familiar face. None of her particular friends were present, and the people she was introduced to all seemed too loud and too cynical without any of the wit that would have made them more congenial to her.

However, she did notice one familiar face—Lady Carew, who drifted through the opulent rooms in her daring, dampened gown, attracting and instantly rejecting the men who flocked about her like feathers from a split pillow.

"Are you admiring Lady Carew?" asked a voice so close behind her that she jumped. It was the Prince Regent himself. "She carries her grief so bravely."

"Grief?" Henrietta repeated. "Oh dear, has her husband died?"

The prince waved one dismissive hand. "He's about to. But I expect you share my love of beauty in all forms. Come, let me show you my favorite collection. I know you will love it."

She found her hand in his arm as he coaxed her away from her mother, who appeared to be deep in conversation with one of the prince's gentlemen. Although she felt a twinge of unease, one couldn't really disobey the Prince Regent. Besides which, he was quite elderly, so it wasn't like slipping away clandestinely with a young man.

Was it? She knew a moment of silly panic as she realized he was actually taking her into another room, and glanced about her in the hope of company. Oddly enough, it was Lord Rudd's eye she caught. He smiled and bowed with a hint of irony, but made no move to follow.

The Regent swept her through a doorway, and though he didn't purposefully close the door, it swung back, cutting her off. "Here are some of my beauties," he said jovially. "Look at this."

The wall of heat and some strange scent was overwhelming, making it difficult for Henrietta to concentrate on the fine works of art the prince showed her with great pride. She would have thought the whole interlude innocent if uncomfortable, had it not been for the way the prince stared fixedly at her as she examined each statuette and miniature and vase. He had got to the level of holding her hand over a porcelain figure to appreciate its texture when the door pushed open.

She had never been more pleased to see Lord Rudd, although she wished he had made his entry five minutes earlier.

"Ah, there you are, Miss Maybury," Rudd said in apparent surprise, as though he had not watched her walk in there. "Your mother is looking for you and about to raise a panic. Forgive me, your Highness, if I deprive you of your companion. I know your other guests are feeling the lack of your presence."

"Oh, very well, very well," the Regent said testily. "You must come another time and view the rest of my collection."

"Thank you, sir." She could bring herself to say no more, merely curtseyed, and walked past Rudd into the main hall which almost felt cool in comparison to the stifling room she'd just left. "And thank *you*, my lord," she added low-voiced. "I had no idea how to extricate myself without blatant flight, and I felt much too dizzy to try."

"Sit here," Rudd commanded, indicating the nearest chair. As she sat, he took the fan from her nerveless fingers and wafted it over her, causing a very welcome, cooling breeze. "A lady shall sit with you while I find you a cooling drink and your mother." His lips curved. "You see, Miss Maybury, I am always able to rescue you."

Despite the heat, she shivered. The whole incident had been Rudd's lesson, perhaps even a punishment for her waltzing with another man at Steynings. He had let her go alone with the prince and given her time to panic before stepping in. A demonstration of his power as well as his greater social skill and knowledge.

For all she knew, he had even made the suggestion to the Prince Regent and caused the distraction of her mother. But perhaps that was ridiculous. She glanced up as a lady sat beside her and had to hide her dismay that it was Lady Carew.

"Rudd to the rescue," she drawled. "Prinny is a terrible old lecher, but I *imagine* he would not actually touch a nobly born maiden. It's the damage to your reputation we must prevent, my feather. Again."

Henrietta regarded her curiously. "Why do you keep my secret?"

she asked bluntly.

"I have no reason not to, and I am famously indolent. Besides, I would do anything for Sydney, as he very well knows."

Henrietta couldn't help asking. "I expect you have known the captain a long time."

"A year or so," Lady Carew replied without obvious interest.

"Before your...friendship ended." She couldn't resist that either, and it won her a look of amused respect.

"My dear child, you will learn a lover's quarrel does not end a relationship but sweetens the reconciliation. You shall meet him again tomorrow evening. And here is Rudd with the welcome parent and lemonade. You are fortunate. Until tomorrow, Miss Maybury." She inclined her head to Lady Overton and drifted away, leaving only her exotic scent behind. And a surge of stupid jealousy that clawed at Henrietta's stomach.

So, Captain Cromarty was in Brighton. The knowledge—or at least the possibility—added a tingle of anticipation to her day, but also anxiety that what Lady Carew had said was true.

Were they really together once more? Had they made-up even before the night on board *The Siren*? She couldn't work out whether their reconciliation was worse before or after. Neither spoke well of his feelings or his respect for Henrietta. Or her own, unforgivable behavior with him.

She was longing for distraction from worries she could do nothing to alleviate when an early morning caller was announced, and Matthew Lacey walked into the salon.

"Why, Matthew," Lady Overton greeted him as he made his bow. "What a pleasant surprise. I did not know your parents were in Brighton."

"They're not, ma'am. I came on my own yesterday, and have made you my first port of call."

"Why?" Henrietta demanded, when her mother returned to her stitching, accepting Matthew as almost family.

"I followed the most beautiful girl here," Matthew said with enthusiasm. His eyes were unusually brilliant. "I thought I might be able to tag along with you so that I can meet her again."

Henrietta blinked. "But Brighton is full of fashionable people right now. *Is* she a lady?"

"Of course, she is!"

"Well, don't get angry with me. Gentlemen frequently pursue females who are not ladies."

"And what would you know of that?" Matthew demanded.

"Enough," she said darkly. "But tell me everything. Who is she, and how did you meet her?"

"Her coach lost a wheel on the Brighton road and I was able to assist. Her parents were most grateful and she has the sweetest smile… Her name is Eunice Blackridge."

The name didn't seem quite worthy of the reverence Matthew accorded it—it hardly rolled off the tongue in a poetic kind of way—but this was hardly the fault of Miss Blackridge.

"I don't believe I know her," Henrietta said regretfully. "But surely if you performed such a service for them, her family would welcome you as a morning caller?"

"Oh, I will call on them, but I can't call *all* the time, can I? I need to meet her in unplanned social situations."

"You do know we are returning to Audley Park the day after to-morrow?"

"Which gives us today, tonight, and tomorrow."

Henrietta wrinkled her nose. "Tonight we're going to Lady Carew's soiree. She invited us, and Mama says we can't get out of it. Do you suppose it's the sort of event your Eunice would be invited to?"

Matthew looked daunted. "I would doubt it."

"Well, we can see," Henrietta encouraged. "Papa is not remotely interested in tenors, so I daresay he would be glad if you offered to be our escort instead."

"Excellent plan," Matthew enthused. "In the meantime, I could take you to…wherever it is ladies go in Brighton. We might bump into her."

This optimistic plan was put into effect. Matthew accompanied them on a shopping expedition and then to make a couple of rather dull calls on friends of Lady Overton. By the time they returned to the house, there had been no sightings of the fair Eunice, and they had established that Lady Overton had never heard of the family. Henrietta began to wonder if they were of quite the rank Matthew imagined, but who was she to judge such things?

"Matthew?" she said as she accompanied him to the front door where they would part until the evening. "Do you know if Captain Cromarty is in Brighton?"

He shrugged. "I haven't seen him. Is there any reason why he should be?"

"Lady Carew said he was, that he would be at her soiree tonight."

Matthew sent her an unexpectedly piercing glance, but said only, "We shall see, then. Until this evening!"

Chapter Thirteen

Henrietta tried not to take extra care over her dress that evening. For one thing, she could not compete with the dashing Lady Carew. For another, she doubted Captain Cromarty noticed such things, and in any case, he was used to seeing her looking like a drowned rat or wearing ridiculous male attire.

All the same, she knew she looked as well as she could. Even her mother nodded her approval. And if there was an excited glitter in her eyes when she gazed in the glass, well, she could keep her eyes demurely lowered. Or strive to look bored, which would serve Lady Carew right.

The thought amused her as they went downstairs to meet Matthew. Her father waved them off with relief at escaping the ordeal, and they set off.

When they entered Lady Carew's spacious drawing room, Matthew suddenly whispered in triumph, "She's here!"

It was only the first surprise of the evening. For after Lady Carew's languid welcome, Matthew all but dragged them across the room to meet the object of his worship. And instead of the unparalleled beauty Henrietta had been led to expect, she found a slightly plain, nervous girl. Her parents, flattered by Lady Overton's attention, seemed to be perfectly respectable, if not of the first rank. The father appeared to be an ordinary country gentleman, much like Matthew's.

For Matthew's sake, Henrietta did her best to make friends with

Eunice, who, however, seemed slightly stiff, with very little conversation. She was different with Matthew, though, and Henrietta discovered she did indeed have a sweet smile, which quite transformed her face from ordinary to pretty for the time it lasted. She reserved judgement.

At last, everyone moved to take their seats for the tenor's performance. As they passed the drawing room's double doors, Lady Carew was talking to one of her footmen, whom she immediately dismissed.

"Ah, Miss Maybury, I've had no chance to speak to you since you arrived. How are you?"

The others, who seemed not to notice she had been waylaid, moved on.

"I'm very well, ma'am," Henrietta replied politely.

"No ill-effects from your affliction at the Pavilion last night?"

"Oh, no. I was fine in cooler air. Thank you for asking."

"I hope you like music. You will love my tenor. Do take your place, my dear, I shall announce him in just a moment." Lady Carew drifted away from the open doors, allowing Henrietta a glimpse into the hallway.

A man in evening dress strolled from the top of the stairs toward a room on the left. Captain Cromarty.

As though drawn by her surge of violent, muddled emotion, he glanced over and saw her. A frown tugged down his brow, which was hardly the reaction she hoped for. But then, she wasn't pleased to see him here either, not when he wasn't a normal guest but a private one making his own way to an entirely different room. As though he were quite at home.

Matthew caught her by the arm. "Hurry up, Henrie, they're waiting for you," he urged, and rather blindly, she followed him to the seat beside her mother.

The tenor was good, so good that he played on her raging emotions, and she had to keep swallowing tears. She was glad when he finished and Lady Carew invited her guests to repair to the dining room for refreshments, although adding ominously that her guest of honor had promised them two more songs later.

Mechanically, Henrietta followed her mother out of the drawing room and into the dining room to the left, where the first person she saw was Captain Cromarty in deep conversation with Lady Carew. She turned hastily away.

But as she let Matthew heap her plate—largely through inertia—she was aware of the attention the pair were drawing. She even overheard several murmurs concerning the fact he was Silford's heir. And connecting his presence to the precarious health of Sir Edward Carew.

"From a disgraced branch of the Cromartys," one lady confided to her friend. "But Silford has no choice but to forgive him."

"Well, it's not the boy's fault his father married a cit's daughter and turned to trade. I just hope he is a gentleman."

"Well, her ladyship appears to think so."

Unable to bear the conversation which she shouldn't even have been able to hear, Henrietta moved blindly away. It took a few minutes before she realized she had lost her mother and Matthew, and looked around for them without much enthusiasm.

A hand stole across her plate and removed one of the elegant canapes teetering on top of the pile. She opened her mouth to tell Matthew off, and instead, gazed up at Captain Cromarty.

"I'm helping you out," he explained, "since you've shown no interest in any of the daunting mountain before you."

The dainty morsel vanished inside his mouth and was gone in a couple of chews.

"Please, help yourself," she managed, offering him the plate.

He took it. "I'll carry it for you. Where do you want to go?"

Home. She swallowed. "Wherever my mother and Matthew have vanished to."

"Are you in trouble?" he asked. "Did word of your unplanned sail get out?"

"Not yet," she said, hastily looking around. "Miss Milsom slept all night and didn't even notice we'd gone. The Villins were so pleased to see us, they asked no questions."

"If they'd been worried, they'd have looked for you. Lily knew you were with me."

"She can't have *known.*"

"Well, she guessed. I'm fairly sure she sent you to me in the first place."

Henrietta frowned. "Why would she have done that?"

"She has her own reasons and means," he said vaguely. "Look, it's quieter through here."

"Are you living here?" she asked abruptly.

He blinked, and she flushed in sheer embarrassment. "Excuse me, it's none of my business. My mouth runs off without my brain's permission."

His eyes laughed at her without rancor. "True on both counts, but since you ask, of course I am not."

It was such a relief, all her other questions died in her throat.

"Why are you here?" he asked more quietly. "She is not a great friend for any debutante, least of all for you."

"She invited us."

"Is Lord Rudd here?" he asked casually.

"Why, do you suspect him of supplanting you?" she snapped.

"Perhaps, but not in the way you mean. What of my delightful cousin Charles?"

"I haven't seen him since he was at the Hart. Why?"

"No reason." He hesitated, then, "I know this will sound rich coming from me, but you should not trust either of them."

She didn't, and yet she refused to let him dictate to her. Lifting her chin, she said carelessly, "Mama expects Rudd to offer for me any day."

His gaze caught hers and held. "Do you?"

"I don't think about it," she said with cool disinterest.

"And if he does, what will you say?"

She raised her eyebrows. "You have no right to ask me such a question."

"I know. But I ask it all the same. Would you marry him, Henrie?"

He was doing it again, making himself the only man in the world who mattered, filling her with trust and confidence in him.

She dragged her gaze free, gazing at the plate he held out to her. "Perhaps," she said, taking a slice of peach, "it would depend on who else asked me."

"Henrie—"

"Ah, there you are, little feather!" Inevitably, it was Lady Carew wafting toward them in a haze of gauze and diamonds.

Cromarty swore under his breath. "Damn, this is impossible!"

Lady Carew held out her gloved hand to Henrietta. "Come! I am charged by your mother to take you to her, since your escort has deserted you for another. Gentlemen are like that—so wretchedly fickle."

Cromarty stood when she did and politely offered the plate. Henrietta glanced at it, then fleetingly up at his face. "You keep it. I find I am not so hungry after all." And she walked away arm-in-arm with the woman she thought she hated most in the world.

Not long after, she was reunited with her mother in the dining room, which was no longer quite so crowded, and the guests were summoned to hear the great tenor's final two songs. Henrietta couldn't help looking around her as she took her seat once more, to see if the captain had gone. He hadn't, but nor did he sit with Lady Carew or with the rest of the audience. Instead, he stood by the wall, his shoulder propping up the doorpost as if preparing for a quick departure. A frown marred his brow, and she wondered whether it was she or something else entirely that was responsible for his anger.

CROMARTY WAS FURIOUS with Susannah Carew, and with himself for falling for her tricks. She had summoned him under a false pretext, and had him shown into the dining room—which was already set with a mouth-watering collation of cold treats—while she entertained her friends of the ton in her drawing room. He was used to such treatment, and merely wished she'd get on with it, while someone warbled on incessantly.

Well, if he was truthful, the man sang beautifully, if he was any judge, but the wretched woman had not brought him here to listen to music. Or had she?

He realized he'd been tricked when she led everyone straight from the drawing room to where he was pacing the dining room waiting for her. Forcing him to be part of her social circle. Now that he was the Earl of Silford's heir.

She came right up to him, smiling.

"Well played, Susannah," he acknowledged. "But it won't work a second time."

"It won't need to. You'll be inundated by invitations from all the matchmaking mamas who want their darlings to be Countess of Silford."

"Think you can cut them out?" he asked insolently.

But she only smiled in the way that had once driven him wild. "Easily."

"Well, the darlings have one advantage," he said. "They don't already have husbands."

As he walked away, leaving her seething, he meant to simply leave the house. If he had not been checked by the unexpected sight of Henrietta Maybury, he would. But she stood alone, for once, looking strangely lost with an enormously heaped plate in one hand. She was peering through the throng of people, as though looking for someone.

He hesitated, for he meant to stay away from her for both their sakes. He told himself she looked just like the puppy she'd found abandoned in the theater, but that wasn't the reason he changed direction and approached her. Nor was her beauty, though he noticed that, too. She shone like a diamond in a wasteland.

Her defensive carelessness, which amounted to rudeness in places, should have amused him. It didn't. But he understood Susannah's reason for bringing her there. She sensed a rival and was telling Henrietta that he was spoken for. Truthfully, it would probably be better for Henrietta if he was, but something was going on he didn't like. He already suspected conspiracy between Charles Cromarty and Lord Rudd. Now he began to wonder if Susannah was not part of it, too.

He had made Henrietta sad, and that bothered him because he wanted so much to make her happy. *"Perhaps it would depend on who else asked me."*

For a moment, he had been unable to breathe. Did she really want to marry him? Even knowing what she did? A wave of happiness shook him to the core, and he had to shake it off to think. He had to talk to her, to resolve this, whatever it was between them. But inevitably, Susannah was there, furious because he had found Henrietta, and her plan had not quite worked.

He should have let it work, he realized as he watched her during the interminable songs. He should have walked away and left her alone. Native cynicism might tell him she was one of Susannah's "darlings", desperate to be Countess of Silford. But he knew it wasn't true. She had put her heart into her kisses and he, utter bastard that he was, had taken them. And still she seemed to want him.

But he was wandering from the important point, which was the conspiracy. Susannah's voracity allied with the violence of the other two, could easily encompass Henrietta. He could not rely on Rudd to protect her. He did not *want* Rudd to protect her, for he did not doubt the man would bring her grief.

And so, when the concert had finally ended, he waited as she and her mother approached the door. She didn't look at him although he was sure she knew he was there. Instead, she seemed to be laughing at something Matthew said. Matthew threw him a quick grin in passing. Cromarty followed them out.

He caught Henrietta emerging from the cloakroom in a moment of quietness and seized her hand. She gasped as he whisked her around the corner into a dimly lit passage. "If you're in trouble, any trouble at all, send for me," he said urgently. "Don't be alone with them, any of them."

She opened her mouth to speak, but already her mother was calling her and there was no time. With an impulse he couldn't help, he raised her hand to his lips and kissed it. She snatched it back and hurried away around the corner.

IT STRUCK CROMARTY, as he took public leave of Lady Carew, that unless her soiree just happened to have coincided with his one night in Brighton, she had known of it in advance. Which meant someone was too aware of his movements. His money was on Lord Rudd, who was famous for having a vast array of gossip coming into him from many sources, great and small. From this, he could sift the information he wanted. The man was serious about Henrietta.

Cromarty couldn't blame him for that. But the combination of Rudd's somehow sinister knowledge and Cousin Charles's determination to be earl was one that worried him. So, he did the unexpected— collected his horse and rode through the night to Steynings.

There were hazards to be faced, travelling at night, but Cromarty had rarely experienced any. On the one occasion someone had tried to hold him up, the highwayman had recognized him, apologized, and shaken his hand before riding off again. On this night, he was aware of a few shadows that made the hair on his neck stand up in warning. But they, too, melted into the darkness.

He slowed, to let dawn break over Steynings as he rode through the ancestral acres. He felt no sense of coming home. Why would he? This had never been his home, and he had never wanted it to be. At least, not after he was eight years old. But he did appreciate the beauty, the sense that the land linked past, present, and future, as did the people sleeping in their cottages, and in the big house looming out of the dawn mist.

He stabled his tired horse before anyone else was up, then went and sat on the bench on the front terrace, wrapping himself in his saddle blanket. Birds' song soothed his tired mind and body and as the sun rose, casting its first warm rays over him, he fell asleep.

WHEN HE WOKE, his grandfather was sitting beside him.

"So," the old man said. "You've changed your mind."

Sydney stirred. "No. I want to ask you something. Two things, really."

The earl waved his stick expansively. "Feel free to do so."

"Is my cousin Charles the reason you are so keen to have me as your heir?"

Lord Silford snorted. "Spotted that much, did you? Charles and the whole parcel of them. Got nothing against Gareth as a parson or as a man. Pleasant fellow. But he's utterly impractical and has the judgement of a flea if his choice of wife is anything to go by. Needless to say, the children all favor her. Charles is petulant, entitled, and stupid. But all the same, he'll inherit all the unentailed land eventually, if you don't come home."

Sydney looked into the distance. "I know money," he said abruptly. "I know trade. I know the sea, and I've made my best friends amongst men who would curl your hair and clear a drawing room in thirty seconds. I know nothing of running an estate."

"It will be harder since you haven't been born and raised with it. But you can learn."

"With respect, you are no judge of that. Which brings me to my next question. What the devil does being earl entail?"

The old man could probably have gone on all day. But once he felt he had the gist of it, Sydney cut him short, rising to his feet and stretching.

"I thought so," he said. "I have neither the ability nor the temperament."

The old man shrugged. "That remains to be seen. Either way, you will still be the Earl of Silford."

Sydney shrugged. "Give me a steward you trust. Any money can go back into the estate. It looks as if it needs it. And I don't. I won't use the title. But who knows? I may yet have children who will."

"Children with whom?" the earl taunted. "The Carew woman? The Maybury chit?"

"More likely some tavern floozie," Sydney said. "And you thought my father made a bad choice. One more thing. I should watch Charles, if I were you. He is really quite keen to be earl, and I doubt he would think twice about promoting your departure from this world. He probably has debts his father can't pay before his inheritance."

The earl curled his lip. "I may be old but that paltry jackanapes could not hurt me if he tried." He caught Sydney's gaze, "You are worth ten of him."

"Oh, at least. And my father was worth rather more. Goodbye, sir."

And he strolled round to the stables, where he surprised the grooms who were scratching their heads over where the strange horse came from.

Chapter Fourteen

Returning to Audley Park made Henrietta more comfortable but could not calm her restlessness. She was glad to see the growing friendship between Eliza and Jane. It did not exclude Horry. In fact, the three of them seemed to have a hilarious time together when the girls were not at lessons. But it seemed to make her less reliant, and Henrietta wrote to her sisters that she had hopes Horatio's next departure for school would have much less effect on his twin.

The good news was that Charlotte and Alvan were hoping to come to Audley Park for a fortnight during August. The bad news was that Rudd was coming to stay first.

"I expect he's coming to make you an offer, Henrie," her father said jovially, when he read the letter out over breakfast.

"Yes, well, we once thought Alvan was coming to make Thomasina an offer," Henrietta pointed out.

"This is different. Fellow's been dangling after you for months. Even *I* noticed that without your mother having to tell me! And it's a good match."

"I know. And I have no wish to disoblige you, Papa," Henrie said anxiously. "But I do not wish to marry Lord Rudd."

Lord Overton cast her an irritated look. Then he sighed. "Girls are trouble. None of you do what is expected."

"But it has worked out well for us," Henrietta pointed out. "At the beginning of the year things looked very different."

"All very well, but what am I to say to Rudd?"

"Nothing. If you can't bring yourself to put him off, I'll give the hint while he's here that marriage is out of the question."

Her father eyed her speculatively. She could almost see him hoping that a few days in the man's company would incline her in his favor. As though some trivial quarrel was merely causing her to be petulant for a week or two.

Her mother's reaction was fairly typical, too. "I suppose we must have some entertainment for him while he is here. Do you think we could risk a small evening party? Hopefully Charlotte will be here by then, and I shall invite Lord Silford. He won't come, of course, but it would be polite. What is his heir's name, Henrie?"

"Captain Cromarty," she said as calmly as she could.

"I shall invite him in the same letter. Though I hope he behaves in a more gentlemanly manner here. I suppose it is difficult for him, having been brought up in trade. Did he seem *very* vulgar to you, Henrie?"

"Not in the least," she managed. "Just a trifle unusual. He won't embarrass you by his lack of manners, if that's what you mean. Though he might put people in their place if they pretend they are superior."

"Perhaps he would not be a very comfortable house guest," her mother worried.

"Well, if Charlotte brings Spring, I should think any discomfort Captain Cromarty could cause would pale by comparison."

"Oh dear, I had forgotten the wretched dog. What if he fights with Minnie? He will have to be banished to the kennels. But perhaps she won't bring him."

Henrietta left her with that fantasy. Her own pleasant imagining was that Spring would annoy Rudd so much he'd leave early or, preferably, take the entire family in disgust.

But nor had she forgotten Captain Cromarty's urgent warning at

Lady Carew's. *Don't be alone with any of them.* She'd known he meant Rudd, Charles Cromarty, and Lady Carew. They were all poisonous in their own way. And it would certainly be harder to avoid Lord Rudd if he was living in the house. Still, she couldn't imagine he or the others would actually try to harm her physically.

Having set her mind on the evening party, Lady Overton sent out cards of invitation to friends and neighbors. Since she planned to call on Mrs. Lacey anyhow, she and Henrietta took the carriage and drove over there with the invitation.

Mrs. Lacey and Almeria were delighted, and when Matthew wandered in a little later and was given the exciting news, his eyes began to gleam. As Henrietta had known he would, he came and sat by her, and when other conversation drowned him out, he pleaded, "Can't you send a card to the Blackridges? After all, you met them at Lady Carew's." Another thought struck him. "Oh dear. Do you suppose your mother has invited *her*?"

"I've no idea, but she plans to ask Lord Silford and Captain Cromarty."

Matthew grinned. "Isn't it great sport, the captain being Silford's heir? Lady Carew is another matter entirely. She either ignores me or looks at me as if I'm her insubstantial dinner. Anyway, you could at least ask your mother to invite Eunice, say you are particular friends or something?"

"She'll smell a hum. I don't believe your Eunice even *likes* me!"

"Oh, she's just shy. Everyone likes you, Henrie."

"Where do they live?"

"Lord knows, but I think they're still in Brighton. Marine Parade."

"I'll see what I can do," Henrie promised, unsure if she was actually doing her friend a favor. She could see nothing in Eunice to inspire his devotion.

But when she suggested the additions to her mother, Lady Overton merely said another young lady would be good for her numbers.

"Though we don't have room for so many people to stay. Why don't you simply invite the girl to come on a visit? Then we shan't have to consider her parents, and she can always share with you if everyone else accepts and we run out of bedchambers. If you like her, I'm she's a good-natured girl."

"Oh, of course," Henrietta said doubtfully, having no idea of Eunice's nature. But she wrote to Eunice that afternoon, enclosing a note from her mother to Mrs. Blackridge, and considered her duty by Matthew done.

As she rose from her desk, she saw, from the window, the children and Miss Milsom heading toward the wood, and hurried to collect Minnie and join them.

Since the boys were home from school, it seemed harsh to keep Eliza and Jane to a strict regime of lessons, so instead, Miss Milsom took them all out on frequent walks or expeditions. Richard deigned to go along on most of these "to help Miss Milsom". Henrietta simply sought distraction from her own muddled thoughts and feelings, and in doing so, rediscovered the fun of her siblings.

That afternoon, walking through the woods to the stream, the children entertained Miss Milsom with stories of Spring, in particular how he had caused havoc while everyone was trying to impress the Duke of Alvan with the sensible propriety of the household.

"But he turned out not to mind in the slightest," Horatio explained. "And he's the only person in the world who can make Spring do as he's told."

"He sounds a rather fearsome beast," Miss Milsom said nervously, which sent everyone into gales of laughter.

They sat by the stream to eat the tea they'd carried with them, and since Minnie had grown so good at coming when she was called, Henrietta let her off the leash to explore. Miss Milsom, clearly feeling obliged to justify the outing, explained to her charges about fresh water flowing down from the hills and into the rivers and from there into the sea.

While they cleared everything up into the basket, Henrietta called for Minnie, who came galloping back along the edge of the stream with her tongue lolling. However, as they set off toward the house, Minnie shot off again the way she'd just come.

"I'll catch up with you," Henrietta said and followed the pup, calling her name. She hadn't gone far when, rounding the bend, she saw a man walking through the trees toward her. Minnie danced around his ankles.

Henrietta's heart leapt. "Captain Cromarty," she managed.

"She's been trying to herd me in your direction. She must be of sheep-dog stock."

"You knew we were here?" Henrietta said, quickly clipping the leash onto Minnie's collar.

"I heard your voices," he admitted. "And then Minnie came to sit with me for a little before running rings around me."

"Are you coming to visit us?"

It seemed unlikely, since he was dressed casually, in old coat and seaman's trousers, rather than as a gentleman.

"No. I was just passing and stopped to rest the horse."

She tried to hide her disappointment, and he said quickly, "How are you?"

"Well, of course. We expect my sister soon. And Lord Rudd comes tomorrow for a week. My mother invited you to our party. Along with Lord Silford."

He blinked at this deluge of news.

"Will you come?" she asked casually.

"I don't know. Perhaps I should."

"Don't put yourself out," she retorted. "It is not a duty, and I am aware you will be heartily bored."

He raised his eyebrows. "When have I ever been bored in your company?"

"I really have no idea."

"Why are you angry with me?"

She rubbed her forehead with her wrist. "I don't know… Very well, I do. I don't want to be nothing to you."

She looked away as she spoke, but even so, she glimpsed the startlement in his face.

"Nothing?" he said quickly and reached for her hand. "Henrietta, I—" Breaking off, he let his hand fall back to his side. "I've gone about this all wrong, haven't I?" he said ruefully. "My brain tells me one thing and my instincts quite another."

She met his gaze, expectantly, but the silence extended. "I'm still angry," she prompted.

He laughed, sweeping back his hat and his hair with one jerky gesture. "I'm thirty-five years old to your eighteen. I'm even older in sin. Even if I weren't a smuggler, I was brought up with family you would regard as vulgar cits, and I have no intention of casting them off. Neither have I any intention of living as the Earl of Silford when my grandfather dies. You are young, beautiful, and enchanting, with the world at your feet and your life before you. I cannot take that from you. And if I did, you would regret it very quickly."

A frown dragged at her brow as he spoke. "How shallow, how fickle do you imagine I am?"

He smiled ruefully. "Sweetheart, I don't think you shallow at all. But everyone is fickle at eighteen."

"You mean you were."

"Yes, I was. Henrie, you only like me because I'm different from the men you know."

"Not as different as you think," she snapped. "You're just as stupid."

A hiss of laughter escaped him. "That, I know. But my poor brain is trying to do the right thing."

Her breath caught. "And what would your instincts do?"

His eyes remained steady although tiny flames seemed to leap from them. "Sweep you off your feet, make you mine, marry you out of hand, and keep you by my side, and to hell with the consequences."

She smiled and heard his breath catch. Her heartbeat galloped as she stepped closer and took his hand.

"There would be consequences," he warned her. "Your family—"

"Would we have fun?" she interrupted.

"God, yes," he said fervently, drawing her against him as though he could no longer resist. She reached up and touched his rough cheek. With a groan, he bent his head and kissed her mouth, long and thoroughly.

"I'm not a child," she whispered against his lips when she could breathe again. "I'm a grown woman. Lots of girls are married before they are my age. And I'm not fickle, Sydney. I love you,"

He groaned again, pressing his cheek to hers, kissing her ear and the side of her neck before returning to her mouth. "God knows why," he muttered against her lips, then sank into them again.

At last he broke free. "It isn't safe for you, though. That's the real reason I'm skulking on your property. I think Rudd's alliance has emboldened Charles, and I really don't trust him. If you were to be engaged to me, God knows what he would do."

"Are you asking me to marry you?" she asked breathlessly.

He rested his forehead against hers. "I'm asking you to think about it over the next few weeks, while I sort out this mess. And then, if you're still of the same mind, we'll talk again. But you must be careful when Rudd is here."

"I will be."

"I'm holding you to nothing, Henrie."

She smiled and kissed his lips. "I understand."

"And we will never live at Steynings."

"I'd rather live on a ship."

He laughed and kissed her until she couldn't breathe, and Minnie had run around them so often they were both tangled in the lead. Sydney scooped the puppy up and unraveled the leash before placing it back in Henrietta's hand. "Now, go before a search party comes back for you."

Henrietta smiled and ran on her way with the dog, waving back over her shoulder. She hadn't believed she could be so happy.

THE INTENSITY OF her happiness helped her face the imminent arrival of Lord Rudd with equanimity. Although she did not want him there, she could easily avoid him, and if she couldn't, she would tell him bluntly not to ask because she could not believe they would suit. In that way, she kept Captain Cromarty out of her reasons, though she was sure Rudd would guess.

Her parents, having learned their lesson earlier in the year about trying to make their family—and pets—behave differently, made no effort to banish the children to the nursery at all times. As a result, they emerged from various doors to witness the arrival of his curricle, which he had driven himself from Brighton, followed by a carriage containing his valet and luggage.

"Good horses," George pronounced, going closer. Rudd, having just stepped down, jerked his head around, probably with a sharp warning not to touch the horses, but Lord Overton was before him.

"Ask permission first, George! Welcome, Rudd, welcome. Come inside and have a drink!"

"He looks a little cross," Eliza whispered in Henrietta's ear after their visitor had bowed over her hand and followed their father inside.

"He isn't cross, precisely," Henrietta murmured. "Just…aloof. And a little pernickety." Odd to think she had once found this manner rather pleasing, as though it raised him above many of his fellow mortals. Now she thought it self-important and just a little ridiculous.

"You won't really marry him, will you?" Eliza asked anxiously.

"No, I won't," Henrietta said with a quick hug. "I promise."

RUDD WAS CLEARLY not as easily beguiled by the family as the Duke of Alvan had been on his first visit. Although he condescended to coax the timid Minnie to come to him, he clearly didn't care when she didn't. He accepted his introductions to the children and their governess without uttering a word to any of them. Later, he was surprised into answering one of George's knowledgeable questions about his horses, but he looked so disdainful afterward that even George was discouraged.

He was urbane and pleasant during dinner, conversing with Henrietta and her mother in his usual manner, which she had once found entertaining. Now it seemed just a little forced and mechanical, and one of his witty stories, Henrietta had already heard before. She found herself wondering if, had she never met Sydney, she would actually have married Rudd. Her mind boggled. Would she really have been so foolish? She hoped not.

Inevitably, after dinner, she was asked to play the pianoforte and sing, which at least served to pass the time, although once when she glanced up from the music, she caught his gaze fixed upon her with a look that reminded her of the kitchen cat with a mouse he had caught. Though it made her shiver, she tried to laugh it off in her mind.

In fact, she looked forward even more to his departure. And there would soon be the leaven of the other guests in just a couple of days. And the Vernes were coming for dinner tomorrow evening.

However, there were many pitfalls to be avoided before then. The following morning, she nearly fell into one of them by walking out the side door with Minnie and turning right into Lord Rudd.

"Miss Maybury." He greeted her with a bow. "I was just taking the air. Perhaps you'd care to join me in a stroll?"

Her heart sank. If he was asking her to go alone with him, he must already have asked her father's permission to address her. Well, it was best to get it over with. A refusal this morning might even see him gone by the afternoon.

Buoyed up by this optimism, she smiled. "I am a slave to this dog at the moment, but please do join us if you wish!"

Since Minnie did not seem to care for Rudd, she was exerting all her growing strength on the end of the leash, tugging Henrietta toward the front of the house.

Rudd's hand closed over hers on the leash, bringing them to a sudden halt. "Would you like me to train her for you?" he asked softly.

"Oh, no. She is *my* dog. But thank you." She met his gaze, smiling determinedly.

After a moment that stretched just a little too long, he smiled back and released her hand. Minnie scrabbled onward toward the voices at the front of the house, and Henrietta let herself be pulled. Rudd strolled beside her.

At the front of the house, Richard stood on the top step with George balanced precariously on his shoulders, peering out over the drive, the view of which was blocked in places by the trees. The twins were dancing about on the terrace below, shouting up, "Who is it? Can you see, can you see?"

Rudd made an ushering gesture in the other direction, clearly suggesting they avoid the racket by walking through the gardens. But Henrietta kept walking toward the children, calling, "What is it? What's going on?"

"There's a carriage coming up the drive!" Horry shouted.

"Well, you'll see who it is soon enough. Although George isn't likely to see anything at all if he falls off there and breaks his skull! It would be much simpler to run down the drive, you know."

"I'm perfectly steady," George said with blatant untruth, grabbing

Richard's hair with both hands. "Don't fuss, Henrie."

"I'm not the one making such a fuss about a mere carriage. It's probably Jane!"

"No, Jane's not coming until later," Eliza said. "She's coming with Lady Cecily tonight and staying with us until tomorrow."

"Oh, dear Lord," Miss Milsom exclaimed, hurrying out of the front door in alarm. "Is that quite safe?"

"Not in the slightest," Henrietta said. "Richard, he's too heavy—put him down!"

But George leapt down himself, crying, "I saw it! It's the Alvan arms! Charlotte is coming!"

"Already?" Henrietta exclaimed. "But that is wonderful! We never expected her before Friday!" She turned to the footman who had stuck his head out the door. "Quick, tell Mama, Gerald! The Duchess is here!"

By then, the carriage, pulled by four perfectly-matched horses, swept around the curve of the drive and onto the terrace. Grooms ran around from the side of the house. The two footmen hurried down the steps after the children to let down the carriage steps, but the door flew open first, and Charlotte and Spring all but tumbled out together and launched themselves into Henrietta's arms.

Laughing, Henrietta hugged her sister whom, she was ashamed to remember, she had once taken rather too much for granted. She and Thomasina had been used to regarding themselves as somehow superior without truly considering what Charlotte had been through in her childhood. Of course, it had been all about saving the family, but none of it had been fair. Only now did Henrietta truly realize what a rock Charlotte had been in the family, and how much they all missed her.

Spring, having slobbered over Henrietta's head, launched himself off her shoulder at the boys. Laughing, Charlotte released her and hugged Eliza and Horatio instead, while Henrietta tuned to welcome her brother-in-law.

Tall and handsome, Alvan was inclined to aloofness, but Henrietta rarely saw that side of him. Now, he grinned easily and kissed her cheek. "How are you, Henrie?"

"Happy," she said honestly. "As I see are both of you! I'm so glad you've come early."

"So is Spring, although your guest seems a trifle uncomfortable."

In dismay—for she had forgotten Rudd—she turned to see Spring rushing at him, bouncing as high as his head. With quick thinking, he stepped back, and on his second bounce, Charlotte reached out and caught him.

"I do beg your pardon, sir," she said, laughing. "We put his ill-manners down to insanity, for he is perfectly goon-natured."

"Spring, sit!" Alvan commanded sternly, as Charlotte set the wildly excited dog back on his feet.

Spring sat, his tail spinning as he waddled forward on his bottom toward Minnie, whom he'd just noticed hiding behind Henrietta's skirts. Minnie emerged, wagging her tail, clearly desperate to talk to the adult dog but understandably wary of his excessive energy. Spring stood up, but without bouncing, and they went nose to nose.

"Good God," said Richard, awed. "Minnie is even better than you, sir. She's tamed him!"

"Not for long," Alvan observed as Spring hurled himself at Gerald and the other footman, who were old friends, and then made a lunge for Lady Overton, who was hurrying down the steps to Charlotte.

This time, the twins caught Spring with a flying tackle and subjected him to the tummy-tickling of his life.

From inbred civility, Henrietta rejoined Lord Rudd, sorry in spite of herself that he had been left standing on the outside.

"What a menagerie," he observed without expression.

Henrietta laughed. "Welcome to Audley Park. Come and meet my sister properly."

Without demur, he walked to the front steps, where Lady Overton smiled at him as though she'd forgotten him and was delighted to find him still here. "Ah, my lord! Charlotte, this is Lord Rudd who is staying with us this week. Sir, my daughter, the Duchess of Alvan, and her husband, the duke. Or are you already acquainted?"

"I don't believe we've ever met face to face," Alvan said, offering his hand. "How do you do?"

Rudd responded in kind, and the adults repaired to the house, although Charlotte could be heard arranging an assignation with the children half an hour hence.

"Maybe you should keep Spring with you for now?" Charlotte suggested. "And perhaps Minnie, too? She is a lovely pup, Henrie."

Chapter Fifteen

Somehow, before the Vernes arrived for dinner, Henrietta had poured out everything to Charlotte, from her first meeting with Captain Cromarty at the theater, through her wager with Matthew, to the recent adventure on board *The Siren*.

Charlotte, who was brushing her hair by the time the long story ended, looked concerned, but did not scold. "I would like to meet this man."

"I think he will come to the party on Friday, but we may run into him before. He is quite…unexpected!"

Charlotte looked thoughtful. "And you love him?"

"More than anything," Henrietta whispered.

Charlotte laid down the hairbrush. "And Lord Rudd? Thomasina seems to think you will marry him."

"I suppose I considered it once, and I'm very afraid that's why he's here. I was about to hint him away when you arrived and threw all such conversation out the window! Mama and Papa would like it, but I couldn't, Charlie, not now."

"No, of course you could not. And there is hope, you know. An earl is a step up from a mere viscount!"

"Yes, but he isn't earl yet and claims he will not live as such even after Silford dies."

"I suspect these things have a way of sorting themselves out," Charlotte said comfortably. All the same, she wore a faint frown of worry she could not hide. Then her brow cleared and she said self-consciously, "I have news of my own. I'm going to have a child."

"Oh, goodness, Charlie," Henrietta said, awed. "That is *very* grown-up." She threw her arms around her sister. "And wonderful! I'm so pleased for you! When will it be?"

"February, we think. I'll tell Mama and Papa, of course, but it isn't generally known yet."

"I shall be discretion itself," Henrietta promised.

That evening's dinner was a complete contrast from the stilted meal of last night. For Charlotte had imparted her news to her parents, and everyone was delighted—apart from Rudd, who knew nothing about it. Nevertheless, he was surrounded by a reunited family in celebratory mood, and he chose to be entertained by the informal fun around the dinner table.

When the men rejoined the ladies in the drawing room, Lord Rudd sat next to Henrietta. "I hope I can induce you to play for us again this evening."

There had been a time when Henrietta had loved to show-off and be the center of admiring attention. But she had learned a lot in the last few months. "My sister is the true musician among us," she said and rose to push Charlotte gently toward the pianoforte.

Charlotte scowled at her, resisting until it would have been ungracious. Even so, she blushed as she sat at the instrument. Henrietta chose the nearest seat beside her mother.

Lord Rudd blinked sleepily at her, clearly aware of her avoidance. But at least he made no effort to pursue her. The rest of the evening passed so pleasantly, the Vernes stayed later than they had intended.

Eventually, everyone spilled out into the moonlight and waved the Vernes off from the front steps.

"A turn in the garden, perhaps?" Rudd murmured beside Henrietta.

"Please, feel free," Henrietta replied. In truth, she was too tired to face this difficult conversation tonight. "I am for bed after all this excitement. Good night."

Eunice Blackridge was expected the following day, so Henrietta wasn't surprised when Matthew appeared during breakfast. He was delighted as always to see Charlotte and was civil to Lord Overton and to the duke and Rudd.

"I knew you were here," he told Charlotte, "when that ball of fluff you call a dog bounced onto my chest at the front door."

"He's calmed down," Charlotte said with more optimism than truth. "How's Almeria? Is she not with you?"

"Still asleep when I left," Matthew replied, accepting his host's invitation to help himself and join them at the table. He took his place beside Henrietta, and under cover of the general talk, asked questions about when and how Eunice would arrive.

Henrietta teased him a little but provided the information. As she glanced casually away from Matthew's ecstatic face, she caught Rudd watching her again. It always made her uneasy.

It was decided they would all take a walk together after breakfast, but as Henrietta ran to fetch her shawl and bonnet, her father poked his head out the library door. "A moment, Henrie."

If her mind hadn't been full of her other visitors, Matthew's romance, Charlotte's baby, dogs, and the fact it was only one day until, surely, she would see Captain Cromarty again, she would have been more prepared. As it was, she walked blithely into the library and was taken aback to see Lord Rudd rising from the armchair.

"I'll give you five minutes," her father said jovially, and whisked himself out of the room.

Instinctively, Henrietta made a move to follow him, casting desperately around for an excuse. But it was time to face this, time to end the uncertainty. It was hardly fair on Lord Rudd to keep him hanging without the truth.

So, taking a deep breath, she turned back and found him right in front of her, as though he'd been hurrying to prevent her leaving.

"My lord," she began, "I beg you will say nothing, for if you speak as I think you mean to, it can only give us both pain."

He raised his eyebrows. "How so? What do you imagine I am going to say?" He looked a little like the cat playing with the mouse again.

She lifted her chin. "I think you are about to offer me marriage, and you should know I have decided not to marry anyone just yet."

"Thank you for the information," he drawled. "But that is not what I was about to ask."

She frowned in incomprehension. There was no other reason for her father to have left her alone with a man not of her family. "Then, what is it you do wish to ask?"

"Nothing," he said, as though surprised. "I am not here to offer, ask, or beg. I am here to tell you what is going to happen."

"Are you? And what on earth is going to happen?"

"You are going to marry me two weeks from today. We shall set off on our wedding trip the same day."

She could not help the drop of her jaw. She wondered if he was actually insane.

"I am afraid you are mistaken, sir. Whether asked civilly or told boorishly, I shall not marry you. Not in two weeks, or one week, or in any other time you imagine. Good morning."

She spun on her heel, but without warning, his hand clamped on her shoulder and turned her back.

"Unhand me, sir," she said tightly.

"Oh, don't be so melodramatic. The sooner you get used to being handled the better. Remember, if you please, that up until a few weeks ago, you were more than happy to flirt with me and keep me dangling.

I have grown tired of it and decided to move matters forward. Your father agrees."

"But I do not!"

"But I think you do. What is it you imagine? That Sydney Cromarty will marry you and make you Countess of Silford when the old man finally turns up his toes? There may even be a lesser title to bestow earlier than that. It makes no difference to you."

"How true," Henrietta snapped back. "I have no such imaginings."

"Liar. But you would do well to be rid of them for a sake of a contented life. We only have a few minutes, so let me say now that you will marry me, and with good grace, because any further attempts at refusal will mean Cromarty's death."

She was trying to tug free of his hand, but at that last chilling word, she froze and stared at him. "What?"

He sighed. "You heard me."

"What, will his cousin send more excise men after him?" she said contemptuously. "The captain can take care of himself."

"Oh, against the imbecile Charles, undoubtedly. I, however, am a very different prospect."

She gazed into his cold, hard eyes and believed him. For it wasn't just cruelty she read there, it was pleasure. He liked hurting her. And he would have no compunction about a mere murder.

"You see, although I would have let Charles take the risk and carry it out had he been able, I can call him off and his cousin will be safe. Or I can send my own men with one snap of my fingers. And they will *not* fail."

Henrietta swallowed, but her throat remained dry. "But…but why would you do such a thing? He means nothing to you."

"But he seems, my dear, to mean something to you."

"You would do such a thing just to spite me?" she said in disbelief.

He regarded his immaculate nails. "Of course not. I would do it to compel you."

"But why?" she asked, bewildered. "What do you want with a reluctant wife who hates you?"

He laughed. "Oh, my dear, you are such an innocent. That, also, I will see to. Suffice it to say, there are many pleasures in the world as yet unknown to you. I find pleasure in compulsion. And I will compel you." He smiled. "I do, don't I? Now, go and tell your eager parents you have accepted me."

"No, wait," she said urgently, as he pushed her toward the door. She felt as if she were in some nightmare from which she could wake if she only tried hard enough. "You cannot mean this!"

He thrust his face close to hers. "A snap of my fingers, *Henrie*," he sneered. "And the man you love is dead. Do you really want to take that chance?"

He was right. She couldn't. At least, not yet, not until she'd spoken to Sydney.

He smiled as though he'd read her thought. "Don't. There will be no further communication with him. You will not write to him or go to him. If you are forced to meet in public—which will not be often, I assure you, given his plebeian preferences—you will merely nod distantly and pass on. I trust I make myself plain, for I would hate you to cry all through our wedding."

"I shall do so anyhow!" she promised with a brief flash of spirit.

"Don't be childish," he said, bored. "To be Lady Rudd is an honor a little trollop like you does not deserve."

Flabbergasted once more, she stared at him, unable to believe he had spoken to her in such a way.

He laughed. "Did you think I did not know about your moonlit escapade at the Hart with young Lacey? Or that it was you who warned Cromarty off landing that night? Well, I believe you must cross Lacey off your list of acquaintances, too."

"If I am a *little trollop*, you should not marry me," she whispered.

"No, I shouldn't," he agreed. "But it so happens I have a soft spot for trollops. Off you go."

THE REST OF the day passed trapped in the same nightmare. Congratulations washed over her, as did questions she could not answer. The only bright spot was that he made no further effort to be alone with her, merely watched her as though prepared to wait for the day she was totally in his power.

She felt sick. And yet she had to welcome Eunice, and ride with her and the others in the afternoon. Afterward, she could barely remember what she had said or done, or even where they had gone.

Only Charlotte dragged her into her bedchamber before dinner. "What is going on?" she demanded. "Yesterday, you swore undying love for Captain Cromarty. Now you're engaged to someone else and it's as if the happiness has drained out of you."

I'll never be happy again. "Oh, it's not as bad as that," she managed. "I've just changed my mind."

"No, you haven't, Henrie," Charlotte said.

"Then how do you explain it?" Henrietta countered.

"I can't," Charlotte said bluntly. "But you don't need to do this, Henrie. You don't have to marry Rudd."

She couldn't help the tiny smile. "Yes. I do."

"No," Charlotte disputed. "I'll stand by you with any threat, any promise you like, and so will Alvan."

"I know," she whispered. "Thank you."

Charlotte took her hands. "I don't know this Cromarty of yours. I don't know if he's suitable for you or if you'd be remotely happy with him. But I do know you're not happy with *this*. End the engagement now before it goes any further."

Henrietta shook her head. She couldn't speak. Already whirling in her head was the expression on Eliza's face as she'd said accusingly,

"But you promised, Henrie, you promised."

IT SEEMED HER only relief could come at night. She could not even cry in her own chamber, for she had to share it with Eunice. And so, she lay awake, waiting for the change in the other girl's breathing that would tell her she was asleep. Only then did she let the tears flow, tears of loss and fear and utter grief, misery over what he would think of her, how much she could hurt him now that he had let her into his heart.

"Miss Maybury?" whispered a voice from the side of her bed. "Oh, please, Henrietta, don't cry."

There was a sound of striking flint and a candle flared to life. Bleary-eyed with tears, Henrietta peered up at Eunice.

"I did not know you cared so for Matthew," Eunice said, distressed. "I never meant to cause you such grief."

"Matthew?" Henrietta was so surprised the tears stopped.

"Is it not so? Have you not agreed to marry Lord Rudd because Matthew has chosen me?"

"Oh, no!" Glad to be able to calm someone's fears, Henrietta sat up. "Of course, I never wanted to marry Matthew. It would be like marrying my brother!"

"Truly? That is what he said, but he spoke of you all the time, and you seemed so close…" One of Eunice's spectacular smiles lit up her face before it quickly faded. "Then why are you so sad?"

"I can't tell you that."

"You love someone else?"

Henrietta nodded. "But please don't ask me anymore!" She reached out and squeezed Eunice's hand. "Thank you. I feel better now and will sleep."

She did, eventually. But at least she woke with an idea. She could not write to Sydney without endangering him. But she could at least get a message to him.

By dawn, she was scribbling a note at her desk. "My dear, please believe that though everything else has changed, my feelings have not." There was no time for more, because the house was stirring and the maids all had duties. She dashed off her name, folded the paper, and wrote the letter S on it, before folding it within a larger paper with Miss Lily Villin inscribed upon it. Then she dashed into the passage and seized Nell the chambermaid.

"Deliver this to the Hart Inn, if you please, right away. I will get someone else to cover your duties. Go!"

Her eyes wide with intrigue, Nell dashed off. Henrietta went back into her room and sank onto the window seat, waiting to see the girl's departure. Wrapped in her shawl, the girl hurried across the terrace.

But someone ran after her in the grey morning light. A man who caught her playfully by the shoulder.

"Hurry, Nell, hurry," Henrietta muttered, and then the man spun around, teasing the girl, and she saw his face. It was Claude, Lord Rudd's valet.

The nightmare went on. Claude teased the letter out of her and hurried on, as if he meant to deliver it for her. But at the sound of the door closing again behind her, he stopped and walked back to the house.

Outraged, Henrietta flew to her feet, meaning to confront him and obtain her letter back. But she wasn't even dressed, and there was no servant to send in her place.

Washed and dressed at last in the first gown that came to hand, she left Eunice to sleep and ran downstairs, meaning to go straight to the kitchen and the servants' hall. Gerald would have her letter out of that vile valet's hands in a matter of seconds, she thought with satisfaction.

But someone fell into step beside her. Lord Rudd. She greeted him only with icy silence. Nor did he speak until she walked past the door to the breakfast room toward the green baize door to the servants' domain.

"I wouldn't bother," he said calmly.

She glanced frigidly over her shoulder and saw that he held her letter in his hand. She flushed with fury, her heart sinking further than she'd known it could go. He held open the door of the breakfast room and she walked straight past him, her head held high.

Annoyingly, no one else was up, so she stood alone with Rudd. Deliberately, he closed the door.

"Who the devil is Lily Villin?"

She stared at him. "The innkeeper's daughter."

"Well, if you want to keep her safe, don't use her as an intermediary any more. You might not have broken the letter of your promise, but you most certainly broke its spirit. This is the only mistake I will allow you. One more and I'll have him killed immediately, and marry you the day after."

But she was growing wiser as to what pleased him. Any sign of weakness or distress made his eyes gleam. So, she merely shrugged and walked out of the room. For once, she took him by surprise and he did not stop her.

FOR THE SECOND time that month, Sydney Cromarty let himself into Lord Verne's library.

It was dusk, and Verne had only just entered the room, walked across the floor, and picked a book off the desk. He spun about at Cromarty's entrance and glared at him. "Will you stop doing that? I'll forget whose house it is."

"I didn't want to disturb your lady."

"She'll be more disturbed by people letting themselves into the house than calling at the front door." Verne's frown deepened. "You can, you know."

Cromarty gave a crooked smile. "Now that I'm an earl's heir?"

"Now your reasons for being here are not totally against the law," Verne corrected. He lifted his brow. "Or are they?"

"No." Sydney paced across the room and back before throwing himself into Verne's winged armchair. "Are you going to this party at Audley Park tomorrow?"

"Yes. Are you?"

"I don't know." He rubbed his forehead until Verne walked to his desk, poured two glasses of brandy, and pressed one into his hand.

Sydney drank. "I'm a selfish dolt," he said abruptly. "All my life, the only path I've followed has been to please myself, not even my parents. And I've looked on it as a virtue."

"Maybe it is."

Sydney cast him a dubious look. "Even the smuggling?"

"Well, it's led to your helping your country."

As though just remembering, Sydney delved inside his coat and took out a folded paper which he threw to Verne. "Message left at the Hart."

"I'll pass it on." Verne sipped his brandy. "I'm going to make a wild guess and ask if this heart-searching is anything to do with a young lady."

Sydney smiled ruefully. "Am I so obvious?"

"You're not yourself," Verne admitted. "Cecily is convinced there is something between you, and she is rarely wrong about such matters."

"She's young, pure, innocent, and I am...*this*." He gestured to himself with loathing. "I have no right to her, and yet I would make her live like me."

"Does she want to?"

He couldn't help smiling. "She says so. And in truth, she would enjoy the odd adventure. But she should be mistress of some fine house, with a stable home and family and every comfort."

"Does it have to be a choice?" Verne asked. "One or the other? Couldn't she have both? Couldn't you?"

Sydney stared at him, frowning.

"It isn't just a matter of selfishness, is it?" Verne pursued. "You have a right to be comfortable and happy, too, whatever form that takes. But actually, I think you'd make rather a wonderful, eccentric earl. I suppose you might have to step back from the smuggling a little, though."

Sydney let out a crack of laughter. "At the very least." He fixed his gaze on Verne's. "You see nothing wrong in such a union?"

Verne shrugged. "I'm hardly the best judge of such matters. But, no, I don't. Not if you love her."

Sydney squeezed his eyes shut. "God help me. After all this time, slain by a chit barely out of the schoolroom. But she is so much more than that, Patrick."

"I know."

Sydney opened his eyes and gave a lopsided smile. "And I can't believe I'm asking advice from a boy I fished out of the sea to preserve from the revenue men."

"Well, there was always more to you, too, Captain! Come and have a glass of wine with Cecily."

Chapter Sixteen

SPITTING OUT SOME of his concerns to Verne helped clarify things in his head. He woke in the morning full of energy and as he went about his business, sending *The Siren* off to Ireland with Kettle, he realized he was almost bursting with happiness. Such an emotion was surely more suited to a youth in the throes of first love, but he couldn't help it. He finally admitted to himself that he longed to see her, that every moment apart from her had become torture. And he would see her tonight.

He suspected he would see his grandfather tonight, too, and perhaps reach some kind of understanding with him. People made mistakes. Who was he to judge his grandfather for hurting his father? He still couldn't quite imagine himself as master of the palatial house at Steynings. He would always be much more at home on the deck of a ship. But with Henrietta, it would all be fun. And there were things he could do, surely, for the people and the land…

He dressed with care in black coat and pantaloons, and a fresh, white cravat with a single diamond pin. A splash of color was added by his tastefully embroidered waistcoat.

"Very handsome," Lily approved as he left his chamber at the inn.

To his annoyance, he actually felt a flush rise to his cheeks. "Thank you."

"Good luck, sir!"

Damn it, did the whole world know of his plan tonight? Lord

Overton was as likely to throw him out on his ear as to entertain him as a son-in-law, and Sydney couldn't blame him. The question was really how to persuade him because he didn't think Henrietta would take well to waiting three years until she was one-and-twenty. They could elope, of course, but while he was prepared to do it, he didn't really want her to begin their married life with such a scandal.

There were ways. There were always ways to do anything.

As he rode up to the house, there were carriages halted on the terrace disgorging their splendid occupants. Sydney dismounted and gave his horse into a groom's keeping before strolling inside.

Compared with Steynings, the house at Audley Park was not huge. But it bore more signs of recent decoration and greater comfort. Sydney followed other guests into the drawing room and was not surprised when several conversations halted and many heads turned in his direction. Word had spread since the ball at Steynings. They knew who he was.

"How good to see you. Mr. Cromarty, is it not?" Lady Overton said, offering her hand. "Or Captain?"

"Mister will do perfectly. Thank you for inviting me."

"Our pleasure, sir. Allow me to present you to my husband, Lord Overton. I'm sure you will find many friends here, including Lord Silford, as I'm sure you know."

Sydney made the correct noises and moved on, his eyes searching out Henrietta. Dressed in diaphanous white muslin trimmed with embroidered red roses, she stood with another young lady dressed in gorgeous midnight blue, and seemed to be chattering excitedly.

Oddly, his first thought was that something was wrong. Her posture, her glittering eyes, the slightly jerky way she swished her fan, all seemed somehow not quite right. But, of course, she was waiting for him. She had no idea what he would do, whether he would speak to her father or carry her off like a damned pirate. God knew part of him longed to.

Her darting gaze found him at last. But there was no surprise in it. She had seen him as soon as he'd come in, and yet made no move toward him. Her gaze slid away again.

Sydney accepted a glass of champagne from a footman and strolled toward her. On the way, he spotted another reason for her discomfort. Susannah Carew, who smiled at him like the coquette she was. He nodded curtly and discovered he stood beside his grandfather.

The old man sat on a sofa, a glass of wine in his hand. Sydney dropped into the place beside him. "My lord."

"Sydney."

"You like her," Sydney said abruptly. "The daughter of the house."

"I think she's just what you need."

"If necessary, will you speak for me to her father?"

The old man's smile was rueful. "Is this a condition of your coming home?"

"No." Sydney got to his feet once more and resumed his path to Henrietta.

But Lord Overton was there already, with Rudd. Overton said something to her and she clutched the arm of the girl in blue beside her. Then her gaze flew beyond them and again connected with Sydney's.

Oh yes, something was very wrong.

A footman rang a small hand bell, and into the surprised silence, Lord Overton said, "Forgive my interruption! I merely wish to welcome you warmly to Audley Park. And at the request of my eager son-in-law-to-be, to ask you to raise your glasses in a toast to the betrothal of my daughter Henrietta to Viscount Rudd."

The blood raged in Sydney's ears. The sound of his life, his happiness falling in on him and crumbling to dust. She did not even look at him but at her father. It was the girl in blue who gazed at him, a frown on her brow.

Dear God, he had been led up the whole garden path, and for

what? A coquettish whim no different from Susannah's? Humiliation seemed the least of his troubles. He had wanted so much. And once he had admitted it, let the happiness in, he had realized the depth, the strength of his unwanted and unlooked-for love for this girl. He'd been going to change his whole way of life, change the world if necessary, for her.

And just like that, she engaged herself to another man, the man who had pursued her all along and allied himself with Sydney's murderous cousin. There were so many betrayals in this engagement, he couldn't count them.

Instead, he eased his way through the guests and out of the drawing room. He abandoned his untouched wine glass on a table in the hall and walked out of the house. He wanted to kill.

SHE COULDN'T RUN after him. Rudd would have him killed. Even Charlotte couldn't help her. The nightmare stretched on, would spread throughout her life, made all the worse by the pain she'd inflicted on the man she loved.

In the meantime, there was this dreadful party to get through. Only two days ago, she had looked forward to this night…

At least Matthew and Eunice seemed happy in each other's company. And Rudd, having made his point, totally ignored her. Not so Lady Carew who deliberately sat down next to her during a music recital and patted her hand with her fan.

"What a clever choice, my dear. I wish you and Rudd very happy. He has a fine estate, and I am sure you will be able to do as you please very soon." She smiled. "Now, you mustn't worry about Sydney. Brutes like him are easily consoled."

He isn't a brute! The words stuck in her throat.

Lady Carew leaned forward. "I should know."

Henrietta turned her gaze away.

"Have I shocked you? You see, you could never have handled him, let alone tamed him. It is best not to care too much when you marry an unfaithful man. In that respect, you and Rudd will work much better. As will Sydney and I."

Henrietta stood up. "Forgive me," she muttered and walked away in search of refuge, any refuge.

Had he really gone?

Another thought struck her somewhat belatedly. Did Rudd's reach really stretch so far? She had no way of knowing, not without talking to Sydney, and that was denied to her. She could not take the chance that Rudd was exaggerating or downright lying. Not with Sydney's life.

SYDNEY WOKE ON the coffee room bench at the Hart. Which was odd. Because although he was weary and bleary-eyed, he didn't think he was drunk. He'd walked and run for miles over rocks and beaches before collapsing in here. He remembered why, though his mind still shied away from that. Instead, he tried to focus on where he had seen the girl now staring down at him.

She wasn't a girl, in fact. She was a lady.

Frowning, he shifted position on the bench and a ball of furry energy landed on his chest. A cold nose was all over his face and ears.

"What the…" He sat bolt-upright, and a small terrier tumbled into his lap before bouncing up with a hectically wagging tail. It leapt onto his shoulders, bounded onto the table and the floor, galloped a quick circuit of the room, and then hurled itself at Sydney again.

The lady caught it with an ease clearly born of long practice, and passed it to a gentleman whom Sydney hadn't previously noticed. But something had clicked into place in his sleep-deprived brain.

"That," he said, pointing to the dog who now sat on the gentleman's boot, wagging his tail off, "has to be the infamous Spring. Which makes *you*..."

"Charlotte," the lady said.

"The Duchess of Alvan," Sydney finished and glanced at the gentleman.

"Alvan," the duke said succinctly.

"I don't seem to have the space to stand up," Sydney said with a wave of one hand. "But consider all the necessary courtesies performed in spirit, and if you're staying, take a seat." He raised his voice. "Lily!"

"We've already bespoken coffee and breakfast," the duchess said.

Sydney stretched his stiff legs. "I expect you'd like me to take my unwashed person elsewhere. Or there is a private parlor you could use."

"We are quite comfortable here," Alvan stated, "since it's quiet, and it is you we have come to see."

"You have?" Sydney looked at him more closely. He was a quietly elegant, good-looking man with cool, rather hard gray eyes. "Did you bring the horsewhips, or do your servants do that?"

"Do what?" the duchess asked, bewildered.

"Never mind."

Lily and Mrs. Villin both came in, carrying trays of breakfast and coffee. Neither of them seemed remotely surprised, let alone flustered to have the Duke and Duchess of Alvan in their house for breakfast, and the duchess called them by name.

"You've been here before," Sydney observed, pouring coffee into three cups.

"Actually, we were married here," Alvan said casually.

"Which is interesting," Sydney allowed. "But doesn't explain why you are here now sharing breakfast with me."

"Henrietta," Charlotte said.

"She's pure as the driven snow," Sydney snapped.

Charlotte looked surprised. "Well, I know that. I want to know what's the matter with her, why she has engaged herself to that man only a day after telling me she wanted to marry *you*."

Sydney's stomach churned unpleasantly. "Ask her."

"I did. She won't tell me."

Sydney shrugged, studiously careless. "Young girls are fickle."

"Yes, but that's the thing," the duchess said impatiently. "Henrietta isn't. She never was. She is loyal to a fault. She was quite prepared to sacrifice herself on the altar of family pride."

"Well, there's your answer," Sydney snapped. "She is pleasing her family."

"No, she isn't. For she told both my parents she would not accept Rudd if he asked, and she told me she loved *you*. So what changed?"

Doubt twisted through Sydney. It had done the same a couple of times last night, too, but he had been too hurt and too angry to pay it much attention.

"Rudd," he said slowly. "He has been a few days with you now."

"He was there when we arrived from Lincolnshire."

Sydney reached blindly for his coffee. "He has compelled her…"

"I asked her that and she denied it. She won't say why she has agreed, just that this is what she wants. But I have to tell you, Captain, it is very hard to make my sister do what she does not wish to. Nor is she easily intimidated. She is no milksop to be persuaded by a stern word or even any threat to her person. She was a fearless child, and I never saw that change."

Understanding swept his breath away. "He threatened *me*. She thinks she's doing it for *me*."

Alvan frowned at him. "*Can* he hurt you?"

Sydney shrugged. "He could make things difficult for me, but no, of course he can't hurt me." He looked at the duchess. "Henrie doesn't know that."

The duchess cut herself a good-sized mouthful of ham. "Then I suggest you tell her before she gets much older and finds herself Lady Rudd."

"I'd make her a widow quickly enough," Sydney said savagely.

Alvan reached past him for the coffee pot. "That's the spirit."

HENRIETTA WOKE WITH a headache that just seemed part and parcel of her misery. But she knew she had to think through it, to find a way to help Sydney rather than simply stop Rudd from killing him. There had to be a way to remove Rudd's power, or at least interfere with it. Her father was still an influential man, but she could not involve his friends without him knowing.

Alvan.

Charlotte's husband was a duke, the most powerful nobleman there was. She lay in bed pondering what on earth use it could be to her while Eunice rose and dressed with the aid of the maid she had brought with her.

"Won't you come down to breakfast, too, Henrietta?" she coaxed.

Henrietta rubbed her head, managing a brief smile. "No, I'm not hungry. But Charlotte will look after you."

"Her grace is very kind," Eunice said warmly. "Shall I get them to bring you up a tray? Or smuggle you a sausage in a napkin?"

Henrietta forced herself to laugh but said, "No, no, truly I don't want anything. Thank you, Eunice."

"Well, we shall ride together later on as we planned."

Henrietta nodded, though she could summon no enthusiasm. When Eunice and the maid left, she rose and opened the window to let in some fresh air before she washed and dressed as best she could without anyone to lace her up. Then, she sat at her desk and tried again to concentrate on a solution to this mess. Rudd had forbidden her to speak of their agreement to anyone, and certainly he had been able to prevent her note from reaching the Hart. But he would never know what she discussed in private with Charlotte and Alvan, and the more she thought about it, the more convinced she was that they could help.

Infuriatingly, the bedchamber door opened after only a few minutes. She was sure she would have had longer in peace.

Trying to squash her irritability, she turned. "Eunice, I hope you didn't hurry on my acc—" She broke off, suddenly unable to breathe, for it was not Miss Blackridge who walked in and closed the door but Sydney Cromarty.

She stumbled to her feet and threw herself across the room and into his arms. "Oh, Sydney, oh, my love, you should not be here. Oh, thank God, I—" The rest was cut off by his mouth as he ruthlessly kissed her.

She clung around his neck, kissing him back, though tears streamed down her face. "You don't hate me," she whispered.

He brushed her tears with his fingers, a tender caress. "Of course I don't hate you, although I confess, I had a few difficult hours."

"You know I didn't mean it?" she said anxiously, taking his face between her hands. "Everything has changed, but not my feelings for you." To prove it, she pressed her lips to his. "But it cannot be, Sydney… How did you get in?"

"The duchess left a side door unlocked for me and gave me directions."

Her eyes widened. "*Charlotte*? When did…oh, Sydney, you cannot be seen here!"

"I admit it would cause quite a scandal. You might be forced to marry me."

She pressed her cheek to his. "Oh, God help me," she said tragically. "I think I'll have to marry Rudd, for I don't see how even Alvan can stop him."

Sydney urged her toward the bed and drew her down to sit beside him, his arm warm and comforting around her shoulders. "You had better tell me what happened."

And so, she did, blurting out in a rush the awful interview that she had imagined she could control, the offer of marriage she had meant to dismiss but which had turned into a threat she could never have foreseen. She even told him about the intercepted note she had tried to send via Lily. Sydney's arm tightened about her, and once his fingers dug briefly into her arm as though he could not prevent the reflex.

"He is a *terrible* man," she finished with despair.

"No, he isn't," Sydney said flatly. "He's a nasty little bully and a flim-flam man."

Her mouth fell open, and he kissed it.

"What did you imagine, my sweet? That he has a network of spies and assassins all over the country, just waiting for me or any other of his enemies to do something he dislikes? That he could instantly mobilize people to shoot me, or poison me, wherever I was, just because you wrote me a letter?"

She searched his face, irritation that he wouldn't take this seriously warring with hope that he was right, that she had been foolish and gullible. "Yes. I suppose that is more or less exactly what I thought. And how do you know it isn't true?"

"Because I actually *do* have a network I can draw on for information—business people, traders, sailors, and friends in all walks of life. And I have asked around. The man has a large circle of gossips who occasionally give him salacious snippets to hold over someone or other. But he has no real influence at all except on his tailor and a few frightened household servants."

Henrietta exhaled slowly. "I suppose I should feel sillier. I did have moments of doubt, but I could not risk you, I *could* not."

It earned her several more kisses that were sweet enough to distract her fears and let them seep away to nothing.

"Then he can't hurt you?" she asked at last, brushing her lips against his.

"Not as much as I intend to hurt him."

"Oh, but you mustn't kill him, Sydney," she said anxiously. "They might hang you."

Sydney grinned. "I never thought I would say this, but I think we should involve the law. Who is the justice of the peace in the neighborhood?"

"Mr. Lacey, Matthew's father. But what on earth can he be charged with? I cannot prove he threatened me."

"Conspiracy, among other things. Hopefully, we can land my murderous little cousin with the same catch." He rose, pulling her to her feet. "Shall we go and see Mr. Lacey together?"

A smile seemed to rise up from her toes. "Oh yes!" Her gown slipped off her shoulder and she blushed, hastily jerking it back it up, "I dressed in a hurry. If you wait five minutes"

"Let me do it," he offered. "It will be quicker."

She hesitated, only too aware of the intimacy of the situation. Then she turned her back. His fingers were sure and efficient, speaking volumes for his past. But there was no room for jealousy of unknown women as his fingers brushed her naked skin. She gasped at the touch of his lips on her back and shoulder and nape.

"Every line, every curve is so lovely," he murmured. "I could drown in your scent."

Nervously, she twisted her head and met his mouth, hot and devouring. Her bones melted. Flames of desire leapt deep in her belly. She gasped and gasped again, and he dragged his mouth free, his breathing ragged.

"Let us go," he said hoarsely, "before I unlace you all over again."

She swallowed, forcing herself to think. "We can leave by the window."

Laughter hissed from his lips. "In broad daylight? It might be fun, but I feel we'd be more discreet leaving the way I came in."

"I suppose most people will still be at breakfast."

Seizing her hat, she went to the door and opened it a crack before peering through. Discovering the passage was empty, she beckoned Sydney, and they ran together to the back stairs. They had to dart into a cupboard to hide from one of the visiting servants laboriously climbing the stairs with a tray for her mistress.

"Susannah's maid," Sydney breathed in her ear.

Henrietta was almost surprised to discover she did not mind. They were having too much fun, and Lady Carew was as much his past as childhood. They ran down the rest of the stairs to the passage below, dodging two of her parents' friends en route to breakfast, and finally made it out of the side door.

"My horse is at the east side of the wood," Sydney murmured.

"I'll meet you there." Henrietta walked briskly round to the stables and gave orders for her mare to be saddled. She met with little resistance when she rejected the offer of a groom to accompany her.

"I have an escort," she said carelessly.

There had clearly been horses in and out already this morning, for no one batted an eyelid. Although she didn't want her family worried, on the whole, she thought she did not care if she ran into any house guests on their journey.

Ten minutes later, she joined Sydney on the east edge of the wood. His eyes gleamed, and she smiled with happy excitement as they galloped off side by side.

CHAPTER SEVENTEEN

B Y CHANCE, THEY encountered Matthew on the road near Seldon Manor.

"Hello!" he exclaimed. "Where are you two off to?"

"Looking for your father," Sydney said succinctly.

"He's in his office, but mainly to hide. Got a thick head if you ask me. Where's Eunice?"

"Going to breakfast when I last saw her." Henrietta frowned suddenly. "Oh dear, we had a plan to ride later. It was to meet you, wasn't it? She'll think I've abandoned her, which I have, only it is important."

"It had better be," Matthew said, scowling. "For Rudd won't like you careering around the countryside with *him*. Or anyone else."

Henrietta smiled. "Well, I have discovered I don't care what Rudd likes or dislikes. In fact, that's why we're going to see your father. We want him to arrest Rudd and Charles Cromarty."

Matthew glanced along the road, clearly torn between love and adventure. "Damn it, I have to come with you," he decided. "This is too good to miss."

Sydney grinned and kicked his horse into motion.

Very quickly after that, Matthew was leading them through a side door that led straight into his father's study. In this way, miscreants could be hauled before him without the chance of them encountering his family.

Frowning, Mr. Lacey glanced up from his newspaper, then

dropped it in surprise and rose to his feet. "Bless my soul, Miss Henrietta! What are you doing here? Matthew, you blockhead, why do you bring her in this way?"

"Oh, we asked him to, sir," Henrietta said quickly. "Mr. Lacey, are you acquainted with Captain Cromarty?"

Lacey's brows flew up. "Silford's heir? No, I don't believe I've had the pleasure." He stretched out his hand, and Sydney stepped closer to shake it.

"I'm afraid we need your help as magistrate," he said bluntly. "And as a friend to Miss Maybury's family."

"I am at your disposal," Mr. Lacey said at once. "Some refreshment? Coffee? Wine?"

They refused politely but took the seats they were offered.

"I wish to report an attempt on my life," Sydney began, and explained the exciseman on the rocks beneath the Hart.

"But you were smuggling," Lacey said bluntly. "Were you not? And you have no witnesses to your story, besides your own men who will hardly count."

"If I was smuggling, it was to cover other comings and goings on His Majesty's business. I believe those protecting the shores have orders not to shoot at my ship. But you will know where to confirm that."

"And there were witnesses," Henrietta told him. "My brothers and I were there. Only one of the excisemen had his weapon aimed at the sea."

"We believe he was paid to shoot me by my cousin Charles Cromarty," Sydney said. "In conspiracy with Lord Rudd, who presumably supplied the fee since Charles's pockets are to let."

Mr. Lacey's mouth fell open. "*Rudd?*" His gaze flew to Henrietta. "Your betrothed."

"I was coerced," Henrietta said firmly. "So it does not count."

"Leaving that aside for the moment, have you proof of such a conspiracy?"

"No," Henrietta admitted, "But—"

"Yes," Sydney said, laying a slightly crumpled paper on the desk before the magistrate.

Henrietta's eyes widened in surprise.

"It's a note from Charles to Rudd," Sydney explained, "requesting funds for the purpose. It's quite explicit."

"How on earth did you find that?" Henrietta demanded.

"I told you, I have many friends, and his household is frightened."

"It's enough to question Cromarty," Lacey allowed. "If he's in the neighborhood."

"He is, and I believe he'll give you Rudd, too."

Henrietta closed her mouth.

Lacey said, "But I need to identify the exciseman in question. For many reasons, not least of which he might identify Cromarty and Rudd. Neither of you are impartial witnesses."

"But you do believe them, don't you?" Matthew interceded, which earned him his father's scowl.

"Exactly what is your interest in all this?" Mr. Lacy demanded.

"Friendship, curiosity, and justice," Matthew said promptly.

Henrietta cast him an admiring glance, although Sydney only grinned.

Lacey grunted and stood up. "I'll go to the revenue office now, and then—"

"Might I make a suggestion?" Sydney intervened. "While you do that, I could bring Charles to you. At the Hart, perhaps, to save further intrusion into your home."

"I'll go with him," Matthew volunteered.

"Hmm, perhaps you'd better, since I doubt I can persuade Miss Maybury to go home. Overton will *not* be happy about her galivanting about with the captain here."

Matthew grinned. "Do you mean I'm their chaperone?"

Sydney stood and clapped him on the shoulder. "You can be Henrie's honorary aunt. Let's go."

Outside, they crossed the lawn to where they had left the horses. At the last moment, Sydney loped after Mr. Lacey to the stables, to make sure he was taking a burly escort with him.

"So," Matthew said to Henrietta. "You and the captain."

"Me and the captain," she agreed, uncaring of her grammar, which would have made Miss Milsom shudder.

"Damned if I know why, but you do seem well suited."

Henrietta smiled and gave him a sisterly hug. "So do you and Eunice."

Matthew hugged her back, and they laughed together in perfect understanding.

ON HER RETURN to Audley Park, Charlotte felt quite pleased by her intervention. She had not been unsure about going to the Hart in search of Captain Cromarty, but it had seemed vital to discover what sort of a man he truly was.

"Is Captain Cromarty here?" she had asked Lily after answering the girl's delighted greeting.

Lily had hesitated. "Yes, but I'm not sure he's fit for polite company."

"Bosky?" Alvan had inquired.

"No, sir, I don't think so, but he's like a bear with a sore tooth and he's only been asleep a couple of hours."

"What's wrong with him?" Charlotte had demanded.

Again, Lily had hesitated and then she said, "If you ask me, he's heartsore."

"For my sister?" Charlotte had asked bluntly.

Lily had lowered her eyes and nodded. She saw things, perceived things other people did not. And Charlotte was growing increasingly sure that she occasionally gave matters a little push in the direction she believed they should go. Like herself and Alvan. And Cecily and Verne. To say nothing of John Coachman and Mrs. Coachman.

"What sort of a man is he?" Charlotte had asked.

"The captain? He's a man you can trust."

"Where is he?" Alvan had demanded, striding impatiently into the coffee room. Catching sight of the figure stretched out on the bench, he'd checked.

"Coffee and breakfast, if you please, Lily," Charlotte had said. "For three."

Although he was a little older than she had imagined, nothing the captain had said or done during their talk had given her cause to doubt Lily's—or Henrietta's—assessment.

"Do you know," she confided to her husband as they rode back to Audley Park, "he might be just what Henrietta needs."

"I certainly prefer him to the snake she engaged herself to," Alvan said bluntly. "Rudd totally ignored her last night after forcing your father's hand over the announcement. It may have been a relief to her, but it was hardly the behavior of a proud or caring man. And if what Cromarty says is true, someone needs to push his teeth down his throat."

Charlotte blinked. "I believe the captain might be before you there, but maybe you could hold his coat while he does it." Alvan laughed, and she stretched out to take his hand. "Thank you for looking after my troublesome family."

He shrugged. "Even if they weren't part of you, I would still like them."

She pressed his hand to her cheek and kissed it.

Several hours later, when most of the overnight guests had departed, Charlotte was with her siblings when, from the window, she saw the agitated arrival of Mrs. Lacey, without either of her children or her husband. She looked distraught enough to send Charlotte hurrying from the room and down to the drawing room, where, refusing to be divested of her bonnet or pelisse, Mrs. Lacey was demanding to speak to both Lord and Lady Overton.

"Fetch his lordship," Charlotte's mother told the footman and tried to placate her guest, although with a rather comical grimace over her shoulder at Charlotte.

Entering the room, Charlotte saw that beside Alvan, only Rudd and Lord Silford were present. "Let me ring for tea," she suggested.

"There is no time for that! I am trying to explain how urgent the matter is and trust me, it will be worse for your daughter than my son!"

"What will be?" Lady Overton asked, bewildered.

"Disgrace! My lady, I am very afraid that Henrietta has eloped with Matthew!"

Lord Rudd stiffened in his chair, looking understandably put-out.

"Nonsense," Lady Overton and Charlotte said together, which only caused Mrs. Lacey to bridle further.

"It is *not* nonsense, and it has been happening right under our noses, mine and your ladyship's. Neither of us knew, for they have been slyer than I ever could have imagined. Matthew never used to be sly."

Lady Overton frowned at this implication that it was somehow her daughter who had imparted the recent slyness, but she let it pass.

Alvan said, "What reason can you have for imagining they have eloped?"

Mrs. Lacey clutched her heart. "I saw them!"

"Eloping?" Charlotte asked, bewildered. "How would you know?"

"They embraced on my lawn, right in front of my morning room window. And they told me at the stables Matthew had ridden off with her."

"Well, they wouldn't ride all the way to Gretna Green," Lord Overton said reasonably, entering in time to hear the last exchanges. "It must be four hundred miles. You have let shock overset your mind, but I guarantee there is nothing to this. Matthew is probably home already." He cast a quick, reassuring smile at Rudd, which annoyed Charlotte. Why were they placating the man?

"Then send for Henrietta," Mrs. Lacey demanded. "And let her tell me what a fool I am. *If she is here!*"

Charlotte rang the bell. "Go up to Miss Henrietta's chamber and ask her to join us in the drawing room," she said to the maid.

Behind her back, she crossed her fingers that Henrietta was there. The plan had been for Cromarty to enter unseen and take her away somewhere to talk, while Alvan kept an eye on Rudd, and Alvan's valet watched Rudd's. They had all trusted Cromarty to behave with propriety.

The maid stuck her head back in the door. "If you please, my lady, Miss Henrietta is not in her chamber."

"You see?" exclaimed Mrs. Lacey.

Lady Overton spared her an irate glance before commanding the maid to find her. "And send Miss Blackridge to me," she added. She scowled direly. "And the children."

"Mama," Charlotte objected.

"Well, it's utter nonsense!" Lady Overton insisted. "But if Mrs. Lacey wishes us to turn our entire household upside down to prove it, I suppose I must, for the sake of old friendship."

Mrs. Lacey looked stricken.

"Truly, I think you are mistaken in this, ma'am," Charlotte said hastily. "Only consider, what reason could Henrietta have for eloping with *Matthew?*"

Rudd curled his lip.

Mrs. Lacey bridled once more. "Are you saying my son is not an eligible husband for her?"

"Hardly," Alvan put in. "I believe in fact, *in*eligibility is the prime cause of elopements."

"In truth, we have been used to regarding Matthew and Almeria as extra siblings," Charlotte said. "And besides, I have reason to believe my sister's heart is given…elsewhere."

Mrs. Lacey regarded Lord Rudd who still sat rigidly in his chair. "They have fooled us all."

Charlotte threw up her hands and turned to face Miss Blackridge.

"Ah, Eunice, my dear," said Lady Overton. "Perhaps you know. Did Henrietta step out for any reason?"

"I have not seen her since before breakfast, my lady." Eunice, who seemed an odd friend for Henrietta, was very stiff and inexpressive. "She said she had a headache and would not come down, although she wished to go riding afterward. When I came back, she was gone." The girl colored. "I confess, I checked, and her riding habit is not there. I can only suppose she went without me."

"I told you!" Mrs. Lacey exclaimed. "She *has* eloped with Matthew!"

Eunice whitened.

"It's true," Mrs. Lacey said sorrowfully. "Dear Lady Overton, I have not told you all because I disliked to hurt you. Matthew told me he was going to Brighton a couple of weeks ago to court a young lady he had met by chance. I paid no attention because you know what they are like at that age, but now I'm convinced he followed *you* there to see Henrietta."

Lady Overton frowned as though going over in her head every encounter.

"And there is more. They have been meeting clandestinely at night."

"Oh no!" Lord Overton roared suddenly. "I have been patient up until now, but that I will not believe! Nor will I have it bandied about my own home or anyone else's!"

The children, who had just trooped in with Miss Milsom, almost bolted out again at the sound of their father's rare anger. But Lady Overton said, "Eliza, Richard, to your knowledge, has Henrietta ever met Matthew in secret?"

The boys shook their heads. Eliza looked stricken and slipped her hand into Charlotte's. But Lady Overton's gaze followed her. "Where is she now?"

"I don't know," Eliza whispered.

"When did she meet Matthew in secret?"

Eliza's grip tightened.

Charlotte said calmly, "I can explain that. It was nothing but a wager, a dare, if you like, since there was no money involved. It was improper most definitely, but not remotely romantic. Henrie already told me about it."

Lord Rudd finally broke his silence, rising to his feet in a decided manner that drew all eyes. "I don't know why we are all sitting here talking about it when we should be out looking for them. If she has eloped, she will be heading north—"

"She has not eloped," Alvan interrupted. "And if she had, it would not be your place to look for her. Rather, it would be your fault."

Charlotte was frequently proud of her husband, but never more so than now. Rudd, who had clearly never troubled to look beneath the surface of the amiable if rather aloof duke, was taken utterly by surprise.

"Your grace has no reason to make such an accusation," Rudd blustered. "It is possible I shall take offence."

"Please, do," Alvan invited. He turned to Lord Overton. "Sir, if Henrietta has done anything foolish—which I doubt—it is because he has frightened her into it with threats of violence to those she loves. I would not harbor him in your home. He is certainly not welcome in mine. Charlotte and I shall find Henrietta—and Matthew if he is with her—and bring them home."

THERE WAS NOTHING for Rudd to do but depart Audley Park in high dudgeon. And it was true he was furious, not so much with Overton, or even Alvan, but with Henrietta who had dared to call his bluff.

Well, he who cried last, cried longest, and that would be Henrietta. While Alvan and the other fools chased her up the Great North Road to Scotland, he would merely go to the Hart. And once the thrice-damned Cromarty was dead, Rudd would elope with her. When all her family and friends cast her off, it would add even more misery to her life. And strengthen her dependence on him. Perhaps this ridiculous start of hers was even for the best.

"Going so early?" Lady Carew drawled as he ran past her down the stairs.

"Dashed dull around here," he managed, slowing up to maintain his bored image.

"Indubitably. But is it true your betrothed has run off with the squire's son?"

"Don't be ridiculous."

"It would serve you right," she mused, as if he had not spoken. "You always had a tendency to overplay your hand, Rudd."

"What would you know? Tied to the same invalid for ten years without any way of getting your hands on his money? Even when he finally turns up his toes, he won't leave you half what you were hoping for. London is full of it. He's found you out at the end, my sweet."

At least it drew a rare flush to her delicate cheeks, which gave him some satisfaction. "You have no idea what you're talking about. But you can still kiss my hand when I'm Countess of Silford and have the world and its wealth at my feet."

Rudd laughed viciously. "Oh, trust me, that dream has passed. Why would the girl elope with the squire's son when an earl's heir is at her beck and call?"

Her eyes narrowed. "What do you mean?"

"Work it out," he advised. "But you're too late. Now, there will be no pieces for you to pick up. Goodbye, Susannah."

CHAPTER EIGHTEEN

CHARLES DIDN'T EVEN see them coming.

Without fuss, Sydney had led Henrietta and Matthew straight to an inn in Finsborough, the nearest town.

"You mean he's just hanging around there waiting for an opportunity to kill you?" Matthew said doubtfully.

"More or less."

"Then you come here often?" Henrietta asked. "And he knows that?"

"I've been here occasionally," Sydney said, dismounting and turning to lift her from the saddle. It was sweet to jump into his arms, feel the grip of his hands at her waist, and from his fleeting smile, he liked it, too.

"Then don't you think we should take Henrietta somewhere out of danger?" Matthew asked nervously, glancing around the windows facing the courtyard. "In fact, you should wait with her. Let me go in. I can speak for my father, you know, that's why he sent me."

"He sent you to keep an eye on me," Sydney said without rancor. "To make sure I stay within the law. After all, he doesn't know me from Adam. As for the rest, it's possible Charles might shoot you by mistake—his aim is erratic from what I hear—but he isn't interested in killing anyone but me."

While the ostler ran to the horses, Sydney drew Henrietta's hand through his arm and advanced to the door of the inn.

"Then you should definitely wait here!" Matthew exclaimed.

Sydney said, "He thinks I'm at sea."

"How exactly has he come to think that?" Henrietta inquired.

"A friend of mine told him."

Henrietta still wasn't convinced. After all, both Rudd and Lady Carew had seen him at Audley Park last night and they could easily have sent Charles word by now. Of course, Lady Carew didn't want Sydney dead. She only wanted her lover back as a husband when her own died. Henrietta wondered if poor Sir Edward was clinging onto life simply to spite her.

But Rudd, unspeakable man, most certainly wanted him dead.

Her fingers dug into Sydney's arm as they entered the building.

"Captain," the innkeeper greeted him, emerging from the taproom with a hint of nervousness and bowing. "How may we serve you today?"

"Perhaps a glass of lemonade for the lady. And a couple of pints of ale." He turned to Matthew and nodded to the empty room across the hall. "Wait for me in the coffee room."

"Not a chance," Henrietta said firmly when Matthew tried to urge her in that direction. From where she stood in the hall, she could see right through the busy taproom, following Sydney's course. And at last, she saw Charles Cromarty, too.

He sat alone at a table, smiling faintly, as though he deigned to enjoy the rough chatter and jests going on around him. But several heads swiveled in Sydney's direction, and Charles eventually looked, too.

He shot to his feet. Even at this distance, Henrietta made out the blind panic in his face. Stumbling backward, he grabbed the greatcoat from the bench and snatched up the pistol that had been hiding beneath it.

"Oh, no!" Henrietta started forward from sheer instinct, but Matthew grabbed her arm, jerking her back as several gasps and warnings rose in the taproom.

There was barely time for them. Before Charles even had the pistol turned around the right way, Sydney sprang forward and snatched it out of his hand. Dropping it on the table with some contempt, he seized Charles's retreating shoulder and yanked him forward.

"A word," he said pleasantly, "before you come with me."

"Assault!" Charles yelped, trying to lash out at Sydney and missing. "Kidnapping! Summon the watch! The magistrate!"

"What a coincidence," Sydney said, pushing him through the taproom door, "that's exactly who we're going to see. After my word." His gaze clashed with Henrietta's. "You'll be more comfortable in the coffee room. My cousin and I shan't be long."

Before she could say anything, he was hauling Charles with him through another door which he kicked shut behind him.

As if nothing untoward had happened, the innkeeper emerged from the taproom with a tray of ale and lemonade.

"This way, Miss," he said cheerfully, leading the way to the coffee room. This time, Henrietta followed.

As she sipped her lemonade, her ears straining for sounds of fighting or screaming, she said abruptly. "Do you suppose he's beating Charles to a pulp?"

"Wouldn't blame him if he did," Matthew confessed. "I should probably go and see."

Henrietta caught his arm and pulled him back down beside her. "That's what I thought at first, but I've been thinking. The men on his ship—most of whom you would not wish to encounter anywhere else!—were all obedient and cheerful, and I saw no signs of violence. I think he can keep men in line without it."

"I hope you're right. It will make a more comfortable journey back to the Hart."

A few minutes later, a door opened across the hall and Sydney walked into the coffee room, followed by a pale, chastened, and distinctly nervous Charles, who made a jerky bow in their direction and mumbled something Henrietta couldn't make out.

"He says, how do you do," Sydney translated, reaching for his ale and taking a few appreciative mouthfuls. He nudged Charles ungently with his free arm.

"I wish to apologize for endangering you and your brothers at the beach," Charles blurted. "I never expected you to be there."

Bewildered, Henrietta transferred her gaze to Sydney.

"He understands a little better the consequences of his actions," Sydney said smoothly. "He's a spoiled little worm but there might be a decent man in there waiting to fight his way out. We'll see. The rest of his life starts at the Hart. Shall we go?"

Sydney may have reduced Charles somehow to temporary obedience, but he took no chances. Although Charles rode his own horse, Sydney attached a leading rein.

"Has he really changed sides so quickly?" Henrietta asked doubtfully as she rode alongside Sydney. "Or is he just scared witless of you?"

"A bit of both. I penetrated his wall of indulged entitlement with a little healthy fear. That's genuine enough, but who knows how long it will last?"

She frowned faintly. "If that is all it took… Why did you not talk to him like this at the beginning? Wouldn't it have been simpler than having him watched and pretending not to be here?"

"Probably." He met her gaze with a rueful curve of his lips. "I did not care enough. I never meant to have any more to do with my father's family."

She left it there, her heart warmed by the implications. For even with all the adventure in the world, he had been lacking something in his life without even knowing it. Stability, perhaps, a responsibility that went beyond a few ships and a bank. A place in the world. A true home. For he had grown up never truly part of either his mother's world nor his father's. Despised by boys and men like Rudd, held at a distance by those supposedly lesser men his father had chosen to live among, he had sought and forged a life of his own, merely tinkering around the edges of his grandfather's business.

She wanted to be what he had been missing. She thought she was.

It was not a long ride back to the Hart.

Jem the ostler ambled across the yard to take their horses, and the large, amiable figure of the innkeeper filled the front door as he welcomed them.

"Is Mr. Lacey here yet?" Sydney asked.

"No, sir. But—"

"We'll need the parlor," Sydney said.

"It's yours, sir, in just a few minutes. We've just had a party of travelling gents in there and my wife's cleaning it up. Go into the coffee room while you wait and I'll bring you refreshment. You'll find their graces there already."

"What, really?" Eagerly, Henrietta rushed into the coffee room and all but danced up to Charlotte and Alvan. "How wonderful!" She threw her arms around Charlotte's neck, whispering, "You sent Sydney to me—thank you!" Then she hugged Alvan for good measure.

"Yes, well," Charlotte said, "whatever you've been up to has just become more complicated, because everyone is now convinced you've eloped with Matthew."

Henrietta blinked.

"*What?*" Matthew exclaimed in horror.

"With *Matthew?*" Henrietta repeated. "But why would anyone ever imagine such a thing?"

"Because Mrs. Lacey saw you go off together—embracing, as she put it—at Seldon Manor."

"We were just congratulating each other on being in love with other people!" Henrietta said indignantly.

Sydney laughed, and laughed all the harder as Henrietta glared at him. Reluctantly, she allowed the smile to break through.

"Very well, it's funny," she allowed, "But what the devil are we to do now? Poor Eunice will be devastated and hate me all over again."

"Ah, Eunice is the object of your passion," Charlotte exclaimed to Matthew. "I wondered what in the world she was doing with us."

"Well, we had enough secrets to discuss without dragging in Matthew's, too," Henrietta said. "This is Mr. Charles Cromarty, by the by, Sydney's cousin. We're waiting for Mr. Lacey to come and question him. Mr. Cromarty, my brother and sister, the Duke and Duchess of Alvan."

Charles's mouth fell open. He barely managed a sketchy bow before Sydney casually shoved him onto a chair.

"Um, I am, of course, delighted to see you again," Sydney said to Alvan. "But if you are here, who is watching Rudd?"

"He was packing, last I heard, in high dudgeon," Charlotte answered. "I expect he's on the Great North Road by now, hoping to catch Henrietta before she reaches Scotland. I have to say, I don't understand the man's motives. You're not a great heiress, and he appears to have no affection for you whatsoever."

Henrietta frowned. "Power. He likes people to cower before him. His greatest possible pleasure in life appeared to be the possession of a wife who hated and feared him." She shivered. "Do you know, I think I would have killed him with my scissors before I ever married him."

Sydney's arm slipped around her shoulders, hugging her to his side.

"Scissors," Charlotte repeated, thoughtfully.

"Well, they are always around and beautifully sharp," Henrietta explained.

"Stop giving your sister ideas," Alvan begged.

Charlotte laughed and kissed his cheek with great natural affection. "Not for you, my dear."

Sydney's gaze lingered on the pair, a faint, fascinated smile playing around his lips. Of course, Charlotte and Alvan had always been a beguiling couple, but Henrietta thought he was wondering about his own future with her and envisioning such happiness. As if he hadn't previously thought it possible for aristocrats.

Charles was staring from face to face in bafflement, as though he thought everyone was insane.

"My father's here," Matthew reported from the window. "With his constables. And they have someone with them. A fat little man who looks terrified."

"Ah, the excise man," Henrietta said with satisfaction.

"Oh, God," Charles said in misery.

"You made a mistake," Sydney growled. "At least face up to the consequences like a man."

A few moments later, Villin, looking none too pleased, ushered in Mr. Lacey and the two constables with their prisoner.

"Forget about the parlor, Villin," Sydney said. "It will be too small. We'll just stay here if that won't put you out."

"Or even if it will," Lacey said sternly. "This is the King's business. Your grace!" he added in surprise, catching sight of Alvan. "Charlotte...I mean, your grace, too! What in the world brings you here?"

"Henrietta and Matthew," Charlotte replied.

"Everyone thinks we've eloped," Matthew said gloomily.

Mr. Lacey frowned. "Thinks you've—" He broke off, shaking his head. "Never mind, we've no time for such nonsense right now. Where's this cousin of yours, Cromarty?"

"Here," Charles said, rising to his feet with conscious bravery. "I'm Charles Cromarty."

"And do you recognize this man?" Lacey snapped his fingers, and his men dragged their prisoner forward.

"Yes. Eric Pollard. I bribed him to shoot my cousin Sydney, and to inform his colleagues where the contraband would be landed."

"How did you know about the contraband?" Lacey asked.

Charles hesitated, looking even more miserable. "Lady Carew," he said at last.

"Dear Susannah," Sydney said fondly.

"And you," Lacey turned to his prisoner. "Do you deny what he says? Did he bribe you?"

"He gave me money, him and the other gent, but I shot wide, sir," Pollard the prisoner whined. "I'd no wish to kill anyone."

"Sit him down there," Lacey said wearily, "while we sort all this out."

"I think we need tea," Charlotte said to the innkeeper's wife, who had just stuck her head in the door. "If you'd be so good."

"On its way, your grace!" Mrs. Villin beamed and departed.

"This is wonderful," Sydney murmured a few minutes later as tea was set out on the tables. Laughter vibrated his voice, making her smile. "A hearing with a tea party. Is life around your family always like this?"

"This is your doing, not mine," she denied. "But we do have fun. Pass the scones, Charlie!"

At that moment, a muffled cry cut through the general conversation. An instant later, the coffee room door burst open and Lord Rudd walked in. Close on his heels came his valet, Claude, with his arm around the throat of the innkeeper's daughter, Lily. And a pistol was held to her temple.

Sydney leapt to his feet. Matthew dropped his teacup with a clatter.

"Dear God," Mr. Lacey uttered.

"Let her go," Sydney said. "There is no need to involve her." He stepped forward, spreading his hands. "Here I am."

"What do I want with you, vulgar cit?" Rudd said contemptuously. "I have come for my wife."

"Did we miss your wedding?" Alvan asked, standing more slowly. "Felicitations."

"Wife, wife-to-be, I think we may regard them as the same thing," Rudd drawled, his gaze finding and fixing on Henrietta.

Already terrified for Lily who stood in the valet's grip with her eyes tightly closed, Henrietta felt an echo of the old wave of revulsion and fear. But it was only an echo, because Sydney had been right. Rudd was nothing but a bully and a flim-flam man.

And she had a pair of sewing scissors in the purse attached to her wrist.

She stood, edging away from Sydney who might stop her. "So, if I come to you, you will let Lily go?"

"Clever girl. I knew there was a reason I chose you."

"Henrie," Sydney warned.

Henrietta kept her gaze on Rudd and continued to walk. "Take the gun away from her head and I'll come."

"An inch back, Claude, and don't touch the trigger," Rudd ordered. "Stand still or she's dead!" he snapped at Sydney who had moved to intercept Henrietta.

Sydney stilled. Only his gaze darted wildly around the room as though looking for solutions.

"It's fine," she said, trying to will him to understand. "Everything will be fine, once he lets Lily go,"

He seemed to relax, and she kept walking slowly toward the still open door. Behind Rudd, she could see Lily's parents wringing their hands with helpless fear. A nightmare for any parents.

"You know if you shoot her, you will hang," Lacey offered.

"I? Hang for killing a tavern wench? I don't think so."

"A trial of your peers won't save you," Alvan said conversationally. "I, personally, will see to that. Let her go, now."

"Don't be silly, my lord duke. You would not convict your wife's brother-in-law. Rather, you will sweep it under the carpet. Hurry up, Henrietta, I don't have all day, you know."

Henrietta drew nearer.

"Let the wench go, Claude," Rudd instructed. Claude released Lily with relief, and Rudd snatched Henrietta's arm. As Lily stumbled forward with a cry, Rudd snapped at his valet. "At the girl, at Miss Maybury!"

But before the valet could obey, a bizarre vision loomed in the doorway. The ancient figure of the Earl of Silford, his cane raised high. It came down sharply on Claude's head and the valet fell forward. As he landed on the floor, the pistol exploded, and several people screamed.

The room was suddenly full. Sydney plunged past Henrietta, battering Rudd into the wall with his hand around his throat.

"Now, now, my boy," Silford said. "Ladies present, you know."

Sydney yanked his captive forward and all but threw him into the chair beside Lacey's constables, with such force that it rocked backward. And then she was in Sydney's arms, clinging, crushed against him. Over his shoulder, she saw Lily with her parents. And her father looking utterly flabbergasted, with Mrs. Lacey staring from her to Matthew. And Eunice Blackridge trailing in behind them, her eyes large and round like saucers.

CHAPTER NINETEEN

WITH AN OBVIOUSLY huge effort, Sydney released her and strode out the door to speak to the Villins.

Beside her, Matthew said, "Dash it, Henrie, that was the bravest thing I ever saw."

"I couldn't let Lily die for us...but I was so afraid Sydney would stop me."

"He might have," Matthew allowed, "even we hadn't seen out the window that Lord Silford and your father had just arrived with your two massive footmen—who didn't get a look-in at the end. Who'd have thought Silford would save the day? Oh," he added unnecessarily, "and my mother is here."

"And Eunice," Henrietta reminded him as they turned together to face the room.

"Henrie, what the devil is going on?" her father exclaimed. "I've been in some odd situations in my life but this is like a madhouse. I must say I'm surprised to see you in Matthew's company after all."

"I'm not," Mrs. Lacey said stoutly. "I told you how it was!"

"And how is it, exactly, Mama?" Matthew dared her, meeting her gaze defiantly.

"Oh, don't look at me like that," his mother commanded. "What are you about to behave in such an ungentlemanly way? We brought you up to be better than this!"

"Indeed, ma'am, he could not have behaved better," Henrietta assured her. "He has been most gentlemanly all day and he could not have been more helpful."

This accolade, meant with the best intentions, struck Mrs. Lacey speechless.

Her husband used the opportunity to say testily, "May we please get on with business?"

Ignoring him, Mrs. Lacey burst out, "Matthew, if you wished to marry Henrietta, why did you not speak to us? To Lord and Lady Overton? Why this vile elopement?"

"Of course I don't want to marry Henrietta," Matthew scoffed.

Mrs. Lacey stared at him in bewilderment. "You don't?"

"No, I want to marry Eunice."

"You do?" Eunice blurted in amazement.

Matthew grinned at her. "Of course I do."

"Then what are you all doing here?" Mrs. Lacey demanded.

"It's a matter of the law," her husband growled, "so anyone who wishes to discuss other matters, please go away, now! Lord Rudd, do you know this man?"

Rudd followed the magistrate's pointing finger to Eric Pollard, the exciseman. "Never seen him before in my life."

"He says otherwise."

"Who cares?" Rudd said coolly. "You have no powers to detain me, sir, let alone try me, so I'll be on my way."

The large figure of the innkeeper loomed in the doorway, shoving Claude inside. The valet seemed to have acquired a cut lip and a rapidly darkening eye.

"He was trying to escape," Villin said, gazing ferociously at Rudd who promptly sat back down.

"I've seen and heard enough," Lacey said disgustedly. "As far as I can see, they are all guilty enough to be committed for trial. The question is, what should we do about them?"

"About us?" Rudd said. "What about the man who has made up all these accusations? The damned smuggler who's pretending gentility. He can and should stand trial!"

Sydney, who had just come back into the room and stood beside Henrietta, laughed.

"Wrong," Lacey snapped. "Captain Cromarty does what he does with government approval."

"What, the government of his bank?" Rudd sneered.

Unexpectedly, Lord Silford roared, "No!"

Everyone stared at him, and he hauled himself to his feet, waving his stick at Rudd. "The government of my country and yours, sirrah! And I have held my peace long enough. What in God's name is wrong with you?" He swung on his grandnephew. "*And* with you? You run out of money so you use someone else's to pay a man to shoot your cousin? Just so you're one step closer to inheriting mine? And you, Lord Rudd, wealthy peer of the realm, seem to think you can freely threaten women to get what you want, to feed your perverse pride or pleasure or whatever unsavory urge possesses you. Yet there you sit convinced that my grandson is beneath you? That *he* is vulgar?"

In his passion, he had stormed across the room and now glared down at him. "You think there are no consequences. Well there are. I am living proof of that. And you, sir, are the excrement under my boot!"

At that, Rudd sprang to his feet, the blood rushing into his face. Henrietta doubted anyone had ever dared offer him such an insult and his persistent pride could not swallow it. Before the constables could seize him, he lashed out.

But his blow never reached Lord Silford. Sydney leapt between them and blocked it on his arm. He stared into Rudd's eyes, and said something soft and challenging that Henrietta couldn't hear. Rudd sat back down with a bump.

Sydney and his grandfather had stood up for each other. It was a beginning that warmed her heart, but when her gaze shifted to the earl, her stomach twisted.

"Sydney," she said urgently, for the old man stumbled and all but fell into the nearest seat. His face was white and twisted in pain.

TWO MONTHS AGO, Sydney could have imagined no scenario in which he carried his grandfather upstairs and put him to bed, let alone one in which he actually cared a jot for the outcome.

But he did care. The sneaking liking had already begun when the little scene with Rudd had somehow made recriminations and apologies unnecessary. Blood, it seemed, was thicker than water, for he stayed by the earl's bed until the doctor came, leaving Lacey to sort things out below as he saw fit. After all, he was the magistrate. Sydney had merely interfered for his own purposes.

Henrietta. Once more in the protection of her father and further away from him than ever.

"Ah, there you are," he remarked to his grandfather, hiding his relief when the earl finally opened his eyes. "I thought you were going to sleep around the clock."

"I feel as if someone's kicked me in the chest. They didn't, did they?"

"No, sir, no one has the guts. The doctor is sent for."

A soft knock sounded at the door. Sydney rose and crossed the room to open it.

Henrietta smiled at him. "How is he?"

Immediately, his heart soared. "He's awake and talking. Sir, do you want company?"

"*She* can come in," Silford said, and Henrietta went to sit by his bed.

"How are you, sir?"

"Tired, but I have no intention of turning up my toes just yet.

What's happening downstairs?"

"They're all being hauled off to the cells in Finsborough for tonight at least. I suspect they will all go free in the end, because my father won't have my name dragged through the courts. But word will get out. Rudd will be socially ruined, the harshest punishment it is possible to give him. Mr. Charles Cromarty is probably savable, according to Sydney."

"Keep him away from his mother," Silford advised. "She may be gently born but the woman is still a harpy."

"I agree," Sydney said from the window. "The doctor has just arrived."

"Damned quack," Silford said ungratefully, although he did not refuse to see him.

Sydney and Henrietta vacated the chamber to give the earl privacy. Mrs. Villin, who had shown the doctor in, hurried downstairs in front of them. Abruptly, Sydney took Henrietta's hand and sat on the stairs, pulling her down beside him. She came willingly, even rested her head on his shoulder, and he ached with happiness.

"I don't want him to die," he said abruptly. "Not yet."

"Because you want this time with him? Or because his death would force you to a decision?"

"Both, I suppose," he said ruefully. "But my decision was made by the night of your party, the night your engagement was announced. I will learn to be the earl."

His declaration was not greeted with the floods of joy he expected. Instead, she searched his face, a frown between her eyes. "Don't do it for me, Sydney," she warned. "I'll go with you anywhere."

He raised her hand to his lips and kissed it. "And I hope you will. But it will be so much more comfortable if we do things this way. Besides, it isn't just for you. I need to do this. For my father's sake and my own. I doubt I will ever be a conventional nobleman, but I can be a decent earl in my own way, if only we can escape occasionally."

She smiled. "On *The Siren?*"

He tipped up her chin and kissed her soft, willing lips. "Perhaps." It was tempting to stay where he was, enjoy a few more kisses and the sheer sweetness of her companionship. But the inn was too full, not least with her family, whom he had no desire to alienate.

So, he pulled her to her feet and they continued their descent.

Lily, carrying another tray of various refreshments to the coffee room, paused to wait for them. "Thank you, Miss," she said to Henrietta. "For what you did."

Henrietta blushed. "I did nothing. It was Lord Silford who saved us all." A moment longer, she regarded the innkeeper's daughter. "I have a feeling the world would be a much less happy place without you."

Lily laughed. "Oh, not me, Miss, it's the Hart. It's a lucky house. And Captain, I'm sure his lordship will be fine."

Sydney opened the door, ushering both women through before following them inside.

Lacey's men had indeed taken away Rudd and Charles, Claude and Pollard. Lacey himself was clearly trying to gather his family for departure, although Matthew lingered by the side of Eunice Blackridge.

"How is Lord Silford?" Lord Overton asked at once.

"He's awake," Sydney said. "But we'll know more when the doctor comes down. Lily, when you've done that, do you think we could have something stronger than tea in here?"

"My father's bringing it now, sir," Lily assured him.

When the doctor finally came in, he looked somewhat disapproving to find something very like a party going on beneath the sick room. Sydney walked toward him.

"He tells me you're his grandson," the doctor said abruptly.

"I am. Come, sit with me over here in some privacy." Sydney swiped up another glass and poured the doctor a brandy before sitting down with him in the corner by the door. "What is your opinion?"

"It's his heart. It's happened before. Minor attacks, and he has always pulled through them. I see no reason why he shouldn't again, provided he has rest and comfort for a few days."

"Should he go back to Steynings? If it's too far, I'm sure the Overtons would take him at Audley Park for a few days."

"He's better where he is," the doctor said bluntly. "If he can be properly cared for. I know the Villins are good people but they have an inn to run."

"I'll send for his valet now," Sydney said. "And anyone else from Steynings that he needs. And I shall remain at least until they get here."

"I've left a tincture in his chamber, to be taken night and morning. Lots of rest, no excitement. Try to keep his mind occupied but quiet if that is possible. I don't want him getting bored and stamping off on a journey before he is fit to travel."

Sydney sighed and clinked his glass on the doctor's. "Thank you."

When the doctor had departed, he arranged with Lord Overton for Silford's valet to be sent over immediately.

"Is there any other way we can help?" Overton asked.

"Perhaps visit occasionally, when you have a moment? He likes Miss Maybury's company, too."

Overton's eyes narrowed. "I think it is you who likes the latter."

"Both of us," Sydney said blandly. "And who wouldn't? But that, I suspect, is a conversation for another day."

Overton scowled at him. "My first instincts concerning my daughters' husbands have always been wrong. But I always worried more for Henrietta. She is too headstrong and too impulsive. I doubt you are the steady man she needs to keep her in line."

"But I shan't bore her. And it's possible we shall keep each other in line."

"Are you offering for her?" Overton asked bluntly.

"Would you agree if I were?"

206

"No." Overton's lips quirked. "Not yet. But you can come to dinner tomorrow evening if you can leave his lordship."

LORD OVERTON WAS only too aware that the happy marriages of his eldest two daughters had taken place more in spite of his efforts than because of them. Still, he refused to be ashamed of using his daughters to further the family interests. It was a long and respectable tradition in noble families, however much personal preference was granted to modern young ladies.

And yet Thomasina, whom he had thought of as the jewel in the family crown, had made a merely respectable match to the comfortable Lord Dunstan while Charlotte, whom he had valued in quite other ways, had made the brilliant match with the Duke of Alvan that he had once sought for Thomasina. Thanks to Charlotte's marriage and Alvan's generosity, his financial troubles were more or less at an end.

He had been relieved that such matters did not need to drive his efforts in finding the right husband for his most willful daughter, and Rudd had seemed the perfect match. Even though Henrie had told him she didn't like him, he hadn't taken her seriously. And that truly frightened him. He had almost tied his daughter to a monster simply because he'd imagined he knew what was good for her.

As a diplomat, he was used to reading character quickly and accurately. And yet, where his daughters were concerned, he was somehow a dismal failure. This severe dent in his confidence contributed to his wild uncertainty about Captain Cromarty.

The heir to the earldom of Silford was undoubtedly an excellent match. But the man's past was checkered to say the least, and while there was nothing precisely ungentlemanly in his manners, they were informal and eccentric. The captain baffled him.

Alvan, whose opinion Overton valued, liked him. So did Charlotte.

And Overton was inclined to think his current care of his ill grandfather had nothing to do with personal gain. The man was already wealthy in his own right.

But could he give his Henrietta to such a man? She was only eighteen years old.

On Charlotte's advice, he took Henrie with him when he rode over to visit Silford at the Hart. To his surprise, when they went up to the room and Silford's valet admitted them, Captain Cromarty, in his shirt sleeves, was sprawled on the side of the bed, with a book between him and his grandfather. They appeared to be alternately reading and arguing over it.

"Now, you can have a second opinion," Cromarty told the old man, standing up and reaching casually for his coat. "But I know I'm right. How do you do, sir? Miss Maybury?"

They did not stay long with Lord Silford, who seemed glad of their company, but quickly grew sleepy. Leaving him, they went downstairs and discovered Captain Cromarty in the private parlor, scribbling hastily on some papers which he shoved into the hands of the waiting young clerk.

"Off you go," he said cheerfully, and the young man bowed and effaced himself with just one awed glance back at Henrietta.

His daughter, however, didn't notice. Her attention was all on the captain, and the smile they exchanged seemed to convey a message that was entirely private and yet perfectly understood by both of them.

It was the beginning of the end to Overton's resistance.

Over dinner that evening at Audley Park and over the next few days when they visited Silford or Cromarty called at the house, it became obvious to him that they cared deeply for each other. It was there in every look, every word. And there were no seedy efforts to get her alone or entice her away. Though the man had a reputation, he was treating Henrietta with every respect.

One morning, earlier than usual, he rode over to the Hart alone.

Cromarty was breakfasting in the coffee room.

"Have you heard the news?" Cromarty greeted him. "Lacey has let them all go. Rudd has retired to his estate and Charles to his parents. And Pollard has been given a post in Cornwall."

"I'm afraid I urged it," Overton said, sitting down opposite him. "I can't have Henrietta's name bandied about in courtrooms, and God knows what that blackguard would say about her in public if he had nothing to lose. As it is, he is finished in society, and frightened enough, I think, to keep his claws well in for a long time." He met Cromarty's unsurprised gaze. "That's what you wanted, isn't it? Dragging the law in was only to frighten them. You always knew it would end like this."

"Well, I think it has worked out quite well," Cromarty said noncommittally.

"How is Silford?" Overton asked after a few moments.

"Much better, I think. He'll be glad to see you." Cromarty signaled to Mrs. Villin for another place setting. "We're traveling to Steynings today." If he was disappointed not to see Henrietta with Overton, he had shown no sign of it so far.

"You're going with him?" Overton asked.

"I'll see him settled and stay a day or so. Then I have business in London I can't put off any longer."

"You're a busy man," Overton observed, and gave in, finally, to the inevitable. "If your time permits, perhaps you'd care to call at Audley Park on your way to London? Or on your way back if that suits you better. I will allow my daughter to receive your addresses."

Cromarty laid down his knife and smiled.

HENRIETTA WAS EAGER to set out for the Hart. She enjoyed spending time with the earl and making him laugh, but she lived for her short

encounters with Sydney. The rest of her day seemed tedious, especially now Charlotte had returned to Lincolnshire with the duke.

Something was missing from her enjoyment of everyday life: Sydney. And secretly, she was disappointed he did not arrange more clandestine meetings when they could be alone. He had even turned her own suggestion aside. Part of her knew he was keeping her father placated, so that they wouldn't have to wait three years to be married. But inevitably, she worried that he was losing interest. After all, what was so unique about her that would keep him?

"Where is his lordship?" Henrietta asked Gerald the footman, on failing to find him in his study.

"He rode over to the Hart, Miss."

"Already?" In dismay, she ran past Gerald and back upstairs for her hat and gloves. She had every intention of riding alone to the Hart, for she was afraid her father's deliberate abandonment meant he was trying to end her relationship with Sydney, and that she would not allow.

Sydney was against an elopement to the border, but now she began to think this might be the only way. On impulse, she pulled a carpet bag from the foot of her wardrobe and dropped in a few chemises and stockings, a day gown and an evening gown. After a moment, she added some indoor slippers and began to close the bag.

The shutting of the bedchamber door made her jump physically. Spinning around, she hid the bag behind her.

But it was not her mother, or even her mother's maid.

"Sydney," she breathed.

With his back against the door, he regarded her. A smile played around his lips. His eyes were warm and predatory. Pushing himself off the door, he advanced across the room. "What are you hiding behind your back?"

"An overnight bag," she said shakily. "My father is on his way to the Hart without me and I'm afraid he's going to try and stop me seeing you. I think we have to elope."

"Your father has already seen me and is now gone to Finsborough to some meeting with the local landowners."

He took both her hands, and she clung to his fingers. "Did he try to send you away?" she asked painfully.

"No. He gave me permission to address you. Not today admittedly, but what difference does a day or so make?"

"He did?" Henrietta squeaked in disbelief, staring at him.

"So, will you marry me, Henrietta, my sweet and only love?"

Henrietta thought the smile would split her face. "Oh yes, you know I will."

He bent his head and kissed her, a long, exploratory kiss that melted into another and then another. By this time, her hat was on the floor and her hair falling from its pins. Both her arms were wrapped around his neck, and he held her so close she could feel every hard plane and muscle of his body.

"When," he whispered against her lips. "How long do you need?"

"Today would be fine."

He smiled and kissed her again. "No, it wouldn't. I have to take my grandfather back to Steynings. And then to London. Five days, and I'll bring a special license."

One more kiss and he was gone as suddenly as he had appeared.

Henrietta collapsed on the bed and began to laugh from pure happiness.

CHAPTER TWENTY

SYDNEY WAS AS good as his word.

Which was why, seven days later, she found herself once more on the pebbly beach below the Hart, being carried into a small boat by her husband, who then picked up the oars and rowed her toward *The Siren*.

The wedding had been a quiet ceremony performed at Audley Park. Henrietta had been sorry Charlotte could not be there, but at least Thomasina had bolted down from London to be her matron of honor. Mr. Kettle, the lieutenant from *The Siren*, had appeared to be Sydney's best man and was given such a warm welcome by the children, that Henrietta was sure her parents would spot they already knew him.

However, everything passed smoothly, and suddenly, she was no longer Miss Maybury but Mrs. Cromarty, and sat down to a family breakfast full of laughter and fun. Kettle left before them, taking Henrietta's trunk with him, for their wedding trip was to begin, with a sail to Ireland and wherever else took their fancy. After calling in at Steynings, of course, for Lord Silford's blessing.

"We did it," Henrietta said, leaning back in the boat. "We actually did it."

"I trust you don't regret your marriage already."

She laughed at the very idea. Something caught her eye on the cliff and she shaded her eyes to see it better. "Someone's waving. I think it's Lily."

"I wouldn't be surprised."

Henrietta waved back, then sat back once more and watched her husband row without obvious effort. There was a contentment in his face she had not seen before. His eyes were curiously distant and yet warm with whatever thoughts took him from her. She ached with love.

Mr. Kettle welcomed her aboard and the crew surprised her with a spontaneous round of applause.

Sydney grinned at this, though after a moment, he growled at them to get back to their duties. "I want to be underway in ten minutes." Then, tucking her hand in his arm, he guided her across the deck and down the ladder to the cabin she and the children had once used.

Her trunk had been unpacked and everything put neatly away. A small vase of roses had been placed on the windowsill, cleverly tied by a ribbon to two hooks in the wood, presumably to stop it sliding about too much with the roll of the ship.

"This is beautiful," she said warmly, turning into his arms. "How good you are to me."

"It was all Kettle. And perhaps Lily. I just issue orders. Though there are some things I prefer to do myself."

He bent and kissed her lips, a quick, smiling kiss that held no threat. It struck her he was giving her time to get used to him, to the idea of intimacy. He would never force himself upon her. But that brief touch of his lips had been enough to set her pulse racing, and she caught his face between her hands, reaching up to kiss him again.

Their mouths fused, and his arms slid inside her pelisse and closed around her. As she gasped with excitement, he deepened the kiss, flooding her with sensation while his hands roamed and caressed. In no time, her pelisse was on the floor and so was his coat, and, greatly daring, she found a way to burrow under his shirt and feel the hot smoothness of his back.

He traced a line of sweet, warm kisses across her jaw to her ear and her neck. He pressed his lips to the galloping pulse at the base of her throat.

She stumbled backward, and he returned to her mouth, his hands busy at her back fastenings. In a disreputably short time, gown, stays, and chemise all spilled around her ankles and he lifted her, carrying her to the bed.

She landed naked on cool sheets. For an instant, he half-knelt on the bed, gazing down at her with something like awe. And God help her, she was not embarrassed. She felt powerful. Raising her arms, she stretched, and he growled deep in his throat. His eyes blazed appreciation as well as humor. "You are a minx," he breathed, tugging off his shirt.

In moments, he lay over her, skin to skin, and his hands and lips roamed freely over her. She could not be still under his caresses, but wriggled and pushed up into him, kissing his shoulder, his hand, his face, whichever parts she could reach. When he touched her intimately between her thighs, she cried out in pleasure, knowing instinctively this was the source of her need. The combination of this caress and his kiss on her breast sent spirals of pleasure rushing through her, and then he was inside her and the world stopped.

"Oh," she said in shock.

"Yes," he agreed breathlessly. He seemed to be trembling with the effort of restraint. "*Oh.* But don't let me hurt you. Tell me to stop and I will. We'll be as slow as you like."

"I don't want to be slow," she gasped, and he pushed further as if he couldn't help it.

"Kiss me," he whispered, and took her lips, rocking within her until the discomfort changed to sweetness and all the remembered pleasure rushed back, expanding and intensifying until her whole body burned with it.

And still he moved within her, bringing her with him on this new journey of strange delight, until she shattered into a million joys all rolled into one. And then he groaned long and deeply, collapsing upon her in release.

IT SEEMED STRANGELY wonderful after that to lie in his arms and talk. To dress slowly, with many kisses, and drink a leisurely glass of wine before going up on deck.

Even more unexpected, the world had not changed. It was still daylight, and they were approaching the harbor from where it was but a short carriage ride to Steynings.

Once, she turned back from the carriage window to find him watching her with a smile deep in his eyes.

"What?" she asked. "Is my hair awry?"

"Have I ever told you, Mrs. Cromarty, how much I love you?"

"You might have to tell me again."

"For the rest of my life," he promised.

On their arrival at Steynings, they found another carriage waiting at the front door.

"He has another visitor," Henrietta observed.

"Hmm." Sydney alighted and handed her down the steps. As they walked the short distance to the front door, a lady emerged, presumably the previous caller.

Henrietta's stomach tightened.

Lady Carew smiled at her, but reserved the most dazzling part for Sydney. "Miss Maybury, what a delightful surprise," she drawled. "Do your charming parents know you are out?"

"Mrs. Cromarty," Sydney corrected before Henrietta could reply. "And since her charming parents just gave her to me in marriage, their permission is no longer required. How are you, Susannah?"

She took the blow well, though the flash of her eyes acknowledged it. "Oh dull, my dear, dull. I'm on my way to visit Edward, who has suffered a relapse, but since I was passing, I couldn't resist calling to see how Lord Silford did. I heard of his illness."

"And how did you find him?" Sydney asked.

She smiled faintly. "I didn't. He was not at home. To me. I expect he is waiting for you. Goodbye, Sydney."

"Goodbye, Susannah."

Lady Carew held out her hand to Henrietta. "Farewell, my dear. It was always your destiny to ruffle my feathers in return."

Henrietta took her hand. "Such was never my motive."

"No, but it makes the defeat easier." And with that, she withdrew her hand and climbed into her carriage.

Sydney and Henrietta were admitted immediately and taken to Lord Silford in his library.

"Don't get up, sir," Henrietta said immediately, seeing him about to rise. She hurried over to his chair and knelt beside it.

He took her hand, and then reached out for Sydney's. "And so, you have tied the knot, my children."

"I know you approve," Sydney said, "so don't pretend to be grumpy about it."

"I'm not yet so bored that I need to resort to that." He squeezed Henrietta's hand. "Thank you for bringing him to see me."

"We brought each other."

The earl transferred his gaze to Sydney, almost as if he was afraid what he would find. "And will you come back?"

Perhaps he thought that having got what he wanted—Henrietta—Sydney would turn his back on "respectability".

"I will come back," Sydney said, like a promise. Then he smiled. "In about four weeks, actually. It's clearly time I licked your land into shape."

The earl emitted a shout of laughter. "Damned insolent jacka-napes! Just like your father! Walters, bring the brandy—the good stuff. It's time I drank to the happiness of my heir and his lady!"

Printed in Great Britain
by Amazon

61782229R00129